Walter Wager

KT-369-488

Telefon

Futura Publications Limited
A Futura Book

A Futura Book

First published in Great Britain in 1975
by Arthur Barker Limited

First Futura Publications edition 1976
Fourth Printing 1977

Copyright © Walter Wager 1975

ISBN 0 8600 7395 5

Printed in Great Britain by
Hazell Watson & Viney Ltd,
Aylesbury, Bucks

Futura Publications Limited
110 Warner Road
Camberwell, London SE5

To
Bernard Korman
and
Bill Frost,
a couple of swells

Walter Wager, a graduate of Harvard Law School and a former Fulbright Fellow at the Sorbonne, has been diplomatic adviser to Israel's Director of Civil Aviation, an editor at the United Nations Secretariat, and editor of *Playbill* and *Show*. A prolific writer, he has contributed articles to sixteen magazines, authored eleven cloak-and-dagger novels under a pseudonym, and written television documentaries for three networks and films for the United States Information Agency. He is currently director of public relations for a music licensing society in the USA.

'Wager develops it in a gorgeous manner and has come up with a doozie of a thriller . . . suspensefully dragging everything out until the reader beings to perspire. It's fun being diddled by so expert a master of hocus-pocus as Wager.'

New York Times Book Review

1

They had the whole house surrounded.

In fact, they had the entire block surrounded.

Gorki Street.

Borisov Street.

Nostamkin Boulevard, known for the excellent puppet theatre.

Tashinevo Street, still adorned with some of the gracious buildings erected before the Revolution.

There were armed men on all four, and on the nearby roofs. Certain units attached to the Committee for State Security—such as those twelve divisions of gray-clad frontier guards—wear uniforms, but the thirty-one agents in *this* K.G.B. raiding party were in civilian clothes. They carried an assortment of weapons under their overcoats—Stechkin machine pistols, Kalashnikov assault rifles (with the stocks folded down) and gas guns—and they were all fine shots. These were experienced professionals, hand picked by Colonel Malchenko himself. They were *his* men from *his* section, the only ones he could trust for this delicate operation. As Deputy Director for Internal Security at K.G.B.-Moscow, it was Aleksei Malchenko's patriotic duty to be paranoid and he did his job well.

Malchenko, a dark bulky man whose face looked older than his fifty-two years, peered down at his agents and saw that every man was in position. *Polkovnik* Malchenko was at his usual command post for such raids, a room on the top floor of the building across the street. In knowledgeable K.G.B. circles, this was as much Malchenko's trademark as the opening salvo of concussion grenades was Strelski's. Malchenko *sometimes* utilized the shock grenades himself, but he *always* attacked from the high ground like the ex-infantryman he was.

He put down the binoculars, glanced at his watch and saw that it was nearly 7 A.M. It was a chilly sunless morning and he'd been up half the night, but he wasn't the least bit tired. He was much too tense for that.

"Time to move," he said to the curly-haired young man beside him. "The children will be out on their way to school soon."

Lieutenant Bogdanovich wasn't surprised. He knew all the scores of Moscow's "Dynamo" soccer team for the past five years, the complete table of organization of Chinese military intelligence and the fact that his superior was very fond of children. It was logical that Malchenko, whose desk mounted large photos of his seven grandchildren, wouldn't risk exposing school kids to a stray bullet.

"Now, Colonel?"

The older man nodded.

Bogdanovich spoke into the walkie-talkie confidentially, almost as if he were afraid that someone in the next room might be eavesdropping.

"Blue Control to all units. Blue Control to all units. Move in. All Blue units move in immediately."

Malchenko saw two assault squads enter the drab apartment house that was Number 108, and even after they were out of sight he knew exactly what they were doing. Three men would be checking out the cellar, two covering the small lobby with machine pistols and seven others on their way up the stairs to Apartment 9. Another team would be blocking the rear exit. He could see it all in his mind's eye quite clearly.

"Alive. I want him *alive*," he thought aloud.

"That's been made clear to everyone, Colonel," assured the thin-faced aide.

Malchenko shook his large head.

"There's always some—what do the Americans say? Yes, some *dumb mother*. Lieutenant, there's always some *dumb mother* who—"

Two short bursts of gunfire amputated the sentence.

"Some *dumb mother!*"

Before Bogdanovich could answer, the beefy colonel was out of the room and pounding heavily down the stairs towards Gorki Street. Shouting. More firing. Malchenko was panting as he charged across to Number 108, and it was mainly rage that helped him bull his way up the three flights of steps. The door to the raided apartment hung askew on one hinge. A dazed K.G.B. corporal with a bright red stain blossoming above his belt buckle sprawled across the threshold. Malchenko leaped over the wounded man with an odd ponderous grace, scanned the drearily furnished room in a single sweep.

"In here, Colonel," said someone with a thick Ukrainian accent.

"Is he *alive?*"

The crew-cut captain in the bedroom doorway nodded twice.

"Oh yes, I saved his life, Colonel."

Malchenko hurried into the bedroom, eyed the doubled-up figure on the linoleum. The man on the floor—the target of the entire operation—didn't move.

"He's all right, Colonel," assured the Ukrainian. "I just gave him a knee in the nuts—that's all. No real *harm* in it."

Now the man on the floor moaned, made a gagging noise.

"A knee in the nuts hurts less than an ungrateful child, Colonel. That's an old Ukrainian proverb, you know."

"I doubt that," Malchenko replied, and the husky captain's grin showed three stainless-steel teeth.

"Like I said, Colonel, I saved his life. Just before I gave him that little knee in the nuts, I sort of jammed my machine pistol into his belly—and this is what he spit out."

Malchenko stared at the capsule in the captain's seamed palm. It wasn't the blue one used by American and British agents. It wasn't the gray pill the Chinese issued. It was green and very familiar and quite lethal. At that moment Lieutenant Bogdanovich entered the room with his walkie-talkie and looked at the suicide capsule that was fascinating his superior.

"That's *ours*, Colonel," he identified briskly.

He was quite right, which meant that something was very wrong.

None of this bothered Harry Bascomb, of course. He was more than six thousand miles away in a pleasant two-bedroom house on the edge of Denver, and he'd never even heard of the Committee for State Security. He didn't care much for spy movies or congressional hearings, being partial to cowboy pictures and telecasts of the games of the Denver Broncos. Sipping his third can of beer of the evening, he waited for the deodorant commercial to subside—confident that Clint Eastwood would soon return to the nineteen-inch screen to demolish the evildoers. He'd get every one of them. He always did.

2

As any cultured Muscovite can tell you, the elegant building at 11 Kropotkin Street houses the Leo Tolstoi Museum where one may inspect the original manuscripts of such masterpieces as *Anna Karenina* and *War and Peace*. Few residents of the Soviet capital are aware, however, of what goes on in the stone mansion four doors away. It is no longer the home of some cousin of the Tsar, but it isn't the Institute for Botanical Research either. The sign outside is a lie. This is the headquarters for the Third Bureau of the K.G.B.—the Committee for State Security—and in its sub-basement, where six thousand bottles of fine wine had once rested, an interrogation team was systematically and expertly hurting the prisoner taken earlier that bone-gray April morning. Aleksei Malchenko sat against the wall in an armchair covered with green plastic, glumly watching and hating the man from 108 Gorki Street who'd scream but wouldn't talk.

"Zagorsk! Viktor Zagorsk!" the captive howled again and again.

"Viktor Zagorsk," said Bogdanovich.

The lieutenant wasn't in the cellar. He was in an office on the second floor, and now instead of a radio he held a bulging brown envelope.

"That's the name on his identity documents," Bogdanovich told the bespectacled moon-faced man across the desk, "but *we* think they're all fake. That's why *we* want you to check them out. After all, you're one of the best documents experts in the business."

It was comical the way these junior officers said "we" to cloak themselves with the authority of their superiors. But Nicolai Dalchimski didn't laugh. He didn't even smile as he accepted the envelope containing the identity papers of "Viktor Zagorsk," for after twenty-three years in the K.G.B. he was used to this sort of thing.

"Thanks for the compliment, Lieutenant," he answered carefully.

"You've earned it. We're counting on you, although the interrogators will probably worm the whole story out of him in three or four days. He's getting the full treatment—the works. Do you know what they found in that bastard's apartment?"

"A transmitter?"

"No—a whole damn arsenal! That's classified, of course."

"I didn't hear a word you said, Lieutenant."

"You're a good man, Dalchimski."

Now the documents expert smiled in gratitude. As the door to the second-floor laboratory closed behind Bogdanovich, another door in the basement swung shut behind Malchenko. The portly colonel nodded to the uniformed guards outside the interrogation room, shook his head and nearly bumped into General Pyotr Strelski.

"You're looking grim, Aleksei," said the white-haired man

who commanded K.G.B.-Moscow, "but then you always do when you come out of *there*."

"I don't enjoy that sort of thing," Malchenko admitted. "Never did. It isn't that I'm squeamish, but all that savagery and screaming depresses me."

"You don't have to apologize to me, Aleksei. I was the one who brought you into this back in forty-six, remember? You were a pretty good soldier before that."

"And you weren't such a bad commissar," Malchenko recalled. Every Soviet battalion had been assigned a political commissar during the war against the Fascists, and Strelski had been one of the best. They'd fought their way into burning Berlin together, riding atop the same mud-smeared tank onto the runway at Templehof.

"You're not saying that just because I recommended you for the medal?" the general asked.

"You know I never gave a shit about medals. I was fighting for the homeland—*long* time ago."

Strelski drew a dark cigar from his jacket pocket, lit it.

"You're still fighting for the homeland—in a slightly different way," he assured him. "How's the interrogation going?"

The ex-infantryman shrugged.

"He's a real fanatic. Takes everything they're dishing out and says nothing except his name—which is almost certainly a lie. I'm having his papers and prints checked now," Malchenko said as he waved aside the offer of a matching corona.

"They're fine Cuban cigars, Aleksei. *Romeo y Julietta,* that's a nice romantic name."

"I'm not feeling that loving, Comrade. Just because they're our allies doesn't mean I've got to smoke their stinking cigars."

They started up the corridor as he told Strelski about the weapons cache and the K.G.B. poison pill. "This isn't some clique of malcontent poets with an illegal mimeograph machine," he judged in bitter tones. "This looks like a real *conspiracy,* and some of our own personnel may be involved. Damn lucky we stumbled onto it."

"Stumbled?"

"Pure chance. The police thought someone in the next

building had a black market operation going, and when they put in the wiretap some idiot plugged into the wrong line," Malchenko explained as they started up the stairs. "Nothing for a week, and then a couple of funny conversations—including two that mentioned Scarface."

Strelski stopped as if he'd hit a wall.

"That's not funny, Aleksei. There aren't that many people who call Marshal Vletska 'Scarface.' Only Red Army staff officers."

"The Red Army staff could be involved in this. So far as we know, Vletska's the last Stalinist left on the General Staff —but there might be others. That son of a bitch downstairs is going to tell us."

The general shook his head, frowned.

"Strelski, old friend, nobody needs twenty-six thousand fucking rounds of ammo to hold up the box office at the Bolshoi. Cases of grenades and explosives, nearly a score of automatic weapons and nine of the latest-model Red Army sniper rifles with night scopes—the *latest* model? What the hell would you say it is—an Armenian folk festival?"

"Not unless you found some musical instruments."

"Not one."

They reached the landing, turned along the corridor that led to Malchenko's office. Concentrating on their conversation, neither heard Lieutenant Bogdanovich approaching behind them.

"We'll find out all about this Zagorsk and his friends," Malchenko vowed, "and we'll exterminate them like roaches. You ever read that Englishman's novel—*1984*? In that book they destroyed enemies of the State completely, even took their names out of all public records so that—for practical purposes —they never existed. That's what I'm going to do to these roaches, annihilate them—names and all."

"Names and all, he said," repeated Bogdanovich that afternoon when he picked up the documents expert's report on the prisoner's papers.

"He needn't bother annihilating the name Viktor Zagorsk," replied Dalchimski. "These identity documents are all forgeries, excellent forgeries—better than the finest C.I.A. or British product. Ink, paper, seals—all nearly perfect. That's all I can tell you at the moment."

"It's all right. That roach in the cellar will tell *us* everything in a day or two," the young officer predicted confidently.

It actually took more than three days—ninety-one hours and some minutes—to break the man who wasn't Viktor Zagorsk, but once he yielded he spoke freely. As Colonel Malchenko suspected, there was a large and well-organized Stalinist plot to seize power. More than two hundred men and women in the government and armed forces were involved, but the ruined prisoner didn't know all the names—just thirteen.

One was the buxom woman who was the secretary to the admiral in command at Leningrad.

Another was a colonel in charge of an armored unit near Odessa.

Still another was Marshal Vletska.

A fourth was a K.G.B. documents expert in Moscow, a man named Dalchimski. Almost all of those identified by the ravaged "Zagorsk" were arrested within the next week, but Nicolai Dalchimski wasn't one of them. He had—somehow—disappeared without a trace. Police and frontier control units across the entire U.S.S.R. were alerted, and normal search procedures were begun.

They all failed.

3

To be fair to the K.G.B., the roundup of Stalinist conspirators during the month after "Viktor Zagorsk" collapsed was highly successful. Some 181 of the plotters were seized by Malchenko and his associates in a series of briskly professional raids that ranged across the Soviet Union from Air Force headquarters at Vladivostok to the Baltic telecommunications center in Riga. Many important individuals in the Party apparatus and the armed forces were taken into custody, and quite a few of these provided useful information after visits to the cellar under Kropotkin Street. Dozens of senior officials—including the Premier, the First Secretary of the Party and nine members of the Politburo—had been slated for assassination, they confessed. There were no public trials this time, no carefully staged "shows" to thrill the press or T.V. audiences. The entire affair was hushed up so efficiently that even many K.G.B. officers never heard of it, and when Malchenko was awarded the Soviet Union's highest decoration it wasn't mentioned in the official gazette.

Imaginative efforts were made to camouflage the executions. Marshal Vletska and eight of the senior plotters died "in the crash of a military transport into the Black Sea," while others perished in "auto accidents" or "fires." There were a number of "heart attacks" and "strokes" and "brain clots"— all neatly spaced in time and geography. It was well done, so well that General Strelski was complimented by the chief of the entire K.G.B. for his organization's "superior performance."

Of course, all these incidents did not go unnoticed in Washington—or to be precise, in Langley, Virginia. The global headquarters of the Central Intelligence Agency is situated in that pleasantly wooded suburb of the American capital, in a massive and totally undistinguished building that is guarded by sophisticated and expensive electronic and sonic hardware, dog patrols and—for all we know—trained alligators, woodchuck teams and killer hummingbirds. Inside this Cold War shrine dedicated to deities whose very names are classified there is a lot more machinery—some $190,000,000 worth of computers and other gear. And there are analysts—not psychoanalysts or urine analysts but intelligence analysts. To be wholly accurate, there are a few psychoanalysts and a couple of laboratory technicians who could tell plenty from pee-pee, but most of the C.I.A. family concentrate on other "areas."

One of these analysts was a trim brunette from Atlanta who'd ranked seventh in Radcliffe College's class of 1966. Her

name was Dorothy Putterman, and she was five feet tall and a
Mozart freak. People sometimes kidded about her height, but
no one ever made jokes about her brain. It was brilliant little
Dorothy Putterman who studied the computer printouts, eval-
uated the unusual death rate in Soviet officialdom the previous
month and soberly concluded that something extraordinary
had happened. Having compiled supporting figures in a chart
covering the preceding thirty-six months, she sent a concise-
precise-carefully reasoned memorandum to her section chief.

Colonel Thomas Stephen Jenkins—T.S. to his colleagues—
was impressed but not surprised. He had a genuine respect for
Dorothy Putterman's fine mind, and they might have gotten
along quite well if he could have suppressed his vulgar sexist
glances at her big breasts. She noticed those looks, and considered them both immature and degrading.

"Fine, very fine," he judged as he put down the memo and
sneaked another optic caress.

"Then you'll send it up to the Sovcom, T.S.?" she responded
purposefully. She saw his eyes flicker carnally again, and for a
moment she was furious until she reminded herself that this
dreary middle-aged man was merely a symbol of a large socio-
cultural problem.

"I'm giving that idea serious consideration," he confirmed
as he decided that the left one was larger.

Colonel Jenkins, who was nobody's fool, took the memo
to the Sovcom—the C.I.A.'s Soviet Affairs Committee—which
met every Monday afternoon. The Sovcom considered the
paper immediately after the report on the implications of the
latest satellite photos of the Smolensk missile complex, and
warily concluded that it was *entirely possible* that *something*
had happened. Before moving on to the obscene pictures of
the Russian ambassador in New Delhi, the Sovcom recommended that the various U.S. intelligence networks in and
near the U.S.S.R. ascertain just what the *something* was.

Zero.

Nothing definite, just speculation and a few pet theories.

This isn't to say that the K.G.B. is better than the C.I.A.
That's the kind of judgment only a syndicated columnist or a
bartender would attempt. No, in this particular furtive con-

frontation—one of about 619 that month—the Sovs prevailed. However, no one at C.I.A. h.q. was discouraged. Dorothy Putterman certainly wasn't. She just added it to her list, humming a fragment of the Mozart Fugue in C Minor and smiling at the delicious challenge.

In Moscow General Strelski had stopped smiling because the K.G.B. had another security problem—in Brussels. There was a certain bank there that appeared to be a perfectly ordinary financial institution, but was actually a front and conduit for funneling funds to K.G.B. agents in Western Europe—including the *apparat* that focused on N.A.T.O. headquarters. Someone had entered at night, gunned down the two guards, penetrated the alarm system and stolen $392,000 in U.S. currency. Much larger sums of francs, marks, pounds and lira had been left untouched.

Why?

What sort of thieves would spurn more than $2,000,000 in hard currencies?

Grinding out a half-smoked *Romeo y Julietta*, Strelski faced the unpleasant fact that either the K.G.B. *apparat* in Belgium had been penetrated by foreign agents or one of the Soviet operatives was a larcenous murderer. Strelski and a lot of other men (no women, because the K.G.B. was even more male chauvinist than the C.I.A.) fretted and sweated in the resolutely devious, wary, dedicated tradition of their chosen profession. Aleksei Malchenko wasn't one of them, not only because his duties were limited to internal security, but also because he was on leave at a Black Sea resort and wasn't due back until June 1st.

June 1st was when Harry Bascomb went crazy.

It was 2:25 P.M. on June 1st, according to the next day's edition of the *Denver Post*. He'd seemed perfectly normal until then, a mechanic at Bascomb's Auto Repair told reporters and the police, and he'd been talking quite healthily about the excellent new pitcher who'd joined the Los Angeles Dodgers that season. There had been a telephone call at 2:25, and when he hung up he "looked sort of funny—real uptight." He'd climbed into the blue Dodge panel-truck—the one he kept locked in the small separate garage and wouldn't let anyone else touch—and driven out to the U.S. Army Chemical Base thirty miles from the city. When the gate sentry routinely asked for his pass, peaceful, well-liked Harry Bascomb had drawn a silenced 7-millimeter pistol and shot him through the head. He'd then put bullets through the heads of two other sentries, firing with the accuracy of a skilled assassin. Bascomb then guided the truck a mile and a half directly to Building M, stepped out and sent the vehicle hurtling into the side of the windowless warehouse.

The tremendous explosion that followed indicated that the truck had been filled with high explosives. There was also a tank of napalm that set off a huge and intensely hot fire. The blaze and the column of oily black smoke were seen for miles. Harry Bascomb was not—not until the evening news telecasts when millions of people saw his body. He didn't look much better than the ruined building. Like it, he'd been pretty well gutted. The Military Police patrol that caught him fleeing from the wreckage just about shot him to pieces with automatic weapons.

It was in many ways rather unfortunate.

For one thing, they never had a chance to apprise him of his constitutional rights or give him a dime to telephone a lawyer.

For another, no psychiatrist ever had a chance to talk with him about his troubled childhood and what made him so unhappy that he committed such a dreadful antisocial deed.

In addition, there was no time to organize a Harry Bascomb Defense Committee to picket the U.S. Court House in Denver.

Still, a lot of very articulate—if not professionally verbose —people issued statements about the strange incident and the Chemical Corps put out its own press release. Like many such documents, it was not wholly complete. It didn't mention that Building M had contained—until seventeen weeks earlier—the newest U.S. equipment for germ warfare. It wasn't a depot for bacterial agents themselves, since all those had been destroyed more than a year earlier on the orders of the President. The Chemical Corps release and the statements of the local police and fire chiefs formed the bases of articles that appeared across the country. There was one on the front page of almost every paper, including the *Washington Post* and *The New York Times*. Those were the two that an Assistant Military Attaché at the Russian Embassy routinely clipped, microfilmed and dropped into the pouch—with many other items—for the diplomatic courier to take to Moscow.

4

The day after the courier delivered the microfilm in Moscow, a member of the Rolling Stones announced that he was converting to Judaism, the Lieutenant-Governor of Alabama was hit with a paternity suit by a nineteen-year-old black girl who was studying marine biology, and there was a terrible air disaster in South America. That week there were the usual strikes—a Paris subway strike, a Rome bus drivers' and postal employees' strike and a total work stoppage by the British dock workers. Two new situation comedies were announced for the next television season, there was a report that Martin Bormann was working as a wardrobe mistress in a Cairo theatre and a 230-pound shipment of heroin was seized by U.S. agents who raided a Los Angeles taxidermist shop. As if that weren't enough, Ralph Nader's fearless consumer group issued a devastating "white paper" on the nine most popular preparations that promised to cure hemorrhoids.

These dramatic and newsworthy events may explain why the attention of the U.S. and world press shifted from what had happened outside Denver. It isn't that journalists are either fickle or shallow, but they are extremely busy and the moving finger—having writ—must move on to goose someone else. This withering of interest in Harry Bascomb was warmly greeted by at least ninety-seven people, all employed by Benjamin F. Adams and Harley R. Greggson. Major General B. F. Adams was in command of the U.S. Army Counter-Intelligence Corps, and Mr. Greggson was the new Director of the Federal Bureau of Investigation. Both of these capable and dedicated men were committed to learning a great deal more about Harry Bascomb and his motives, and neither of them placed much stock in the press theory that Bascomb was either a super-pacifist or a lunatic. "The idea that this guy was just a weirdo is a lot of horseshit," said General Adams, whose terse, direct prose made him so respected by the Chief of Staff. Mr. Greggson was somewhat less colloquial, but he too believed the case "looked suspicious" and he meant the F.B.I. to have the honor of solving the mystery. While public interest focused on new sensations, both of these federal agencies pursued their large and careful investigations.

They spared no effort or expense.

These weren't routine name checks in the computer file, but "full field investigations" with plenty of knocking on doors and questioning of the subject's former schoolteachers and long chats with his neighbors and garbage collector. Many of those who spoke to the earnest federal operatives were openly astonished that a man as placid and ordinary as Bascomb could ever become a "subject" since all the "subjects" in television melodramas were visibly mean, rich, crazy or nasty to women. Bascomb wasn't any of these. He was a regular church-goer, a better-than-average bowler and a registered Republican who contributed annually to all the major charities. He wasn't rotten to anyone. "He was a good-natured guy who always gave me presents at Christmas or my birthday," confided the chemical redhead whom Bascomb had "visited" two or three times a week for the past twenty-nine months. From the warm gleam in her eyes, he'd been good at "visiting."

During all the years he'd been in Colorado he'd never had an auto accident or received a traffic ticket.

He'd always paid his taxes on time and to the penny, local and federal.

He was a very moderate drinker, did daily calisthenics and

usually spent one afternoon each weekend at the Western Gun Club where he polished his marksmanship with both rifle and handgun.

He had no known associations with radical or black militant groups, drug addicts, homosexuals, folk dancing societies, gamblers, strange cults, consciousness-raising outfits, poets, psychoanalysts, lefty priests, sadomasochists or organic food types—and he had no library card or interest in foreign films. It was—as one investigator noted—a miracle that he hadn't been elected to the state legislature, but then Bascomb wasn't much of a speaker and he wasn't that handsome either.

The twin probes continued, with the Army digging into his service record and the F.B.I. rooting deeper into his financial affairs. The F.B.I. found that there was a three-year gap in his tax payments which immediately preceded Bascomb's arrival in Denver. As a matter of fact, there was a curious three-year hole in all the records and nobody could explain this vacuum. Bascomb had been a bachelor, and both his parents and his older sister, Irene, were dead. What the Army discovered was even more puzzling and bothersome than the three-year mystery. Harry Bascomb had perished in an auto accident in Ohio *seventeen* years earlier, and his life insurance company had paid $15,000 to his mother just a month before she "passed away."

"I knew that son of a bitch was a son of a bitch," rejoiced General Adams, "and now we've got to find out who the son of a bitch really was." Comparison of the fingerprints established that the deceased who'd said that he was the Harry Bascomb who'd been born in Dayton in 1930 and served as an infantry corporal during the Korean War wasn't the Harry Bascomb who had fought in Korea at all. Then the F.B.I., which is certainly thorough as well as neat, discovered that the signatures on the pre-gap tax returns didn't exactly match those on the returns filed later from Denver. The entire question of the man who hadn't been Harry Bascomb was discussed at some length at a meeting of counter-espionage experts representing various branches of the U.S. intelligence community, and after the usual acrimony the case was given to the F.B.I. to complete.

That was on June 19th.

On the 20th a thirty-nine-year-old woman named Ruth Alice Mintzer disappeared. She was the owner of Ruth's Booth —second most popular beauty shop in Augusta, Maine—and she had just finished tinting the hair of Mrs. Marie Rioux when the telephone rang. Five minutes later Ruth Alice Mintzer drove to her bank and removed a package from the safety deposit box she'd been renting since she came to town from Albany, New York, twelve years earlier. According to bank records, she left the vault at 11:50 that brisk morning.

She was never seen again.

Her car was found on a back road, not far from the area where the fires consumed almost all the fuel at the jet fighter base. Fortunately there was no threat of hostile bombers striking the northeastern United States during the next four days, since there was a temporary hole in America's air defenses—a small temporary tear in the costly umbrella—until the fuel trucks arrived on the afternoon of the 24th. Technical experts of the U.S. Air Force's Office of Special Investigation came to check into the fires, but no one associated the disappearance of Ruth Alice Mintzer with them.

Not yet.

5

Lac du Flambeau is roughly a thousand miles west of Augusta, an easy pan for any aspiring film-maker with an 8-millimeter camera and a set of Fellini posters. There aren't any aspiring film-makers in Lac du Flambeau, however, for it's just a small town in the northern Wisconsin woods with an Indian reservation about twenty miles to the west. These Indians aren't particularly colorful or militant, and few hunters or tour-

ists who pass this way bother to visit them. There's also the
Rainbow Reservation to the east and the Willow Reservation
to the south, and, quite frankly, there's nothing terribly special
about them either. Chippewas are Chippewas. The Lac du
Flambeau area is quiet and scenic and relatively unspoiled, the
only significant intrusion the large but unobtrusive Torrance
Naval Communications Station. It was named after some dead
admiral who'd been an Annapolis friend and World War II
colleague of the crusty character who'd been Chief of Naval
Operations in 1959 when Torrance was built.

Perhaps "dug" would be more accurate, for the key to this
unusual installation was some 118 miles of wires buried in the
ground. This enormous and ingeniously designed grid formed
a gigantic antenna engineered to transmit extremely shortwave
signals to America's Polaris submarines on patrol four thousand to twelve thousand miles away. Messages sent over the
Torrance grid could not be intercepted or jammed, a vital factor in the Pentagon's policy of deterrence. Should it ever be
necessary for some President of the United States to order a
retaliatory strike in some future exchange of thermonuclear
horrors, the order to launch the undersea rockets would reach
the mobile submarines immediately. Few Americans knew
about the wires in the Wisconsin woods, but the Chinese and
the Russians did—and they respected them. So did the U.S.
Department of Defense. Torrance was ringed by three electri-
fied fences, and the perimeter was guarded by numerous sentry
posts and jeep patrols as well as a mine field. All day and all
night helicopter gun-ships flew along the fence on schedules
that were changed at irregular intervals.

Nobody in Lac du Flambeau minded or really cared much,
since the Navy people rarely came into town. The communications technicians had their own movie theatre and bowling
alley and store and mini-hospital out at Torrance, and when
they came or left it was often by plane from the station's landing strip. There were few airfields in the region. The population was sparse and the Chippewas didn't have the money to
fly, and the fishing and hunting enthusiasts who came in from
Duluth or Milwaukee preferred amphibious planes that could
touch down directly on the well-stocked lakes that dotted the

area. All the pilots knew that the air space over Torrance was "restricted," but that was no problem because there were so many lakes and so much empty sky that it was easy to bypass the base.

Carl Hassler certainly knew about the "restricted" air space. He'd been operating a small charter service out of Duluth for years, and he'd landed hunters or fishermen on lakes in the area—including Lac du Flambeau—hundreds of times. He was quite familiar with the region, for his wife was half-Chippewa and they often visited her relatives—perhaps half a dozen times a year. On the morning of the 26th he was out in the garage behind his house refueling his lawnmower when the telephone rang. Some ninety seconds later, his wife came out to tell him that a Dr. Edward Granville had called to remind him about the 4 P.M. flight to Lake Tomahawk.

"You're sure that's exactly what he said?"

"Word for word, Carl. I know how you count on me to get messages right," she replied with a wifely smile.

"I'd better check out the plane."

He seemed very preoccupied—almost grim. Still, he paused long enough to kiss her goodbye—with considerably more passion than an eight-hour absence ordinarily inspired. The pilot wasn't usually very demonstrative, and this unexpected warmth pleased Annie Hassler. Maybe they could talk again about that baby Carl had put off for so many years.

Carl Hassler drove down to the seaplane base in his 1969 station wagon, checked out the amphibian very, very carefully and took off just before one o'clock. He didn't wait for Dr. Edward Granville, and he didn't wait for 4 P.M. either. He filed a flight plan for Lake Tomahawk, set off on the normal route to that fisherman's paradise. He didn't turn off to circle around Torrance as usual, however. Instead, he took the Grumman down suddenly to one hundred feet and raced into the "restricted" area at top speed. As he crossed the fence, the new low-scan radar picked him up and bells sounded and a Marine Corps private at Sentry Post 9 grabbed a telephone.

"Hot Pistol! Hot Pistol!" he shouted. "Unidentified aircraft heading directly for command post. Bearing Delta, closing fast at low altitude."

"Hot Pistol" was the code phrase for a *real* alert, not one of those dry-run tests they pulled every couple of weeks. There had never been a "Hot Pistol" at Torrance before, and for about three seconds the lieutenant in the command post wondered what to do. It was very probably one of those dumb-ass charter pilots. It was almost surely some stupid civilian, for no hostile military aircraft could get within a thousand miles of Torrance without being detected by U.S. or Canadian radar. At the end of three seconds the young officer shrugged and did what he'd been trained to do.

He hit a button on the console facing his desk, and klaxons began to sound insistently all over Torrance. It was a horrible battering sound that couldn't be ignored. Some nine hundred yards from the command post Sergeant O. J. Darby didn't ignore it. He scooped up his "Redeye" missile launcher, jerked it to his shoulder and looked towards the perimeter.

"Gawddam," he said to nobody in particular in his rich Arkansan drawl as he spotted the plane charging across the treetops.

At that moment the lieutenant was speaking urgently into a microphone, trying to find the plane's radio frequency to order it away. Either he didn't find it or the pilot wasn't listening, because the amphibian kept boring in straight towards the building that housed the command post and key radio equipment.

"Gawddam," Sergeant Darby repeated.

Then he fired the "Redeye" rocket, and the surface-to-air missile blasted the Grumman into a ball of fire. There was a terrific explosion just before it hit the ground, and chunks of hot metal were scattered for half a mile. Then there was another very large explosion, one that gouged out an extraordinary crater more than ninety yards in diameter and a full two feet deep.

The official word—the story given to the press—was that a twin-engine Grumman amphibian had caught fire in the air on a charter flight to Lake Tomahawk, and that the civilian pilot had tried to make an emergency landing on the Torrance strip. There was no mention made of the cargo of explosives, or the other peculiar details being investigated by the Office of

Naval Intelligence. The Navy's public relations specialists were both uneasy and embarrassed by the entire incident, for if the civilian flier had simply strayed over Torrance during this peace-time period of no special international tension it might outrage the public to hear what had actually happened. General Louis Bellingham, the Marine Corps Commandant, had a very different reaction.

"Get that Darby on the horn," he told his aide.

It took about four minutes.

"Sergeant Darby, this is the Commandant."

"Yes, *suh*."

"Darby, the Navy public relations people here are out to rip your ass for what you did this afternoon. Now you tell me *exactly* what happened, and don't shit me—hear?"

"Yes, *suh*. I was out in my position, *suh*. Kind of a crappy little sand-bagged hole sort-of-bunker. See-curity position, suh. I was on see-curity duty, General. In-teerior see-curity, suh. Post nahn-teen, 'bout half a mile or so from the C.P., suh. Nothin' much happenin', if yo know what I mean."

"You were sitting in the hole scratching your ass. Then what?"

"Keerist, the gawddam klaxon went off—and it wasn't no gawddam test signal, suh. It was the real fuckin' thing, *suh*."

"It certainly was. Go ahead."

"I grabbed up the Redeye, saw this son-a-bitch come bar-reling in hell-for-gawddam-leather right over the treetops. Didn't look like no joke, suh. Not a bit. I sighted my piece, suh, an' I let him have it. Those were mah orders, suh. When the klaxon goes like that, I'm s'posed to kill airplanes—and that's what ah did."

"Beautiful," commended the general. "Beautiful shooting. One round, and you blasted that bastard right out of the sky. That's real Marine Corps shooting, Sergeant. I'm proud of you, and don't worry about your ass."

"Thank you, *suh*."

"I don't want you talking to any reporters out there, Darby. Get your ass on the next plane into Andrews. If there's nothing moving east tonight, you tell them to lay on a special bird for you. That's an order."

Three hours after Sergeant Darby reached Andrews Air Force Base near Washington, Lieutenant Ivan Bogdanovich brought Colonel Malchenko the results of the documents "audit" that had been going on since Dalchimski's disappearance. This count was one of the last items on the checklist, one of the final details to be attended to before the conspiracy case could be considered closed.

A number of items were missing from the documents vault.

Malchenko looked at the report silently, reread it and then reread it again.

Then he swore several old soldier's oaths that he hadn't used in more than twenty years, and he dialed Strelski's private line on the telephone.

"General Strelski's in a meeting," explained the woman captain who was his aide-de-camp.

"I don't care. Get him out—now."

"There are some senior officers in there, Colonel."

"I don't care if Lenin's mother is in there. This is extremely important—a matter of the highest priority."

Strelski came to the phone some ninety seconds later.

"What's the crisis, Aleksei?" he asked. "Captain Drina says that you spoke of a matter of the *highest priority*. Have you found some new Stalinist plot?"

"Worse."

"Worse? What could be worse?"

The colonel glanced at Bogdanovich, gestured him to leave.

"Aleksei, what the hell is it?" pressed the general impatiently.

"Just a second . . . all right, I'm alone now. Listen, do you remember that project you and I worked on fourteen or fifteen years ago—the one we called Telefon?"

"No one forgets that sort of thing."

"Well, we've finally completed our documents audit. The Telefon Book is gone!"

6

Click.

The face that filled the screen was tanned, open, even-featured. Male, white, mid-thirties, American haircut and necktie. Grigori Tabbat registered all that in a fifth of a second, the time it would take him to recognize the silhouette of a Mystère fighter-bomber or a Polaris submarine. He was quick, experienced and clever, and his American-English was as perfect as his marksmanship.

"Well?" asked Malchenko in the darkness.

"Zero," Tabbat replied. "He's nobody to me."

Click.

"*She's* another nobody as far as I'm concerned," announced Tabbat. "Who are they—ours or theirs?"

Click, click.

The projector was off, the lights were on and General Strelski looked very grim. "The operation began fourteen years ago just after the U-2 spy flights," he said, squirting out the words in a bitter burst. "We thought they were looking for targets. A nuclear war seemed quite possible, so we started this operation. Code name: Telefon."

Tabbat shrugged.

"Never heard of it, General."

"You weren't supposed to. It was more than Top Secret, *much* more. It was based on the finest deep-cover agents any country ever produced. They were to infiltrate and burrow deep, waiting patiently for the strike signal. They had to be *perfect*."

Tabbat lit a filter-tipped Tarryton, inhaled. Foreign ciga-rettes were one of the privileges that made K.G.B. service worthwhile.

"What is the *perfect* deep-cover agent, Grigori?" challenged Strelski.

The fact that he didn't wait for an answer hardly surprised Tabbat. Generals rarely did.

"The *perfect* deep-cover agent," continued Strelski in almost savage tones, "is the one who doesn't know he or she *is* an agent. It was a brilliant idea, Aleksei—*brilliant*."

"It made sense at the time," Malchenko admitted modestly.

"It was *brilliant*," Strelski insisted as he ground out his cigar. "Hypnosis. We collected four hundred and thirty first-class English-speakers who'd never been outside the country, drilled them in every detail of American life and then hand-picked the cream for drug-assisted hypnosis. The money and time spent on each one were enormous, but it worked. When we were finished with them, every one of them really believed that he or she was the American whose papers he or she carried. We sent them off, and every single one of them got through!"

"Fantastic," acknowledged Tabbat.

"They were all in excellent health, thoroughly trained in sabotage. *Not one* was detected entering the United States," boasted the general. "*Every one* of them had a strategic military or naval target, and *every one* infiltrated the target area successfully and settled in. Consciously they had no idea as to why those places or towns seemed so attractive to them, but they went and they waited."

"For what?"

"The trigger phrase," Malchenko explained. "Each agent had—buried in his or her mind—a coded trigger phrase. It was to be used only in case of a nuclear war, and only the Premier could authorize a Telefon attack. Some of these agents had missions that offered little chance for survival."

"They were all ready to die. That was buried in their unconscious too," Strelski added. "After a year, each one of them mailed a picture postcard to a prearranged address in Canada or Mexico, and later each one was sent a package which his unconscious made him hide."

"Explosives and detonators?"

"Exactly. Every six months we'd simply check on whether they were still listed with the local telephone company. There was never any direct communication, for obvious reasons. Nothing was to blow their cover."

Tabbat, who had the lean good looks of an actor and the analytical mind of a homicidal accountant, reflected for several seconds before he nodded.

"Perfect agents in a perfectly planned operation—completely watertight," he judged admiringly. "When did you bring them out?"

"We didn't," said Malchenko.

"There was no way to get them out without terrible risks," Strelski pointed out in tones that were simultaneously aggressive and defensive, "and there was no good reason to do so."

"They're *still* there?"

Malchenko sighed, and that was answer enough.

"Those two faces you threw up on the screen?" Tabbat wondered incredulously.

"She was known as Ruth Alice Mintzer in Augusta, Maine," said the ex-infantry officer, "and in Denver people called him Harry Bascomb. Two of the best. They're both dead—within the past month."

"They died bravely."

"They died senselessly and terribly, Pyotr," Malchenko corrected harshly, "as others will if we don't recover the Book. Tell him—now."

They both looked at Strelski.

"It's quite simple," he said in flat, controlled tones. "All the names and phone numbers of all the deep-cover agents were kept in a small book."

"With the trigger phrases," added the colonel.

"Yes. There were three copies of this book. One was kept by the Rezident who directs all K.G.B. operations in the United States—in an attaché case with instant destruct equipment. The second one is in the private safe of the Red Army Chief of Staff, under round-the-clock guard."

"I know what you're going to say, and I don't *believe* it," Tabbat said with a shake of his head.

"Shut up. Believe it. That's an order," Strelski snapped in pure "general" tones. "The third one was here in the special burglar-proof steel vault where we keep the most important and secret K.G.B. papers. That vault is protected by every modern alarm and security device."

Tabbat shook his head twice more.

"Stop that, dammit. All right—it's gone!"

At that point General Pyotr Strelski was either so angry or so frightened that he was temporarily incapable of further speech. He sat and stared and swallowed and stared some more.

"We think we know who took it," Malchenko said slowly.

"Who?"

"A man called Nicolai Dalchimski who was a senior documents expert here. We think he took it when he ran. That was in April. He just disappeared, probably because he'd heard that we were closing in on his group."

"C.I.A.?"

"No, Stalinist. They were planning to kill the Premier and a lot of other people."

"Oh—the usual thing."

"*Da*—the usual thing. Well, we know that Dalchimski took several passports and the drawings of the security and alarm system of our bank in Brussels. They're missing, and so is a lot of U.S. currency that somebody took from that bank. That somebody murdered two guards."

Tabbat lit another cigarette with his silver Ronson.

"A real pussy-cat," he jibed.

"A mad dog."

"So you think that this mad dog used the money and passports to escape, Colonel?"

"With the Telefon Book. We believe that he's in the U.S.A. with the damn book right now. There are two things that we don't *believe*, we *know*. We ran a computer name check on all reports from the States since the bank robbery, and we've found that Harry Bascomb was shot to pieces by guards at a U.S. Army chemical warfare base on June 1st—after completing his mission. We've learned that there was a big fire at a jet fighter base in Maine—the day that Ruth Mintzer vanished."

"So he's setting off your human time-bombs one by one?"

Malchenko nodded.

"And what the hell do you want *me* to do about it, Colonel?"

"Find him, Grigori."

"Find him and kill him," corrected Strelski viciously.

"And bring your book back before he starts World War Three?"

Both the colonel and the general nodded.

"How many of these wonderfully perfect agents are there left?" asked Tabbat.

Strelski eyed him warily.

"Many . . . perhaps ninety," he finally replied.

"There are a hundred and thirty-six, Grigori," Malchenko announced bluntly, "scattered all across the country."

Tabbat was on his feet, pacing and calculating and puffing on the cigarette.

"If absolutely necessary, we can tell you where they are," Strelski offered grudgingly.

"Very goddam generous of you, General. Could you also tell me where in the fifty United States—a country with two hundred and twenty million people spread across three goddam million square miles—I might find this bastard?"

There was no answer.

"You must think I'm a magician, General."

Strelski shook his head.

"No . . . but I think you'd better draw a pistol from the weapons section, comrade. You're leaving for the U.S. tomorrow."

7

The argument began immediately.

A lot of people think that no one ever argues in the Committee for State Security. They imagine that the entire staff consists of disciplined, beefy, beetle-browed men exuding almost tangible menace, Russian prototypes of the most brutal and cunning thugs imaginable. They see the K.G.B. as a Soviet version of the Hollywood version of the Mafia, only with different accents and a lot of heavy political talk. In fact, the great majority of those employed by the K.G.B. aren't into ideological discussions at all. They're not that deep. They spend a lot more time talking about the lousy switchboard service and the stupid new forms just issued and the decline of the food in the cafeteria. The K.G.B. is a government agency in a country afflicted with one of the more ridiculous bureaucracies. It is the most powerful police unit of a rigid and ruthless regime, which means that there are plenty of frightened men and bored-inhibited men on the staff. There are also brutal and cunning types capable of great savagery, but they don't debate Marxist dialectic. They do argue with each other about methods, not on a moral but on a practical level. Morality—in either ethical or sexual terms—certainly had never bothered Grigori Tabbat. Any woman in K.G.B. headquarters could tell you that.

This argument—not a very long one—was about whether Tabbat could find Nicolai Dalchimski without the assistance of every Soviet agent in the United States, and all those of the Communist countries.

"Preposterous," said the general. "You might as well ask the F.B.I. to join the search."

"That's the best idea I've heard this morning," answered Tabbat.

"I'm sure you'll find a better one," Malchenko soothed in an effort to ease the acrimony.

"I appreciate your confidence, Colonel."

"Grigori, we know that this will be extremely difficult—for one man or a thousand—but we really have no choice. We simply can't risk letting any significant number of people know about either Dalchimski or Telefon," Malchenko explained.

"I understand the logic, but the mission is crazy. I'd be crazy to go. It would make more sense to jump off the Kremlin bell tower."

Strelski stood up, pointed an index finger like a pistol.

"We're not *asking* you to go. We're *telling* you. That's a direct order."

"From General Strelski himself?" Tabbat asked resentfully.

"From the head of the K.G.B. and the Red Army Chief of Staff. Is that good enough for you, comrade? Go or die!"

"Now wait a minute," protested Malchenko.

Tabbat smiled.

"It's all right, Colonel. I appreciate General Strelski's frankness. Yes, General, that's good enough for me. You talked me into it. You've got a great gift for handling people, General."

"And you've got a big mouth. Get the hell out of here, Tabbat. A car will pick you up at your apartment at five tomorrow morning. Don't bother to pack a bag."

Tabbat started for the door, stopped.

"Won't it look suspicious at Kennedy when I arrive without luggage?"

"You're not going to Kennedy. Goodbye, comrade, and good hunting."

Malchenko shook hands with Tabbat, walked him to the door.

"I suppose you think I should have told him all the details of his trip, Aleksei?" the general asked a few moments later.

"No, but you were kind of tough with him. He's not just a top assassin, you know. He's one of the finest agents in all of Soviet intelligence, and he's already completed five missions in the States."

"*Da*, agreed. That's why I accepted your proposal that we send *him*. I've never liked him, though. A woman chaser, cocky, does everything his own damn way. I'll bet he's laid half the women in this building."

"A *fifth* at most, Pyotr. Don't worry about that," Malchenko urged. "After all, we're supplying him with a woman so he won't have to waste any time on chasing."

Strelski lit a fresh cigar.

"Frankly, that's not my main worry at the moment, Aleksei. What I'm much more concerned about is the Americans. How long will it be before they discover that these 'accidents' aren't accidents at all, and what will they do then?"

Some 3,462 miles away—if you took the polar route—Major Maurice Spanbock was puffing on a cigar in his office on the second floor of a building known as T-83. It was one of many "tempos," temporary structures erected near Washington during World War II and somehow still standing. This one in Virginia housed several laboratories of the Air Force's Office of Special Investigation. Major Spanbock didn't have General Strelski's access to fine Cuban *Romeo y Juliettas*, so he smoked a rather ordinary thirty-cent Bering as he studied the report just handed to him.

NO-9s, beyond any doubt.

It was the timing mechanism that made the identification definite. The phosphorus didn't mean much because more than a score of incendiary devices used by SovBlock intelligence outfits worked with phosphorus compounds, but this particular timing device was unique to the NO-9. This sabotage device had been designated the NO-9 at a 1958 meeting of N.A.T.O. counter-espionage agencies, the NO reflecting the fact that the weapon was produced at a plant in Noginsk east of Moscow and the 9 label indicating there were eight previous gadgets in the series.

"I don't get it," Major Spanbock confessed-complained.

Nobody on this side of the Curtain had seen an NO-9 since 1966, when even the Viet Cong had stopped using them. There were a couple in a glass case at the Navy's Explosive Ordnance Disposal School at Indian Head, Maryland, but solely as historic curios. Perhaps someone else could make sense of it. Spanbock would send the report along to A-2 in the Pentagon, and maybe those "big brains" would figure how and why pieces of several NO-9s were found near burned-out fuel tanks at a fighter base in Maine.

There couldn't be any Viet Cong in Maine. It was much too cold for them, and that war was over anyway.

8

Malchenko picked him up at 5 A.M., but not in one of those black Moskvas that were practically a K.G.B. trademark. The colonel had too much sense for that, Tabbat reflected as he climbed into the small Pobeda. The streets of the capital were nearly deserted at this hour, and they passed only a dozen cars on the drive out to the airport.

"You've memorized the entire list, Grigori?" the ex-infantryman asked.

It was typical of Malchenko to check and recheck. He was a careful man. Even now he was driving a cautious five kilometers below the speed limit.

"Yes, Colonel. All the names, addresses and telephone numbers."

Malchenko nodded, still going down his mental list like a housewife in a grocery store.

"Good. And you have the green pill?"

"Yes, Colonel. I'm properly equipped to kill myself for Mother Russia—if necessary."

"Very good. . . . Oh, I'm sorry. I didn't mean that the way it sounded. I hope it won't ever come to that. It's just that there's always some risk that you might be captured, and that list cannot fall into enemy hands."

Tabbat barely suppressed a grin.

"Of course, Colonel. I realize that the list is much more important than I am."

Malchenko saw the sign, turned the car up the right fork.

"You're a very important man to the Soviet Union and the K.G.B., Grigori. Please don't think that we don't value you highly."

"Almost as much as the list. I'm flattered, Colonel. Don't worry. I have no intention of getting captured. My ass is very precious to me. It comes a very close third—right after my devotion to Karl Marx and Telefon. You could say *very, very* close."

"I didn't know that you were such a devoted Socialist, Grigori," Malchenko replied drily.

"Every morning when I wake up I recite a quotation from *Das Kapital.*"

"To the blonde in bed beside you?"

"Sometimes it's a brunette. But Marx always comes first. Sometimes I throw in a few lines of Lenin too. Goes over very big."

"I'll bet. I'm sure that you'll be pleased to hear that your contact in the U.S. is reported to be quite pretty—and extremely practical."

"I'm crazy about practical women, Colonel—but I hate females who argue."

"She'll obey your orders. This is your mission, Grigori, or—to put it in your language—your ass."

Now they could see the roofs of the hangars up ahead.

"I hope that you've reserved me a seat by the window, Colonel," Tabbat joked as he ground out his cigarette in the ashtray.

"We've done a lot better than that—a lot better than that. You can have any seat you want, my friend."

When he boarded the big Ilyushin jet Tabbat discovered that Colonel Malchenko hadn't been jesting. There were no other passengers. The whole plane had been reserved for Grigori Tabbat, and his baggage. There were two suitcases of drab gray plastic, presumably containing American clothes and some additional weapons or equipment. Someone had adorned the side of one bag with an "X"—two strips of tape.

"We take off in three minutes," someone announced over the cabin loudspeaker. Tabbat looked up, suddenly became aware that there was no steward or stewardess in the entire passenger compartment. He was completely alone. No member of the crew was to be allowed to see him. Security, no doubt. The plane rose smoothly, headed west. Twenty minutes after it was airborne, the metallic voice sounded again.

"There are two thermos containers and food in a box on seat twelve."

Tabbat found the sealed container, tore it open and saw the envelope taped inside the lid. He checked the thermos bottles, discovered one was filled with strong tea and the other brimming with black coffee. Using the cap of the latter as a cup, he drank several sips of the coffee. It wasn't very good, but then he'd soon be drinking some of the excellent Colombian available in the States. They'd forgotten the sugar, but someone—probably Malchenko, who thought of everything—had provided two packs of Tarrytons and three books of paper matches. The matches advertised the virtues of the American Hilton hotel chain. Nice touch. Tabbat opened the envelope, scanned the instructions. He reread them several times before he tore the single sheet into strips, then into bits. Using the ashtrays of four seats, he burned the bits into ashes and then leaned back to sleep.

He was awakened by the speaker three hours later.

"You may wish to eat now. We are proceeding on schedule, and will give you a one-hour alert before we make our descent. Current altitude is thirty-one thousand feet, and no turbulence is expected."

Tabbat ate a piece of bread and a chunk of sausage, only nibbled at the apple. He ignored the cookies for a while, finally consumed two with another thermos cup of bitter coffee. He looked around the strangely empty cabin, shrugged and decided to use the lavatory. At least he wouldn't have to wait to get in, an improvement over usual airline conditions. When the voice said, "One hour . . . one hour to descent," he opened the suitcase marked with the "X" and found the parachute. It was a familiar model, one he'd jumped with a dozen times before. Then he opened the other one, saw the scuba gear. It would be his size. You could count on Colonel Malchenko's orderly mind to attend to these details.

Tabbat looked at his watch, took out the parachute and placed it on a nearby seat. Then he began to undress, carefully folding his clothes and placing each item in the now empty case that had enclosed the chute. When he was down to his undershorts, he glanced up and down the cabin again and laughed. This was probably the first—and the last—time the regular Aeroflot flight from Moscow to Montreal had carried a single passenger, let alone one who wandered around in his shorts. He took them off, tried a few dance steps in the nude and decided that his mambo was still pretty good. Then he put on the scuba gear. It fit perfectly, and not one piece of it was Russian-made. Every item bore the trademark of a big Italian firm that sold all over the world—including the United States.

So far, so good.

"Thirty minutes to descent. Thirty minutes. We will fly at special altitude for ten minutes. Repeat, ten minutes."

It was typical airline jargon. They never said anything simply or directly. No doubt eighteen hundred feet was a fairly "special altitude" for a commercial flight on the North Atlantic, but it certainly could have been stated less gingerly. Feeling mildly irritated by this linguistic gentility, Tabbat wrapped his Colt .32 in a plastic bag, knotted the top tightly and placed it in another plastic bag which he sealed the same way. He put the whole package in an over-the-shoulder pouch which he belted shut, and then he looked at the waterproof diver's watch Malchenko had provided.

"It ought to work," he said to the empty cabin.

If the parachute didn't malfunction.

If the mini-transmitter attached to the harness operated properly.

If *they* were on time and on station.

According to the plan, the big plane would slide down to eighteen hundred and then reduce its air speed to just above stall. Cabin pressure would be lowered, Tabbat would open a door and jump. The door had been rigged with a cable so that it wouldn't open more than a few feet, and presumably two of the stronger crewmen could pull it shut before the plane climbed back up above thirty thousand feet for the last 275 miles to the Canadian coast. A military aircraft might have been easier for the jumping, but the arrival of a Red Air Force long-range transport or bomber in Montreal would certainly have aroused a huge amount of U.S. and Canadian curiosity. That danger presumably outweighed the risk that Tabbat might have his brains smashed out against the tail of the Ilyushin—at least for General Strelski.

"Five minutes to descent. Cabin pressure about to lower."

Tabbat felt his chest, was reassured by the bulk of the waterproof packet of false identity documents taped to his ribs. He took a seat by the door he was to use, waited and experienced the sensation of the transport's dropping rapidly in a semi-dive. The change in cabin pressure was more than noticeable. It was unpleasant, painful to the ears.

"Leveling off at special altitude . . . on course and on schedule."

"Screw you," Tabbat said to the speaker—and felt better.

The plane was slowing down steadily, and it was almost time to jump. Tabbat put on the chute, checked the harness and straps carefully. He walked to the door, opened the catch and rotated the crank that the K.G.B. had installed to pay out the cable slowly. When the door was about two-thirds open and the wind was hammering him fiercely, Tabbat rechecked his watch again.

It was time.

He jumped, and he didn't hit the tail. He flew past the rear of the plane, counted five and pulled the ripcord. The parachute blossomed with a jerk that knocked most of the air out of him, but he drifted down swiftly into the sea. It was green-black, choppy and cold. It was terribly cold despite the protection of the rubber suit. It was numbingly, frighteningly cold. He splashed, swam, paddled, swallowed icy water and coughed on the bitter salt. He swore and he flicked on the mini-transmitter that was to beam his location, and he hoped that *they* were within the fifteen-mile range of his sender. Even in the scuba outfit he probably couldn't survive this icy water for more than twenty minutes.

He didn't have to.

There *they* were—only half a mile away.

With deck almost awash and only its conning tower visible, the sleek nuclear submarine cut through the seas towards him. As it drew closer he could make out two heads protruding from the conning tower, each looking like the face of some monster because of its weird eyes. It was only as he swam alongside that he realized that the weird eyes were binoculars, and by that time he didn't care. All that mattered was getting inside the submarine, out of the chill, battering waves. The sea carried him onto the deck, and he climbed the ladder up the side of the conning tower. The two men stepped aside to let him enter.

It was warm. The column of hot air rising from within the hull felt good, and yet he started shivering.

"You all right?" one of the men asked as he reached for the hatch lever.

Before Tabbat could answer, the questioner slammed and bolted the hatch. The other man picked up a microphone/telephone. "Passenger aboard. Hatch secure," he reported. The undersea craft began to dive almost immediately, and by the time Grigori Tabbat was accepting a cup of mediocre vodka from the captain, the submarine was ninety feet beneath the surface of the North Atlantic.

9

There are all kinds of chic on Long Island. Nassau County, which is next to New York City, has plenty of expensive homes and Caddies and marinas in addition to all those split-level pueblos built by Messrs. Levitt and other canny developers—but it is basically more comfortable than chic. There isn't much real chic until you get beyond Riverhead in Suffolk County, and then really only when you reach the Hamptons. There are several Hamptons on the South Shore of Long Island, the side that faces the Atlantic. There's Bridgehampton, Westhampton, Southhampton and East Hampton—and after that there's Amagansett, where so many successful writers and painters cut capers all summer. Southhampton still has some of the old chic, the rich WASP chic of the brokers and ex-polo players. East Hampton has the frenetic new chic of advertising executives, Park Avenue psychiatrists, T.V. directors, affluent clothing manufacturers with good art collections, middle-aged public relations tycoons, literary and talent agents who speak casually about the Coast and prosperous attorneys who play pretty fair tennis.

The beach at East Hampton is crowded with clever and worldly people on any summer Saturday, and on this one—the third of July—it was swarming with tanned wit, well-oiled perceptions, attractive women who wondered whether their husbands fully appreciated them and a lot of highly articulate people who glowed with the wonderful after-effects of three Bloody Marys at a late brunch. The sun was bright and the sand was clean and the beach buzzed, and the swimmers looked fine in their new designer bathing suits. Broadway playwrights and network vice-presidents exchanged obscene jokes that were far more amusing than any you'd hear on the Jersey shore, and actors whose faces you'd recognize laughed with assurance. It was a fine, comfortable Saturday afternoon. Everyone was almost relaxed, for East Hampton was a wholly appropriate place to spend the July 4th weekend, even if both Edward Albee and Truman Capote were further down the coast at Montauk. East Hampton had its own celebrities—fine, responsible types who played in special revues and all-star softball games to raise money for George McGovern or hungry American Indian children. Their own children weren't hungry. They were muscular, good-natured, energetic and all over the beach this splendid afternoon. Some were in the water, swimming well despite the rolling waves. A few were snorkeling with the face masks and breathing tubes they'd tested in Barbados and Jamaica the previous Christmas.

Just before five o'clock a figure in scuba gear surfaced some sixty yards off the beach. Nobody paid much attention, for men in wet-suits with compressed-air tanks and flippers were nothing special in the Hampton waters. The scuba diver looked around, dropped back beneath the water and then surfaced again about twenty yards from the shore.

"Gregg! Gregg! Where've you been?"

The woman who called out was about twenty-eight or thirty, and she had a fine rounded body that did wonders for her mini-bikini. She had pretty glowing face that radiated vitality, and her eyes beamed a cool intelligence that was immediately noticeable. She stood at the edge of the sand, facing the rubber-suited man with open impatience.

"For God's sake, Gregg, get out of the water. Hurry up, will you?"

The scuba diver walked out of the sea with the odd ponderous steps that the flippers required, and then he took them off and removed his facemask.

"Hiya, hon," he acknowledged.

He was a handsome man, and he smiled as if he knew it.

"Gregg, the Kesslers are going to be *furious*," she pressed. "This will be the third time that we've been late, and Ginger Kessler is going to *poison* us."

"Arsenic in the martinis? That isn't Ginger's style, is it?" the man from the sea asked as he zipped open a foot of the rubber suit. "Next you'll tell me she sleeps with the help."

"How about her analyst? Does he count as help?"

He shook his head, and they started towards a car.

"No, hon, he's supposed to help all right—but he isn't *the* help. He's a helpful father figure," Tabbat explained.

"Ginger Kessler balling with her father? Doesn't surprise me a bit—and I'd imagine that it doesn't *entirely* surprise you either."

She stopped, picked up her large straw purse from the sand. Tabbat assumed that the short-range transmitter that had guided in the submarine to within a mile and a half of the beach was in that attractive tan "box"—but he didn't ask. He could wait. It was all going well—as Malchenko had planned. They reached the edge of the sand, strolled along a road marked "Egypt's Lane" for a minute until she stopped at a maroon Mustang convertible.

"Don't tell me you've forgotten your car, Gregg?" she teased.

"I've even forgotten your name," he confessed.

She slid behind the wheel, raised her left hand to show the triple gold-band on the meaningful finger.

"Barbara. I'm your ever-lovin' wife Barbara," she said.

He entered the Mustang, moved close to her.

"Ever-lovin'? I like that."

She smiled as she started the motor.

"I thought you would, dear husband. Why else would they have code-named you Romeo?"

They drove past something large and old called the Maidstone Club, cruised a delightful tree-lined street adorned with handsome "country" houses and then slowed for East Hampton's small shopping area before turning onto Route 27. The motel where she'd rented a room was ten miles down Route 27 towards New York. It was a classic motel room, with lots of plywood and Formica and foam rubber and air conditioning just about five degrees cooler than necessary.

"It's good to be back in the States," Tabbat said amiably. "Now all I need is a cheeseburger and a chocolate malted."

"Would some malt Scotch do?"

She nodded towards a green wedge-shaped bottle on the table beside the table, and Tabbat smiled in recognition.

"Glenfiddich will do just fine, Barbara, and I'll bet you will too."

"Barbi," she corrected as she offered him a wax paper-wrapped water tumbler.

"What?"

"You call me Barbi, Gregg."

He poured two inches of the unblended Scotch, took a long sip and shuddered contentedly.

"Barbi? That's terrible. Do I have to?"

She prepared her own drink.

"I'm afraid so. That's the kind of guy you are, Gregg," she teased.

"I must be a real creep."

She laughed—very attractively.

"Oh no, my husband Gregg is a *swell guy*—pays his taxes, obeys the speed limits and does terrific things with a patio barbecue."

He zipped open the wet-suit, stripped it off. She studied his splendid body, nodded again.

"*Swell*. You've got a *swell* body, Gregg. You're in great shape."

"Glad you like it. Have I got some great clothes to go with it?"

She finished her Scotch, jerked open the closet to show him a blue suit and a grey suit and a yellow blazer and three shirts. Folded over the black loafers on the floor was a set of underwear, and a pair of dark socks rested on top.

"They radioed your sizes," she explained. "I hope my choices weren't too conservative."

"Not too bad. When I get some money I can buy more in town."

She opened her straw bag, handed him an expensive-looking morocco wallet.

"There's $2,000—half of it in hundreds."

He counted the money.

"Don't you trust your own ever-lovin wife?" she asked.

He didn't bother to reply. He braced himself, ripped off the pouch taped to his lower chest and swore. Then he removed all the documents from the plastic packet and put them in the wallet.

"Driver's license. Social Security card. American Express and BankAmericard. Passport. Blue Cross and Blue Shield. AAA. Kinney and Air Travel cards. And here's my favorite—my Red Cross blood donor's card."

"I told you that you were a swell guy, Gregg."

He poured himself more of the Glenfiddich, sipped it thoughtfully.

"Gun. I need a gun, Barbi. I left mine in the submarine. It made an awful bulge in the wet-suit."

She opened a drawer, took out an airline bag. A moment later she handed him a small .22 revolver and a screw-on silencer.

"You're a great wife, Barbi," he complimented. "I'll bet you're terrific in the sack too."

"Why don't you shower first?" she parried. "I'll go after you."

"Oh no—ladies first."

She took off the bathing suit, walked into the bathroom. As she showered, Tabbat searched her bag and then went over the room very, very carefully. It was routine, of course. They'd trained him that way. As he checked for hidden "bugs" or cameras, the submarine was transmitting a coded message that "Romeo arrived on schedule." The message was much too brief for anyone to get an accurate fix on the location of the sender, but two men did try. They were technicians on a U.S. Navy patrol plane, one of those lumbering turbo-props crammed with thousands of pounds of electronic gear and numerous "black boxes" whose very names were classified. Even though they couldn't quite pinpoint the transmitter, the technicians consoled themselves with the thought that it would probably interest some intelligence office at Atlantic Fleet headquarters in Norfolk to learn that a foreign submarine was cruising within fifty miles of Long Island.

It did.

10

She stepped out of the bathroom, finished drying herself and put down the towel. She was naked and she was humming something almost as pretty as she was, something that reminded Tabbat of one of those Brazilian songs Sinatra had recorded eight or ten years ago. Jobim. Antonio Carlos Jobim. Sinatra had done an entire album of his melodies, and it was one of Tabbat's favorites. As she reached for a pair of minute blue panties, she noticed his smile of approval and she blew him a kiss.

"Hope you don't mind," he said.

"Course not. You're just a typical American tourist—enjoying the sights."

"They're *terrific*," he replied truthfully as she pulled on the panties.

"Thanks. The second show's at midnight."

"I don't know if I can wait."

She blew him another kiss, slipped on her gold-and-tortoise-shell wristwatch and waved it at him.

"Right, time to move," he agreed. "Rule Number Six: Evacuate the infiltration area as soon as possible."

"Glad to see we read the same books. I'll be dressed in two minutes."

She was, and while he was putting on his new clothes she went out to pay the bill. There was no reason for the motel clerk to see Tabbat's face at all, and if he didn't he could not describe it to anyone later. By 5:40 they were in the Mustang heading towards New York in light traffic.

"You've handled this type of car before," she judged.

"I've driven fifty kinds of cars. It was part of the training," he acknowledged.

"And thirty-eight types of boats and helicopters," she guessed.

"Thirty-nine if you include light planes. My real specialty is guns—all the handguns and small arms of the armies of eleven peace-loving powers. The television's the worst, though."

"Television?"

"Every goddam six months they make me watch twenty goddam hours of tapes of the most popular T.V. shows, the American and then the British and the French and the West German. I'm supposed to be able to talk about them the way the natives do. I can take Walter Cronkite and Johnny Carson and *Kojak*, but those medical shows—too much."

"You've done a lot for Socialism, Gregg," she teased.

He shook his head, turned right at the sign marked Riverhead and New York.

"Not enough, they tell me. I must be deranged. Certainly no sane man would take on this thing."

She didn't answer.

"You don't know what this thing is all about?" he guessed.

"I'm only your sweet, loving wife, Gregg. I don't have to know."

He nodded, turned his head three inches and saw her smiling.

"Spare me the cute stuff, will you? It's enough that some imbecile has tagged you with that dumb-ass name, Barbi. *Barbi?*"

"Your English—or should I say American—is very good, Gregg."

"It's perfect, but what the hell has that got to do with anything? Listen, there's no reason for you to know the whole story. It's a *terrible* story, and this is a *terrible* mission. Well, maybe *stupid* would be more precise."

"I'm sure you're right, hon."

"Don't humor me, dammit—and don't get any jerky ideas about reporting my lack of enthusiasm or respect in some fucking furtive report. I made my views absolutely clear before I left Moscow. They have no illusions about me at all. They didn't pick me because I'm such a good boy. They chose me because they thought that I might be able to pull this damn thing off somehow."

There was a moment of silence, and then she crossed her legs—riding the miniskirt up even higher. His eyes were on the road, but he noticed that. It was the sort of thing Tabbat always noticed.

"Do you have any idea as to why they picked you to work with me?" he asked as a red Ferrari barreled past.

"Probably because of my sense of humor. I'm known for my swell sense of humor."

"That's not a bad answer. You know the B.B.C. once phoned Frank's lawyer—a very smart guy—and asked whether Frank would tape some remarks for a show they were doing about Bing Crosby. The lawyer said that Frank wouldn't because he didn't like cheddar cheese. What's that got to do with it, the B.B.C. guy asked. Well, said the lawyer, if you don't want to do something any excuse is good enough."

There was another moment of silence.

"Who's Frank?" she asked.

"*Frank*—the Chairman of the Board."

"You mean Sinatra?" she wondered.

"That's him."

She took a pack of cigarettes from her purse, extracted one.

"You a friend of his, Gregg?"

"Just a fan. I've got every album he ever cut."

She bent low out of the wind to light the cigarette, puffed twice before she sat up again.

"Don't brood about it," he continued. "They know all about it in Moscow. They've probably got a list of the records in some file."

"You're kidding?"

He shook his head emphatically.

"Hell, no. They send people in to search my apartment two or three times a year when I'm away—routine security crap. They put in new bugs, and I disconnect them a couple of weeks later. I don't wreck them—just disconnect them. Don't want to destroy property of the State."

"And you're just crazy about the State, right?"

"Well, we respect the hell out of each other. It's a good working relationship. . . . Listen, there's one thing that I can tell you about this operation. I'm here to find a man—one of Ours. He's armed and probably crazy."

The sign announced that it was four miles to the Long Island Expressway.

"Crazy?" she repeated.

"Vicious, homicidal, a traitor. A genuine Enemy of the State. This isn't some neurotic who can't give up smoking because his mother weaned him too soon. This is a monster, a fiend—tricky and bitter."

"Where is he—in some C.I.A. 'safe house' near Washington?"

"No, he's playing his own weird game—*somewhere* out there. Could be anywhere. Miami or Seattle or Gopher Crotch, Arkansas. Maybe even up in Montreal."

It was true. With Canada integrated into the main U.S. direct-dial system, Dalchimski could strike from any of thousands of telephone booths north of the border. It was all quite simple—and thrifty. The hating Stalinist could easily set off World War III with $60 or $70—in dimes and quarters. That would be after 6 P.M., of course. It would cost more earlier in the day.

"What are your instructions?" Tabbat demanded in an abrupt change of subject.

"To assist you in your mission, and to obey your orders without question. That's what the Rezident said. The entire U.S. *apparat*—"

"Forget that. I can't trust any of them."

"Are you saying we've been penetrated by American counter-espionage?" she challenged.

"Of course. How many agents in the various networks the Rezident is running? Two hundred? Five hundred? It doesn't matter. Once you get up into numbers like that, I've got to assume that you've been penetrated. I don't mean you *personally*, dear bride."

He wasn't leering, but the look on his face was unmistakable.

"I just love it when you talk dirty, Gregg. A filthy young man was what I've always dreamt about."

He shrugged.

"We're not talking about dreams. The reality is that I can't use your people—not one of them."

"You want me to tell *that* to the Rezident?"

"I don't want you to tell him anything. You are to have no contact with the Rezident or any other of our agents. That's an order. All I ask of you is instant, absolute, unquestioning obedience. Just do exactly as you're told, and we'll get along fine."

"Yes, SIR!"

"Spare me the female fury. Just remember that you belong to me now, like the pistol you gave me. We operate alone. If you make any effort to contact the Rezident, you're fired."

"Do I get any severance pay?"

"A bullet in the head. Is that clear enough, Barbi?"

She studied him for several moments.

"You've got a terrific way with women, Gregg."

"The candy and flowers come later," he promised. "Don't worry. I'm not such a brutal bastard all the time. I just wanted to make the ground rules absolutely clear, to paraphrase our former leader."

"*Our* leader?"

"Didn't you see my voter's card, Barbi? I'm a registered Republican!"

Then he turned on the radio, and something wonderful happened. It was the mellow voice of the Chairman of the Board sailing silkily and joyfully through "You Make Me Feel So Young." Tabbat smiled in instant appreciation, and she found herself smiling too—both at him and with him. The handsome assassin beside her sang along effortlessly, relishing the record that he knew so well. ". . . Spring has sprung," he exulted and then he winked at her. He could be quite charming—if he wanted to, she judged. And he could kill her at any moment—if he wanted to.

Tabbat was still beaming when the record ended and the

Pan Am commercial began, but Colonel Malchenko wasn't. Sitting in his office in Moscow—a city that was a certain target for the first salvo of U.S. missiles if Dalchimski succeeded—he looked at the two message forms that Bogdanovich had just delivered. One brought word of the attack on the Torrance Naval Communications Center at Lac du Flambeau. The other reported that "Romeo" was ashore safely.

The race was on, and there was nothing that Malchenko could do to help. He couldn't pray because he didn't believe in that superstitious rubbish—so he cursed in frustration for nearly a minute. Then he picked up the telephone to call Strelski. That wouldn't help either, but it was his duty to keep the general informed and Malchenko was a man who always did his duty. As he heard the phone ringing, Colonel Malchenko suddenly remembered a fragment of a prayer that his grandmother had often spoken—just a fragment.

He swore again.

11

"I live on Seventy-sixth Street," she said as the Mustang emerged from the Queens-Midtown Tunnel onto the steamy streets of Manhattan.

"Not this month," he replied while he waited for the Third Avenue traffic light to change.

"Don't you want to stay in my apartment?"

"If I had my choice I wouldn't even stay in the same borough. How the hell can I know what mistakes you've made —or whether you've made any at all? Maybe some foxy U.S.

crew has had you staked out for three months, or maybe the Rezident's keeping an eye on you."

The light turned green, and he swung the Mustang north on Third.

"You're very shy, aren't you, Gregg?"

"A girl like you could bring me out of my shell. Tenderness and understanding—that's all I need."

"And instant, total obedience?"

He nodded as he slowed for a moment to avoid a station wagon.

"*Very* good," he complimented. "I'm sure that your apartment's fine, but we'll stay at the Drake on East Fifty-sixth."

"That was the phone call you made from the gas station?"

He nodded again, and ten minutes later they were alone in Room 818 of the Hotel Drake. He began unpacking his suitcase immediately, carefully arranging his new wardrobe in the closet so that the wrinkles might hang out by morning.

"We'll get some of your clothes after dinner," he announced as if he'd read her mind. "First I'd like to celebrate with one of those big steaks at The Palm. A medium-rare sirloin, some great home fries and a couple of bottles of dark Löwenbräu and I'll be ready to come out of my shell. Shall we go?"

They went to the restaurant on Second Avenue and they ate and drank both amply and well, and the woman who called herself Barbi this week found the stranger who was answering to Gregg amiable and amusing. He was almost gallant, and if he didn't quite make it, she forgave him because it is impossible for a man who's checking and rechecking all the people around him to be truly gallant. Only a professional would have noticed what Tabbat was doing; she noticed. It was nearly eleven o'clock when they climbed back into the Mustang.

"Must still be eighty," she judged the July heat.

"The humidity's even higher. Next time don't be so damn *chic*. Get an air-conditioned sedan instead of a convertible. This is almost as bad as the Congo," he grumbled.

"You've been everywhere, haven't you?"

"Twice."

He drove north on Third Avenue again, turned west on Sixty-sixth Street and said nothing until they were halfway through Central Park. She'd said over coffee that her apartment was on the second floor of a brownstone just three doors in from Riverside Drive, 284 West Seventy-sixth Street.

"Two-eighty-four?" he tested.

"Yes. Why?"

"I'm computing. Look, I'm going to swing through the neighborhood once or twice to check it out first."

"You really think that I've been burned?" she asked sharply.

"How would I know? Be sweet and indulge my paranoia, Barbi, and we'll enjoy a long, happy marriage."

"I'm not arguing with you, Gregg."

"I should hope not—not on our honeymoon."

Up Central Park West to Seventy-third, then across to Riverside Drive and up to Seventy-sixth. He circled the block twice before he finally dropped her off at the corner of West End Avenue and Seventy-fifth.

"I'm giving you exactly fifteen minutes to pack a suitcase—two bags if necessary. At 11:25 I'll pull up outside your building, and you'll be coming out the door. Clear?"

She nodded, and they checked their watches. As she walked back towards Seventy-sixth, he drove the car over to Broadway and parked. Ignoring a pair of tarts in high wigs and short skirts, he sauntered towards the building where he was to meet her. He scanned both sides of the street as he approached 284, looking for the traditional delivery van or telephone company truck used for surveillance jobs. The fact that he didn't see one proved nothing, he reminded himself as he unbuttoned his jacket, for the watchers could be on some nearby roof or even in 284 itself. He saw a bedraggled scrawny man sipping from a paper bag that almost surely contained a pint of cheap port, and he paused for a moment in automatic caution. The wino wandered into a doorway.

That was when Tabbat heard the footstep behind him.

He tensed, turned quickly to face a thin dark-complexioned man of about twenty-four or -five. He could have been a Latin or a light-skinned black or even a swarthy Caucasian, but that hardly mattered. What counted was the knife he held in his left hand.

"Don't scream or I'll cut you."

"I won't scream," Tabbat promised truthfully.

"Good. Be a nice dude, and you won't get cut. Just give me your wallet and your watch."

It was a hot night, and under the best of conditions Tabbat wasn't known for his patience or tolerance.

"You're making a mistake," he said generously.

He was trying to avoid trouble, really trying.

"Don't jive me, man, or I'll cut your face," threatened the man with the knife.

Tabbat shrugged in resignation. All the reports were apparently true. American society *was* beginning to unravel. Crime in the streets was everywhere, and decent people weren't safe in the hearts of major cities.

"Idiot!" he judged.

The man with the knife lunged in anger, and Tabbat stepped aside in automatic reflex. He grabbed the wrist that held the weapon, twisted sharply until he heard the crack of the joint breaking. Then he kneed the mugger in the groin. The man screamed, doubled up and reeled towards the outer wall of 275 West Seventy-sixth. Tabbat reached him in one tigerish leap, seized him by the shoulders and slammed his head against the side of the building—three times. The mugger's face was bruised and scraped, and blood trickling from his mouth suggested major dental problems in the immediate future. Tabbat glanced up and down the street, saw no one. He noticed a flight of metal steps leading down into some backyard or alley, so he pushed the man over the edge and watched until the semi-conscious body thudded onto the cement at the bottom.

"You made a big mistake," Tabbat announced.

His eyes swept the windows on the sides of Seventy-sixth, then the doorways and the parked vehicles. A taxi was turning the corner at Riverside Drive now. Tabbat walked on casually to the Drive and then north to Seventy-seventh before circling back to the Mustang on Broadway. The two prostitutes were chatting with a gray-haired man in his late sixties, and Tabbat heard the word "party" as he unlocked the car door.

At 11:25 the Mustang swooped to a halt in front of 284 W. 76 Street, and shortly after midnight Grigori Tabbat came out of his shell in their room at the Drake. He was a firm but tender lover, so aware and adroit that she probably couldn't have helped responding even if she had wanted to resist. They cuddled and talked, and then he reached out for her again. It was nearly 2 A.M. by the time they fell asleep. He hadn't said a word about the man with the knife during the rambling intimate conversation, of course. The woman beside him was pretty and uninhibited and sophisticated in so many ways, and she was very giving—but that certainly didn't mean that Tabbat was about to trust her. She was attractive and convenient. For the moment that was all he needed. Her perfume smelled good as he finally slid off contentedly into exhausted sleep, smiling at the anticipation that it might still linger on her warm skin in the morning.

12

They awoke at eleven the next morning, and it didn't surprise Tabbat that she was smiling. He wasn't the boastful sort, but he couldn't deny that he was a handsome man who was more civilized than most and highly talented in bed. He accepted the fact that he had a way with women, a skill that was almost as important as his expertise with all those different cars and small arms. On the basis of his considerable experience with women in some thirty countries—white women, black women, yellow women, brown women and assorted blends thereof—he expected that a female who awoke beside him would be smiling. Sometimes he'd be smiling too. This was one of those times. He was smiling and he was hungry, so he ordered a large breakfast to be sent up to the room. Her hair looked wonderful and her skin glowed and her eyes beamed—all the usual signs of a contented female. He knew that the release of hormones had done most of that, but that awareness didn't reduce his appreciation of her loveliness.

"You're quite a little beauty," he said admiringly.

The smile widened, and the shine in her eyes grew warmer.

"That was good last night—without a lot of talking," he told her.

"You communicate very well without words, dear," she answered.

He reached out to pat her head.

"We're going to get along fine," he predicted.

She put her hands around his neck, and they kissed.

"Just fine," she agreed a moment later.

They kissed again, and probably would have returned to bed if both hadn't realized that the waiter would soon interrupt with the wheeled breakfast cart. Their estimate of the Drake's room service proved correct, for she had barely donned a sheer yellow robe and finished her face washing and hair combing when they heard the discreet rap-rap at the door. Tabbat added a 20 percent tip to the bill before he signed it, and at 11:20 the two secret agents sat down to enjoy a cozy breakfast. It wasn't until they finished their grapefruit that she noticed the look in his eyes had changed.

"You're working," she guessed.

"Most of the time."

"On a national holiday like the 4th of July, Gregg?"

"That's how you get ahead in business," he explained as he reached for the apricot jam.

"Can I help?"

"You could pour another cup of coffee. . . . Thanks."

He added sugar to the black-brown brew, sipped and sighed.

"I wasn't trying to put you down, Barb," he explained between bites of the jam-covered toast, "but I can't quite figure out who's going to find this son of a bitch for me. Try the jam. It's excellent."

She obeyed, nodded in agreement.

"Why don't you offer a reward?" she suggested archly.

"To whom? Don't worry. I'll work it out in a day or two.

Maybe he's taking the day off himself. Maybe he's at the beach, or watching some patriotic parade in Boston or Philadelphia. He's crazy enough to do anything."

Dalchimski wasn't at any beach, and he wasn't observing any parades. He was taking a shower in a room in the "good section" of the Beverly-Wilshire Hotel—the new part, not the section that faced onto Wilshire. He'd spent the previous night in a motel near Chicago's O'Hare Airport, and he found this hotel much more pleasant. He'd always wanted to visit glamorous Beverly Hills to see the beautiful women and ostentatious decadence, and now that he was here he felt sorry that he could only remain for one day. Still, he couldn't violate his rule never to stay anywhere for more than twenty-four hours since the K.G.B. had undoubtedly discovered that the Book was gone and was surely searching for him. They'd be sweating back there in Moscow, he thought happily. They'd be getting more desperate by the hour, more frightened as they wondered helplessly. The panic would be seeping into the Kremlin itself, scourging the cowardly rogues and traitors who had sold out to the West.

While they suffered, Dalchimski finished his shower and got dressed and had breakfast in a hotel coffee shop named Hernando's Hideaway. Afterwards he sunned himself beside the pool, and then swam for forty minutes in water that was just a bit too warm. At 10:35 he returned to his room and dressed to go out for a walk. He sauntered a dozen blocks in the glaring heat before he found a telephone booth. First he piled up a heap of coins, and then he took the small black plastic notebook from his pocket. He was about to dial when he saw the girl. She was standing less than two feet away, a trim blonde in a bare-midriff outfit adorned with some sort of hippie necklace. She grinned at him through the glass of the booth, pointed at the telephone. He opened the door.

"Going to be long, man?"

She had splendid skin and teeth, and was certainly pretty enough to be a starlet.

"Just a minute," Dalchimski assured her.

He closed the door, dialed swiftly.

At six that night Tabbat and his "wife" were watching the *Eyewitness News* on the color T.V. set in their room. The first item was a report of what had happened in Chanute, Kansas, earlier in the afternoon. There had been a series of mysterious explosions at the telephone company's main switching point for the entire nation, knocking out all coast-to-coast circuits and scores of other key lines—including those used by the three big television networks. Roadblocks had been set up within a fifty-mile radius to "apprehend a man observed fleeing the scene on a blue motorcycle," and according to the latest reports state police had the man surrounded on a farm three miles outside the town of Thayer.

"Let's hope they kill him," Tabbat said with startling savagery.

She didn't understand the fury, but she knew enough not to ask any questions. There was a reason for Tabbat's fury. She had no doubt of that. She had no idea that the saboteur had been an artillery captain named Dmitri Krivoy, although not in recent years. Now the screen filled with a not very close view of a house and barn, and an invisible speaker explained that this was an on-the-spot report from Kansas. The camera panned slowly to survey some forty, perhaps fifty, state and local police strung out in a wide ring. Then it zoomed in swiftly for a tight, close view of a window beside the front door. It happened so fast that you had to blink in reaction, and a splitsecond later the crisp, tough, fast-talking reporter was rattling off facts with the urgency of a man who knows that a Volkswagen commercial will run him over in ninety-five seconds. Tabbat leaned forward, cursed. The curtain moved, and a dozen shots sounded as the police resumed their barrage.

"Kill him! Kill him, dammit!" Tabbat demanded.

"That isn't the man you came to find, is it?"

Tabbat shook his head.

He couldn't tell her that the poor bastard was a victim, another one. He couldn't explain why it would be better for everyone—including the saboteur in the house—if police bullets silenced him before he could be interrogated. The Stalinist maniac would be delighted if they took Krivoy alive, and was probably out there somewhere enjoying the entire spectacle on T.V. himself.

This time Tabbat was right. Dalchimski was sprawled on a bed in his air-conditioned room in the Beverly-Wilshire, savoring the scene in full color on a big twenty-one-inch set. When the report from Kansas ended, Dalchimski turned off the television and changed back to his bathing suit. He just had time for another half-hour in the pool before packing for his flight East.

The news would reach Moscow by morning.

They'd sweat.

13

"There has to be a pattern," Tabbat decided as they paused in front of the bookstore window on Fifth Avenue.

"To what?"

He didn't really hear her words. He'd been almost completely remote since they left the Japanese restaurant, listening only to his thoughts as he concentrated on analyzing the situation.

"There has to be a pattern because that's the sort of mind he has. That bastard's the meticulous sort, the kind who always works from a plan. Everything I've learned about him points to that. He's one of those who make lists and schedules —nice and tidy. No, nasty and tidy."

"That man in Kansas—"

"I can't see the pattern though," Tabbat continued inexorably. "It's something nasty and tricky, but I just can't figure it out."

"Happy birthday!" she said cheerfully.

He blinked, looked at her sharply.

"What the hell are you talking about?"

"I thought I'd say something jolly. I didn't realize that you were paying any attention," she replied.

"Sorry. . . . The man in Kansas? Don't worry about him. They've probably killed him by now, or he's killed himself. All for nothing, dammit. Why him? That's the question. Maybe it's a random pattern. Maybe the pattern is no pattern."

He shrugged, swung his attention to the window display.

"There's the book that got the first-page review in the Times," he noted. "I didn't believe it. Who the hell would write a four-hundred-page book titled *Chicano Rabbi?*"

"A Chicano rabbi, Gregg."

"And that other book—the memoirs of the woman who ran the ladies' can in the Senate Office Building for thirty years—that's for real too?"

"I think so. The review made it sound rather amusing."

Tabbat shrugged again.

"Light reading for summer," she explained. "They always publish that sort of thing at this time of year. Good for the beach or wherever you vacation."

He seemed to be focused on large volume titled *I Was Hitler's Chiropodist,* but the glazed stare suggested that Tabbat's thoughts might be elsewhere.

"I may have to change my plan," he announced, and started walking south towards Fifty-sixth Street.

"I didn't know you had a plan."

"If I do, I'll need a lot more money—fast. Ten, maybe twenty—perhaps thirty thousand right away. Can you get it?"

"From the *Rezident,* but I thought that you didn't want to have anything to do with our people here."

"I don't. You'll get the money. If you've been burned by the Americans, well—you can't be burned twice. Either they've spotted you or they haven't. Make it thirty thousand—in twenties and fifties."

Traffic halted for the light, and they sauntered east across Fifth. Her eyes flicked to the dresses in the Bonwit Teller window—very briefly.

"There's a Monday drop," she told him. "If I leave a message there tomorrow morning you might have the cash by Tuesday."

He hesitated, nodded.

"I hate blind drops," he told her, "but we'll have to risk it. Once you leave the message, stay away from me until you pick up the money. Check into another hotel. When you've got the cash, phone me at the Drake and leave word for me to call Mr. . . . Mr. Mark Sheldon. Exactly two hours after you call, start walking south on Fifth from right here—this corner. Down to that cathedral—what's it called?"

"Saint Patrick's?"

"Right. Down to the cathedral, go in to pray for ten minutes. If I don't meet you there, walk west to Thirty Rockefeller Plaza—past the ice skating rink. That's the N.B.C. building, and there's always a bunch of boobs from Buffalo lined up to take the dollar-sixty-five tour. That's your second check-point. I assume that you'll be watching to see whether anybody's tailing you. You can shake them there—in the crowd."

"Is that it?"

"No. There's a charming little bistro over on Seventh Avenue at Forty-eighth, or Forty-ninth. The Metropole—topless go-go dancers shaking their tits for world peace."

"You couldn't make it the Palm Court of the Plaza instead?" she proposed.

"Some other time. Let's get home to bed."

She was smiling again the next morning, but Tabbat couldn't ignore the ghost of a frown that flickered underneath. Perhaps she was nervous about the drop herself, or maybe she didn't relish the prospect of a night away from him. It might help if he showed some interest.

"Where is the Monday drop?" he asked as she buttoned her blouse.

"None of your business."

"Need to know?" he chuckled.

"You're damn right. You're great in the sack, Gregg, but I can't see why you need to know these details of our local operation."

"You can't even be sure I'm the right scuba diver, can you?" he joked.

She thought about it for several seconds.

"There could have been a switch," he challenged.

"I don't think so. Take care of yourself, Gregg."

Her kiss at the door was a bit less passionate than earlier when they'd awakened, but there was enough warmth so that Tabbat could be sure she still believed him. Her complete trust and unquestioning obedience would be essential. He turned on the television set, walked into the bathroom to brush his teeth. Tabbat couldn't understand why anyone brushed before breakfast, for that would leave food particles in one's gums all day. He took care of his gums and the rest of his body as diligently as most people attend to regular maintenance of their cars.

It was as he finished his ablutions and turned off the tap that he heard the bad news. Some N.B.C. reporter completed an account of a skyjacking in Brazil, and then announced that Kansas and federal police were still trying to piece together what had happened in Chanute the previous afternoon. "The suspected saboteur, who was badly wounded in a shoot-out, remains on the critical list at the military hospital at Fort Leavenworth where he was delivered by helicopter last night. He is still unidentified," said the reporter, "but authorities are currently tracing the registration of the blue motorcycle he was driving."

Shit.

Why couldn't he die the way he was supposed to, dammit?

A military hospital—that wasn't going to be easy. If Krivoy survived, there was always the risk that he'd crack. They might use sodium pentothal or some other drug, and then the whole damn story might come pouring out. Even if Krivoy knew nothing of the other agents or their specific targets, the Americans would guess that they existed, so somebody would have to silence Krivoy before he could talk. They'd have him heavily guarded. It would be an extremely difficult, probably suicidal mission.

Shit.

Why didn't he swallow his green pill?

Tabbat finished dressing, walked to Bloomingdale's where

he bought three shirts, additional underwear and socks, a seersucker sport jacket, tan wash-and-wear slacks, white canvas "deck shoes" and brown loafers. On his way out onto Third Avenue he saw some handsome solid-color ties of raw silk, and at $9 each he had to purchase a red one and a blue one for his wardrobe. He told himself that they were just right for his role, and besides they looked better than anything he could buy in Moscow. After dropping off the clothes at the hotel and re-checking the room for those sub-miniature electronic listening devices in which the Americans so proudly excelled, Tabbat wandered not so casually down to St. Patrick's Cathedral to reconnoiter the interior. Although he'd enjoyed the blessings of a sound atheist education, religious institutions didn't bother Tabbat at all. They were—like railroad stations, all-night cafeterias and supermarkets—useful and impersonal places where one might make a "drop" or shake off a "tail." From the cathedral, he took a taxi to the zoo. Well, Grigori Tabbat called it the zoo. It wasn't the one in Central Park or the even bigger one up in the Bronx. In fact, it wasn't a zoo at all in a strict sense. Still the weird people who patrolled and haunted the Forty-second Street block between Broadway and Eighth Avenue were such odd animals that Tabbat felt wholly justified in describing the area as a zoo.

Runaways, addicts, whores of all four sexes, dazed adolescents who seemed either retarded or lost, homeless old women in rags with all their possessions in plastic shopping bags, assorted patrons of pornographic bookstores, alcoholics, raw-boned and acneed hustlers, porky sadomasochists, curious tourists eager to observe the freaks—they blended unpleasantly like garbage in a sewer. Tabbat walked west just quickly enough to discourage any contact, ignoring their eyes and the smell of the pizzas and frying onions until he crossed Eighth Avenue to the gun shop. The window was filled with a strange assortment of weapons, Gurkha knives, British Lee-Enfield rifles and even semi-automatic carbines that appeared to be cousins of the U.S. Army's M-14. Tabbat wanted a hunting rifle with the punch to kill a man at two hundred yards, and he had no difficulty in purchasing a Winchester .270 with a variable Redfield scope that offered magnification up to nine-power. He bought a shoulder-sling gun bag and two boxes of shells, and left without being asked any questions.

In Duluth federal agents were asking Carl Hassler's widow questions—for the ninth time. All of his canceled checks for the past five years were heaped in stacks on the dining room table, and Mrs. Hassler was doing her best to cooperate with these official representatives of her government. She didn't understand why they were so interested in the background of the pilot's life before he married her and why they kept probing about where he'd grown up, but she did her best to answer. After all, her widow's pension under Social Security was going to be important and she couldn't afford to offend anyone connected with Washington. She repeated to them what Carl Hassler had told her, that he'd gone to high school in Minneapolis and learned to fly up in Canada during the two years he'd spent at the University of Toronto.

"Bullshit."

"Just a lot of bullshit," repeated Colonel Thomas Stephen Jenkins in reply to Dorothy Putterman's inquiry about the weekly meeting of an inter-agency intelligence committee that assembled in the Pentagon under the vague title of Working Group Six.

"Anything new on Hot Rod or Cotton Candy?" she asked, referring to the operations by their code names.

"Nothing we didn't already know. Some clown from O.N.I. tried to show off with a report about a sub cruising off Long Island. They had a tape of a radio signal about somebody or something called Romeo. The N.S.A. boys had decoded it and they were mighty proud, but I couldn't get too excited about it."

"You weren't rude?" she wondered solicitously.

"Hell, no. I was just as sweet as pecan pie, honeychile."

She glared. The sly son of a bitch knew she hated that put-on Southern talk, but he simply couldn't control himself. Now he was scanning her new bra. He was hopeless, a social cripple maimed by machismo.

"Army wanted to brag about some Chicom outfit they'd

tagged in Hawaii, and the Air Force had some more pictures they'd shot from a million feet up. That's about all they can do is shoot pictures. Couldn't bomb an outhouse from a hundred yards, but they take great pictures from way up there. Don't worry, I was a real gent. Nodded a lot and looked impressed, and didn't say any of the wrong things. Fed 'em a few crumbs about the new Polish air attaché coming in and that transmitter in Tijuana—just enough to keep them happy."

He winked, gave her that wonderful Boy Scout grin that had helped elect him vice-president of the University of New Mexico's Class of 1959.

"Any messages or crises?" he asked.

"There was a call from Coltrane."

"Nice fellah," judged the colonel as he reached for a cigar.

"Ben Coltrane happens to be a total turd as well as the personal assistant to the Director of Central Intelligence."

Jenkins lit the cigar, nodded.

"That's what I said—nice fellah. What did he want?"

"He said that the D.C.I. wanted to know whether we had any word from your cousin."

Jenkins puffed twice.

"What did you tell him, Dorothy?"

"That we'd keep him informed."

"Gooood. Say, you don't mind me calling you Dorothy, do you?"

"Names don't mean much to me. It's relationships and respect that count."

The colonel nodded again.

"I'm with you. I didn't want you to think that I was getting too personal," he explained.

Then he took another radar sweep of the new bra.

14

Tabbat didn't take the rifle back to the Drake. He found an Avis office on West Forty-second Street, waved his magic American Express talisman of blue plastic and charmed the dimpled blonde behind the counter into surrendering an air-conditioned Dodge wagon. After he locked the gun and shells in a concealed compartment in the rear section, Tabbat drove off into the steamy pollution with a cheery "Hiyo, Silver!" Even though the blonde was taking night courses in avant-garde theatre and child psychology, she would never guess that the Lone Ranger was a Cossack—on his mother's side.

He went shopping, spreading his purchases among many stores as a routine precaution. An hour and a half after he rented the Dodge, he checked into the Howard Johnson motel on Eighth Avenue with a new suitcase filled with his acquisitions. Unlike most visitors, who wished to avoid the traffic noise, he asked for a second-floor room—lying about a fear of elevators. If he had to flee, Tabbat was in good enough condition to drop that far with only minor discomfort. This room would be his "safe house"—an alternate base of operations in case something made the Drake dangerous. He opened the valise, removed the four Motorola walkie-talkies, the battery-powered AM-FM radio and the $210 shortwave receiver. After he put away the extra set of toilet articles and the work clothes, he picked up the tool kit and started modifying the AM-FM unit. When he had fixed it so that he could pick up the frequencies used by the F.B.I., he listened for several minutes before he smiled in satisfaction. Then he set out for the range on West Twentieth Street.

It was almost dawn in Moscow, and the two men in Strelski's office overlooking Kropotkin Street were puffy-faced with fatigue. The room stank of cigar smoke. Even the general was vaguely depressed by the odor now, so he opened a window.

"That's better," Strelski said as he sucked in the fresh air. "The place smells like a Polish whorehouse."

"It has for the past three hours," answered Malchenko.

The general nodded, took another deep breath.

"Yes, that's a lot better . . . You think I smoke too many cigars, Aleksei?"

Malchenko managed to shrug.

"I think we ought to make a decision about that poor bastard in Kansas," he replied, "although it probably doesn't matter."

Strelski rubbed his eyes, then fingered the stubble on his chin.

"Of course it matters," he replied irritably. "We've been sweating this mess all night. It matters a great deal."

The colonel stood up, walked to the window and stood beside his old comrade-in-arms. He inhaled several times, grunted.

"You're right that it smells a lot better here, Pyotr," he said, "but you're wrong about the other thing. He's probably made the decision by now. Decisions are one of the things he's good at, you know."

"Who the hell are you talking about?"

"Tabbat . . . I wonder why expensive Cuban cigars should make the place smell like a Polish whorehouse. It's terrible, just terrible."

Strelski turned, stared at him as if he were six feet instead of six inches away.

"Tabbat has decided *what*?" he demanded harshly.

"*Who* should kill him! The only question is whether Tabbat should do it himself or call in someone else for the job. We'll never get Krivoy out of an Army hospital, and it wouldn't be worth the effort anyway."

"What do you think he'll decide?" Strelski asked.

The crack of the Winchester echoed loudly. The shooting range on West Twentieth Street was almost new and built with the latest sound-absorbent materials, but the battering sound of the rifle still jarred everyone in the chamber. Tabbat adjusted the sight slightly, fired again.

Bull's-eye.

Dead center.

He looked into the open box, saw another magazine. The Winchester was sighted in now, but he would shoot again and again just to make certain that the .270 was precisely "tuned." He reloaded, aimed and fired.

Bull's-eye.

Bull's-eye.

Bull's-eye.

Bull's-eye.

Bull's-eye.

The shiny shell cases littered the floor at his feet.

"Nice shooting," said the bald man in the tan sport shirt.

Tabbat couldn't hear him because of the ear-protecting headset, so he squeezed the trigger again.

Bull's-eye, and the magazine was empty. He took off the "ear muffs" now, and heard the man speak again.

"Very nice shooting, especially with a gun like that. What do you hunt with it?"

"Bear . . . werewolves . . . alligators. I just fool around," the K.G.B. agent responded with his finest All-American grin. It was pure country boy, worthy of a shaving cream commercial. There wasn't a professional football player in the nation who could beat it, and only a handful who'd even tie it.

There were the amenities, and as a serious shooter Tabbat felt obliged to respect them. You simply didn't leave those shell cases, no matter how wealthy you might be. You picked up the cases to reload—to reload very carefully—if you were a serious marksman, and even if you weren't so meticulous that you reloaded your own shells, you'd save the casings for another shooter who did. Only a goon wouldn't, so Tabbat half-filled the empty box and handed it to a range employee on the way out a few minutes later.

Then he returned to his room in the Howard Johnson Motor Inn, washed up and checked his watch. It was nearly time—his time. If Moscow had a message for him, it would come in exactly three minutes on the prearranged frequency in the daily shortwave news broadcast. Tabbat turned on the Hallicrafter receiver, found the frequency and waited for the "futbol" scores that would end the news. He listened carefully, nodded.

"Thank you very much," he replied in courteous acknowledgment. "Yes, I'll take care of it promptly," he said to the room as he took a sheet of writing paper from the desk drawer. He made a list of the names of the Telefon operatives who'd already been triggered, and then glanced at the U.S. road map he'd picked up at the gas station on the way in from East Hampton.

"Colorado . . . Maine . . . Wisconsin . . . Kansas," he identified as his finger tapped the places where the defector had struck. There was a pattern here somewhere, but he couldn't see it. He looked at the list of the American cover names of the agents, then at the column that held the names they'd been born with in the Soviet Union. Nothing. He tore the sheet of paper into pieces, burned it and flushed the ashes down the toilet. At four o'clock he turned on the other radio— the one that picked up commercial stations—and found WCBS. WCBS was a great convenience, for it offered a steady stream of news around the clock with five minutes of network news on the hour. Unlike some American politicians, Grigori Tabbat trusted network news broadcasts—especially those on CBS. It was one of the strange and amusing charms of the United States: you could believe the network news.

"The Senate hearings will resume tomorrow at ten A.M. . . . From Kansas, CBS correspondent Tom Ralston reports on the latest developments in the puzzling case of the Chanute saboteur."

Tabbat lit a cigarette, hunched forward intently.

"Two days after someone blew up the main switching circuits of the telephone company's long-lines operation and knocked out much of U.S. television, authorities here are still trying to find out more about the man who apparently did it.

Stuart Diller, who was gravely wounded by police in a shoot-
out after fleeing the scene of the explosions on a blue motorcycle, is still unconscious and under heavy guard. That much is
definite. Efforts to locate Diller's family or possible associates
have run into a stone wall, and some police doubt whether his
real name is Diller. The Federal Bureau of Investigation has
refused to discuss the case, standard F.B.I. procedure in situations where an investigation has not been completed. While a
large task force of federal agents—at least twenty, it appears—
continues the probe, local police and citizens openly wonder
who the man everyone knew as Stuart Diller is and why would
he commit such a crime. Sunday School teachers just don't go
around blowing up things, and Diller had been a Baptist
Sunday School teacher for eleven years. . . ."

The man who walked out of the sea heard the first few
words of the latest warlike manifesto from Cairo, flicked off the
radio impatiently.

"A Sunday School teacher?" he wondered bitterly. Somebody in Moscow had a grotesque sense of humor, and this was
the sort of joke that didn't move Tabbat at all. It was cheap
and adolescent. It certainly didn't bear Colonel Malchenko's
touch, and was probably the work of some smirking junior
officer who'd handled minor details. There was really no point
in getting agitated, however, since Krivoy might well die before
anyone could question him.

And then he might not.

Tabbat picked up the telephone book, found the number of
T.W.A. and dialed. After eleven rings a cheery-cheery voice
answered.

"T.W.A. Miss Bleich. May I help you?"

He asked her about flights to Leavenworth, was told that
the nearest city T.W.A. served was Wichita. The airline offered
five flights a day to Wichita from LaGuardia Airport, plus two
others from Newark.

"Can I book you a seat, sir?" asked the reservations clerk
courteously.

"I hope not," Tabbat replied truthfully a moment before he
slammed down the phone.

He really should have given Miss Bleich a chance to say

"Thank you for calling T.W.A.," he realized as he took another look at the terrible framed print across the room. She'd undoubtedly been trained to say "Thank you for calling T.W.A." by the same conscientious people who taught her not to pick up the phone until it had rung nineteen times. There were such people in the personnel departments of airlines around the world. Miss Bleich was probably frustrated, perhaps even hurt. She'd been cheery-cheery, and he'd behaved badly.

"Up yours, Miss Bleich," he said maliciously and he felt just a little bit better.

15

Some thirty-odd years ago there was a global struggle which some people called the Great War. Each generation seems to enjoy its own Great War, of course, which is rather stupid since there's nothing that great about any war. Well, during the Great War of thirty years ago—often referred to as World War II—significant numbers of miserable draftees spoke of a certain U.S. Army base in Alabama as the Ass-Hole of the Universe. This lyrical description was founded on pride of ownership, and glum young men sweating at other military installations in Mississippi and Arkansas often claimed that same glorious title for their own training centers. To keep the record straight, it should be noted that certain lads conscripted out of the better colleges were somewhat more circumspect, and merely stated that if God wanted to give the world an enema, this was where he would stick it in.

All of the bases competing for the honor were extremely hot and humid. Now Fort Leavenworth isn't at all humid, but it is so boiling and so dusty that it should be rated a worthy contender for any divine efforts in the field of proctology. Set out on the searing plains of Kansas, it is one of

those unbelievable places that only a deranged cavalryman
would select for a base. Fort Leavenworth was once a cavalry
base, but the horses have long since been replaced by aspiring
and perspiring majors and light colonels attending the Command and General Staff School. Even with the fairly modern
buildings and the excellent air conditioning, summer is a
grisly experience at Fort Leavenworth and can be justified only
as a character-building exercise. This afternoon—as Tabbat
paced his motel room in New York—the outside temperature
at Fort Leavenworth was 101.

It was a more comfortable 70 degrees within the hospital,
but no one in Room 211 appreciated the difference. The man
in the bed was in acute discomfort. He had several terrible
abdominal wounds as well as bullet holes in his chest and
right shoulder and his left ear had been shot off. The various
tubes and pipes plugged into his semi-conscious body didn't
help. Still, of the seven other people in Room 211, only Gloria
McInerney and Herbert B. Peyser cared about his distress. She
was a tall thin nurse with delightfully blue Irish eyes, and
Peyser was a major and a surgeon with a wife who couldn't
understand why neither the Juilliard String Quartet nor Jean-
Pierre Rampal ever gave concerts in this part of Kansas.

Shea certainly didn't care. Ted Shea was the earnest and
practical F.B.I. man who ran the Wichita Bureau, short on
hair but brighter than most people guessed. If Shea didn't care,
Monk surely didn't. Charles Monk was a boyish Tennesseean
who worked under Shea, and he was loyal. The rangy Counter-
Intelligence Corps colonel whose name-tag said "Frohlich"
was completely focused on a report he was reading, and his
aide—a black lieutenant who'd been fifth in his class at West
Point—was much too busy with his tape recorder to consider
the patient. As for the seventh person, his face and eyes showed
no emotion. He had his own tape recorder and documents
that identified him as Assistant Chief of Security of the telephone company, Mr. Arnold Thayer of New York City.

The man in the bed made a low guttural sound that was
barely audible, and the others all looked at the electronic gad-
get whose screen displayed the patient's heartbeat as a series
of moving white dots. The senior F.B.I. man frowned.

"Don't let him die," Shea ordered.

Major-Doctor Peyser shrugged. Perhaps his mother had been right. It might have been wiser to go into psychiatry. He'd have a nice two-couch office on Park Avenue by now as well as a summer and weekend house in the Berkshires. He wouldn't have to cope with colonels or federal agents.

"We're doing our best," Peyser replied with as much courtesy as he could mobilize. He was tired, fed up and quite uncertain as to whether the patient would survive.

"He mustn't die before we talk to him," insisted Shea. His aide nodded in devout agreement.

"What do you think, Major?" asked the C.I.C. colonel.

"Don't know. Damn miracle he's still breathing this long. You gents really shot the crap out of him, didn't you?"

"Listen, Major—"

"Constitution of a bull," Peyser continued. "Ordinary man would have checked out hours ago."

Then the man in the bed spoke—one word.

"Edna," he sighed.

The military intelligence men and the F.B.I. team pressed closer, but he said nothing more.

"Edna?" repeated Shea. "Now what the hell does that mean?"

Nurse McInerney, who did wonders for her uniform and a certain X-ray specialist whose wife didn't appreciate him fully, considered the question—briefly.

"Don't know," she replied with the truthfulness that was such a source of pride to her mother back in Brooklyn.

"Couldn't be his wife," contributed Frohlich alertly. "She's dead, three years now."

"Her name was *Betty*," the younger F.B.I. man pointed out scornfully.

The nurse looked unimpressed.

"His birth certificate and high school diploma and discharge papers from the Navy are all *fakes*," the black lieutenant whispered to her.

She was still unimpressed.

"Edna," repeated the gravely wounded man who'd blown up the telephone switching center.

The full phrase in the Telefon Book was "Edna Norris says you want to sell your cottage," but the only person in the room to whom those words meant anything was in neither the mood nor the condition to explain them. The dots on the oscilloscope screen showed no improvement in the heartbeat.

"Hang in there, baby," urged Major Peyser. "I'd like some of the rest of you to clear out now."

"This case may involve *national security*," protested Shea.

"We're staying too," Colonel Frohlich announced righteously.

"You've got to keep him alive, Doctor," the senior F.B.I. man insisted. "We've got to talk to him. He may have been part of some vicious *conspiracy*."

"Like James Earl Ray?" wondered the nurse.

Both of the federal agents shook their heads very slowly and soberly, plainly disappointed. Then Shea and the colonel departed, each leaving behind his aide to watch and to listen and to protect his interests. The black officer sat beside the bed, tape recorder at the ready. He knew that the attaché case of the younger F.B.I. agent contained another recorder—probably a Nagra or a Uher—and he wondered why it had to be concealed.

"Going to get something to eat," announced the man from the phone company ten minutes later as he rose and reached for the door. That was true. He was hungry, but his name wasn't Arnold Thayer and he didn't live or work in New York. As a matter of fact, he wasn't employed by the American Telephone & Telegraph Co. or any of its divisions, branches, affiliates, subsidiaries or holding companies. He worked for an even more gothic and monolithic organization that was much less tolerant of error.

They *never* gave your dime back, even if it was their fault.

They had terrible personnel policies too.

They killed people, all sorts of people, for mistakes.

At this moment they were deciding what to do about the patient in Room 211 of the U.S. Army Hospital at Fort Leavenworth, Kansas—where the outdoor temperature had just risen to 103.

16

The grenade arched through the air, and four men died.

The heavy machine gun in the bushes hammered like some pneumatic drill, scything another five in the first burst.

The second chopped down three more.

Now a whole salvo of grenades burst among them, one detonating a truckload of ammunition with a terrific explosion. The lead car in the column crashed into the ditch, its driver gutted by .50-caliber slugs and fire flickering perilously at its fuel tank. A machine gunner on a half-track was firing back at the attackers, but Tabbat knew that he'd be picked off in a moment. He was. The Japanese never fared too well in these low-budget movies about heroic U.S. and Philippine guerrillas in World War II, and this picture was no exception.

It was stupid to watch such junk at 11 A.M., but Tabbat had no stomach for game shows or kiddie cartoons and he'd never enjoyed *I Love Lucy* that much. He flicked off the television set just in time to catch the eleven o'clock news on the radio. There was no further word about the wounded saboteur. Of course that didn't mean anything. The F.B.I. might be playing it cute. They might have wormed plenty from the poor bastard by now, using drugs that counter-espionage organizations on both sides of the Iron Curtain applied routinely.

Then there was the *Rezident* in Washington. Tabbat had no illusions about the sort of people who rose to senior positions in intelligence agencies, but this man who ran the K.G.B. network in the U.S. from his "cover job" at the embassy was one of the few people Tabbat actively disliked. It wasn't that he was devious and ruthless, for Tabbat expected a K.G.B. *Rezident* to be devious and ruthless—but this Armenian was too ambitious. He was surely aware of the dangerous situation at Leavenworth, and there was no telling what he might attempt. If his achievements during the three years he'd served as *Rezident* in Istanbul were any clue, the man who passed as the Assistant Cultural Attaché was likely to do something violent.

When?

How long would he wait?

How much time did Tabbat have?

Tabbat glanced at his watch, descended to the bustling lobby and used a pay phone to call the Drake. There was a message from Mr. Mark Sheldon, who'd called at 10:40. Good. She would start down Fifth Avenue at 12:40, and the midday crowds of shoppers and office workers on their way to lunch would provide a useful screen. He had no doubt that she'd be both prompt and careful, for all his instincts told him that Barbi's skills went beyond the bedroom.

She was on time. At 12:30 she emerged from the Doubleday bookstore between Fifty-sixth and Fifty-seventh with a package under her arm. The middle-aged guard at the door to thwart shoplifters found her round rump and miniskirt so intriguing that he couldn't help smiling, and he missed seeing a white-haired gentleman pilfer a $25 "art book" of erotic sculptures of India. She missed nothing, for her eyes were sweeping back and forth like a warship's radar as she sauntered south to the Hallmark Card Shop at the corner. She wandered into the store—still checking for watchers. After five minutes of not-so-aimless wandering through the displays, she left and crossed to the east side of Fifth Avenue at 12:39. One minute later she started walking downtown.

The street was crowded despite the midday summer heat, alive with executives, office workers, affluent tourists chatting in seven tongues including Texan, and a few chic ladies en route to lunch at Brussels, "21" or Caravelle. Pausing now and then to scan the Puccis and Guccis in the windows, the secret agent who called herself Barbi Gordon used each stop to search for furtive followers. She escaped the heat for two minutes by stepping into the Air France office for a brochure, and then walked on past the cathedral to enjoy five cool minutes studying the new perfumes available at Saks. At 1:05 she walked up the steps of the great church and entered St. Patrick's. She dipped to one knee and crossed herself and did all the things a good Catholic should, although she was neither good nor a Catholic.

At 1:15 she walked out into the glare of July in New York, keeping a firm grip on the package and weaving through the crowd like some skillful football player. She made her way between the tall buildings on Fifth, down past the offices of El Al Israel Airlines to the sunken skating rink that was now abloom with umbrella-shaded tables as a summer restaurant. She pressed on to 30 Rockefeller Plaza, and found in the lobby the crowd of tourists waiting to tour the N.B.C. television studios. It was just as Tabbat had promised, and she could see no hint of American surveillance. Unlike the man who'd come ashore at East Hampton, she wasn't worried about the *Rezident* at all. She was confident that he wouldn't interfere, but the C.I.A. or F.B.I. were another matter. They could be trouble, could menace the entire operation.

Through the crowd and out the south door on Forty-ninth, she strode west past the jewelry stores and the cheap hotels and the whores in the doorways to Seventh Avenue. She took one glance at the sign promising topless beauties, entered the dark cave that was the Metropole. A three-piece band was blasting rock, using its amplifiers like Indian clubs to assault the dozen men seated at the long bar. Two young women were dancing gracefully but mechanically. One was a blonde of about twenty-one or two, a slim girl in gold bikini-panties and matching shoes. The other entertainer was three or four years older, darker and bustier. Both were sort of smiling, topless and agile.

Tabbat wasn't smiling. He was on a stool at the far end of the bar, one eye on the teats of the brunette and the other zeroed in on the door. He saw the husky assistant manager moving towards his courier, waved to her before the man could say "No unescorted ladies" or anything else. She joined him at the bar.

"Having a good time?" she asked archly.

"You've got the line wrong," he told her and sipped his vodka and tonic. "It's supposed to be 'Show you a good time,' isn't it?"

She shook her head.

"Drink?" Tabbat offered.

"Does it have to be here?"

"I think so—unless you want to attract attention by leaving so fast. Try a vodka tonic."

It wasn't that bad.

"You've been in here before, I gather?" she asked-derided after a few sips.

"Yes. I've been in topless bars, saunas, mosques, bowling alleys, morgues, cat houses, progressive kindergartens, shrines, lesbian joints, oil refineries, convents, pizza parlors and mental institutions—love 'em all. This is one of the better topless bars in New York. You can recommend it to your friends and family."

The trio was improving the chord structure of "Spinning Wheel"—spoke by spoke. The dancers were undaunted, the men at the bar delighted. "They really shake tit," said one to his companion who chuckled at his witty observation. Tabbat paid the fleshy female bartender, guided a grateful Barbi out and west to his motel room.

"You're not so good, you know," she accused as she put down the package and began to remove her blouse.

"I'm very good. You getting ready for bed?"

"I *saw* you. Spotted you at Fifty-third Street."

He shrugged, took off his jacket and tie.

"Don't be an idiot, Gregg. I've got your cash here in a money belt, dammit. Count it."

He counted it . . . very carefully . . . twice. He didn't trust her on general principles, and he had excellent and specific reasons not to trust that sneaky Armenian *Rezident*.

"It's all here. Thanks. Any problems?"

She shook her head, sat down on the edge of the bed.

"Did he ask questions?" demanded Tabbat.

"Sure, but he didn't get any answers. Can we get something to eat now?"

"Afterwards," he promised, and then they undressed completely.

"You are very good," she admitted half an hour later as they lay in each other's arms.

"So are you. Let's have lunch."

He kissed her again, and it wasn't until they were finishing their rum cake desserts at the neighborhood Italian restaurant that he mentioned what Miss Bleich had reported about flights to Wichita.

17

Wichita is not a jerkwater cow-town, hasn't been for forty or fifty years. That Wichita you saw in the old cowboy movie—Joel McCrea, wasn't it?—hasn't existed for a long time. Today's Wichita is the dynamic heart of Sedgwick County, with a population of some 280,000 fine people and regular service by four airlines. It has five hotel-motels, three on East Kellogg and two on West Kellogg. When the Joffrey Ballet spent three days at the Wichita Symphony's Century II Concert Hall in 1974, the *Prairie Journal* gave them a fine review and Loren Reyher of the *Wichita Eagle and Beacon* reported, "Wichita became an exuberant, scintillating axis of music and motion." The coverage by KAKE-TV and KARD-TV was simply outstanding.

Unfortunately, Mr. and Mrs. Gregg Gordon didn't get to enjoy the many advantages of today's Wichita. Within half an hour after the T.W.A. jet touched down at the Wichita Airport, the K.G.B. team was in a rented car en route to Leavenworth. Now there's no point in knocking Leavenworth. Leavenworth, which has a distinguished federal penitentiary and a population of twenty-five thousand, doesn't pretend to be a cultural center like Wichita. The Cody Hotel at Fourth and Shawnee has eighty-four rooms, sensible rates and an ex-colonel as the manager. The beds are good and the air conditioning works, and double rooms rent for $18—European plan.

The drive east—northeast, to be precise—from Wichita was uneventful. Some people might call it boring. The woman who sat beside Tabbat was one of them. Actually, that description was inadequate and unfair to a wonderful state. It was hot and boring.

"Why didn't we fly into Topeka?" she asked about eighty miles out of Wichita.

Tabbat turned on the radio, dialed without much hope and was not surprised. He couldn't find one station playing Sinatra.

"Shit," he said dispassionately.

"What?"

"I've got nothing against Charley Pride or Elton John," he continued truthfully. "A lot of people like country and rock, I suppose."

"Topeka is much nearer to Leavenworth than Wichita is," she noted.

He nodded.

"No direct air service from New York," he explained, "and I've got a hunch that it might be safer coming in from the west. Just a hunch."

"I'm not arguing with you, Gregg."

"Didn't think you were. Topeka's not too bad, you understand. *Three* Holiday Inns—quite civilized."

"Would you mind if I don't laugh?" she asked as she lit a cigarette.

He took his right hand from the wheel of the Dodge, patted her thigh with possessive affection.

"Don't sweat it, honey," he advised. "I'm just as uptight as you are. It's going to be a tough hit, and hitting people has never been my favorite sport. . . . Want to stop to powder your kidneys?"

She couldn't help grimacing at this awful jest. They stopped for coffee and toilet facilities at a roadside diner, then drove on directly to the Cody. The room was cool and clean, and some thoughtful person had left a copy of *The Leavenworth Times* on the double bed. They began to unpack.

"Home, home on the range," he sang softly as he hung up his blazer. "That's the state song," he added.

"And the state flower's the sunflower," she replied.

"What about the bird?"

"The Western Meadow Lark."

"*Very* good, hon. You've got a wonderful mind," he complimented.

She had just removed her dress and was standing in her mini-briefs, so it was difficult to tell whether he meant it. Well, it was her assignment to keep him happy. She blew him a kiss.

"Wheat, sorghum, cattle, aircraft, oil and helium are some of the main products of Kansas," she recited in schoolgirl tones.

"Fabulous. What can you tell me about Fort Leavenworth?"

She faced him squarely.

"It's got one helluva military cemetery—where you might get space if you blow this," she warned.

"Where *we* might share space," he corrected. "Don't worry. We won't. I'm not suicidal. If we can't do it without a decent chance of walking out, we'll split. Did I tell you my plan?"

"I didn't know you had one."

"Honey, I've always got a plan. Sometimes two."

But he didn't tell her what it was that night, nor did he explain it the next morning before he left with the cardboard box. It was 6 P.M. before he returned, carrying the same flat container.

"I was getting worried," she confessed.

He patted her head.

"I think we've got a chance. Spent the day at the fort, and I managed to get into that hospital."

He pointed at the box.

"Rented a lieutenant's uniform from a costume outfit in New York," he reported. "In my soldier suit I had no trouble getting into the base—and out—on the Army shuttle bus. They could improve their security at the gate. Hospital was a bit tougher, but I went in the back."

"Where is he?"

"Second floor. They've got security up there. Two M.P.s at the head of the corridor, and a couple of men in civilian clothes outside his room. F.B.I., I suppose. I sure hope they're F.B.I.," Tabbat brooded.

"Why?"

"If they're F.B.I., then everybody probably thinks our boy's just a nut or weirdo radical. But if those men aren't F.B.I., we could be up to our collective ass in trouble. They could be C.I.A., and that would mean that somebody's starting to suspect something."

He sat down, took off his shoes and then his shirt. His undershirt was damp with sweat, and he shivered in the powerful air conditioning.

"Hard to tell about the goddam C.I.A.," he grumbled. "Bastards work in all sorts of outfits—sometimes in Army uniforms. The law says they can't operate inside the continental United States, but they don't give a shit. No respect for anything or anybody. Bunch of goddam gangsters."

She took two beers from the refrigerator, opened them and looked for glasses. He reached out impatiently, drank from the can like a truck driver.

"That's good. Thanks. Hot as hell out there," he said.

"They're probably F.B.I., Gregg."

He shook his head, sipped again and wiped the foam from his lips.

"F.B.I.'s no picnic either, and if they are F.B.I. you can bet your ass there are more than two around. They travel in herds, ten or twenty—sometimes more," he reminded her.

He shuddered again.

"Ninety-seven goddam degrees out there," he complained, "but they won't sweat. F.B.I. men don't sweat. They're a special breed, like those creepy turkeys that are all white meat. . . . Well, someone will have to go in for the hit. He's still on the critical list, and the shades are closed. Best damn sniper in the world couldn't touch him, and I don't believe in farting around with his medicine or oxygen. That may work in the movies, but it isn't safe in real life. Thousand things could go wrong."

He emptied the aluminum can, squeezed it out of shape. He walked to the refrigerator, started on a second beer.

"Nothing fancy. Clever—but not fancy," he reasoned aloud. After several seconds he looked at her appraisingly.

"Could *you* do it?"

"I've had the course," she answered.

"All that fancy crap with cyanide bullets and poison darts?" he challenged. "This'll have to be much quicker and cruder. An icepick, or maybe a hypo full of air. Yeah, that might be best. Air bubble, no trace. . . . You ever hit anyone?"

"Once."

He saw the expression in her eyes.

"And you didn't like it. Well, hon, nobody normal does. Only the psychos like it. Can you do it again?"

"If I have to. . . . If you say it's necessary, Gregg."

"I think it is. A woman—a woman in a nurse's uniform— might get in there a lot easier."

"Tonight?"

He shook his head.

"That's when they're expecting trouble. No. Tomorrow, in broad daylight. Lots of people moving around. One more nurse is less likely to be spotted. . . . Okay?"

She hesitated for a full ten seconds.

"Okay," she finally answered.

"You scared?"

"Yes."

"That's good. You ought to be. Now let's talk about that nurse's uniform."

It took two days to find out about the exact room and to secure the uniform. She used the same trick, entering Fort Leavenworth on an Army shuttle bus. By the time she walked into the hospital she was no longer frightened—only tense. All the training she'd had took over, and now she was a professional intelligence agent on a mission. When she got to the second floor, she found a telephone and dialed Room 211.

"Allison," said the nurse in the wounded man's room.

"Major Walker here. Would you please report to the Personnel Office? I'll send up Lieutenant Russo to take over for fifteen minutes," said the spy.

Four minutes later "Lieutenant Mary Russo" entered Room 211. Unlike the armed guards outside the door, she perspired —but she did what she had come to do. Less than fifty minutes later, she was seated in the rented car beside Tabbat as he drove towards the Topeka airport. She stared silently out the window at the highway traffic.

"Don't brood about it," he advised. "You did what you had to do, and it was important. He'd probably have checked out anyway."

"That wasn't what I was thinking about. I was thinking about why you sent *me* to kill him instead of doing it yourself."

"I told you why."

"Balls. You sent me because it wouldn't matter to your manhunt if I got caught—because you think *you're* more important," she accused.

"Because my mission is more important," he corrected coolly, "and because you couldn't complete the mission and I have to. Don't look so furious, hon. I never promised you a rose garden."

"You never promised me anything, you son of a bitch. . . . Well, maybe he would have died anyway. He was probably terminal."

Tabbat sighed, shrugged.

"We're all terminal, Barbi. From the minute we're born, we're all terminal."

"And some are more terminal than others," she completed. "Okay, what do we do now?"

On the horizon a transport plane was starting its descent into the Topeka landing pattern.

"Now we try to find the homicidal maniac who caused this mess," Tabbat replied without the slightest idea as to how they would do so. He turned on the radio, heard the strong voice and smiled.

Tony Bennett.

Not Sinatra, but very fine in his own way.

Like Tabbat, one of the best in his business.

A dedicated pro, with a lot of style and talent.

The record ended, and the news broadcast reported that the suspected saboteur had died of his wounds in the Fort Leavenworth Military Hospital. At least the vicious *Rezident* hadn't meddled in his usual violent way, Tabbat thought, and no one would know that the two K.G.B. agents had even been in the area. There was nothing to alarm the U.S. counterespionage units about the death. Tabbat drove on, wondering where and when Dalchimski would strike next. It would be soon, he reckoned.

He was right.

18

Quite a few people were pleased by news of the death of the saboteur who'd once been Captain Dmitri Krivoy.

That's the kind of world we live in—brutal.

Among those delighted by the demise was the man who'd pretended to be Arnold Foster, and he didn't conceal his enthusiasm when he called his superior more than twelve hundred miles away.

"Doug? This is Arnie. It's all over here," he reported in cheerful tones.

"You sure?"

"*Dead* sure."

"That's not very funny," said the intelligence supervisor whose name wasn't Doug, "but I guess it'll do. Was there any trouble?"

"I don't think so. I don't think they know what happened."

"And he didn't say anything more?"

"Not a word. Can I clear out of here?"

"The sooner the better. I'll pass the word along."

When the *Rezident* heard the news, he grinned and drank two double-shots of mediocre Crimean brandy before he coded the message for relay to Moscow. He would have preferred a good French cognac such as Remy Martin, but he was one of those super-patriots always eager to demonstrate his rabid loyalty to the Motherland. In any case, the dispatch reached the Third Bureau of the K.G.B. the next morning and there was relief and joy on Kropotkin Street.

"I knew that we could count on Tabbat," celebrated General Strelski exuberantly.

"Pyotr—you've never trusted him at all," Malchenko corrected.

"No, I've always despised him as a human being—but I've respected him professionally."

"And do you still despise him?"

Strelski looked puzzled.

"Of course," he responded without a moment's hesitation. "He's decadent, devious and has practically no principles at all."

Malchenko waved away the curl of cigar smoke creeping towards him from across Strelski's massive desk.

"An almost perfect agent," teased the ex-infantryman.

"A son of a bitch."

"I'm glad we agree on definitions."

There were also a number of people who were much less enthusiastic about the death of the saboteur. Most of them were at the U.S. Army Hospital in Fort Leavenworth, Kansas. Most disappointed of all was the head of the Wichita Bureau of the Federal Bureau of Investigation, for it was going to be unpleasant to explain how the "suspect" had perished during the few minutes that the agent on duty had stepped into the adjacent lavatory. The F.B.I. would have been even more troubled if Colonel Frohlich had shared the hospital's report about the phone call and the nonexistent "Lieutenant Mary Russo." The colonel shrewdly suspected that Nurse Allison might have invented the yarn to slip out for a fast smoke or a quick grope with her lover, and even if she hadn't, Frohlich was confident that the Counter-Intelligence Corps could/would find the truth without those cocky and super-critical F.B.I. types. The autopsy had shown no signs of poison, strangulation, blunt or pointed instruments, but Frohlich was certain that the F.B.I. eager-beavers would come up with some wild theory of foul play.

While the conscientious colonel sought to protect the reputation of the Army, the F.B.I. was still very much on the case. In its own official prose, the investigation of the late Stuart Diller was continuing and a certain Assistant Director of the F.B.I. was pondering some of the "data." He was pondering and wondering, weighing why Stuart Diller's papers and identity were fake and why the papers of that other man who'd attacked the Army base near Denver were fakes of the same high quality.

There could be a connection.

It might even be a *conspiracy*, perhaps a radical conspiracy involving an *extremist* group of interracial *terrorists*. One of the things the F.B.I. did best was to uncover and destroy conspiracies, and the capable new head of the Bureau agreed that this "case" seemed to offer "a real challenge." The Assistant Director correctly translated those words to mean that the F.B.I. would plough ahead energetically on its own, without giving Army's heavy handed G-2 or C.I.C. too much opportunity to meddle or hog the credit. The fact that the F.B.I. and the Army weren't sharing all they knew wasn't extraordinary, and—while nothing to cheer about—reflected the traditional rivalries between and within government agencies and schools and business firms in many lands. In the words of Beaudelaire, there are schmucks everywhere.

Including Huntington, West Virginia. Of course the percentage of schmucks in Huntington is no greater—or less—than in Nashville, Tennessee (known as Music City, U.S.A.) or Beckenham, Kent, at the edge of London, or Kawasaki, Japan, where the good times ride. One of the many solid and responsible residents in Huntington was a building contractor named Malcolm James Bryans, a rugged man who stood six-feet-one-inch tall and no nonsense. Mal Bryans had been a mine foreman when he'd moved up from Kentucky in 1960—or was it

'61?—and he still owned one small mine about eleven miles out of Huntington. The hole wasn't worth much, hadn't been worked for several years. Nevertheless Bryans spoke of resuming coal production when the price was right, and it wouldn't be too long now with oil so expensive. He often discussed this with Norm Aikens, the Huntington chief of police with whom he hunted so regularly. Bryans and the chief were close friends, both simple and honest men who believed in law and order, neatness, private property, hard work and the other traditional values that made the U.S. of A. great.

On the afternoon of July 11th Bryans was closing up his warehouse of construction supplies for the night—it was half-past five—when he was called to the telephone. He climbed into his four-wheel-drive jeep a few minutes later, headed out south over a road that soon dwindled into a rutted track past some abandoned mines. There wasn't much up this narrow valley, except Headset. Headset was the code name for a subterranean command post which the U.S. Joint Chiefs of Staff might use in case of war, a bomb-proof and gas-proof and germ-proof bunker with elaborate communications gear. Dug and equipped in 1958, Headset was kept in a state of constant readiness by a small force of security troops and radio technicians. Officially, it was just an old mine in which the Army stored surplus ammunition. That fiction justified sealing off the end of the valley, barring most of it to private vehicles.

Bryans didn't point his jeep directly towards Headset. He took it up towards the top of the ridge, stopped near the skyline to park under overhanging branches of a pine forest. He walked on through the woods for another mile and a half, found the clump of underbrush and fought his way through the thorns to the camouflaged metal box.

It was 6:14 when he rammed down the detonator, and then the mountain fell. The explosion sent more than one thousand tons of earth and rock crashing down the slope, bulldozing the two small surface buildings at Headset into scrap and plugging the openings to the command post. Tons of rubble thundered into the bunker, smashing through heavy metal doors as if they were aluminum foil. There were sixty-three men on duty at Headset when Malcolm James Bryans—whose younger brother was Leningrad's top theatre critic—hit that plunger. Fifty-one died within minutes, and seven others perished in the hospital by the end of the week.

Neither the number of casualties nor the secret of Headset was released to the press, which had to make do with a brief announcement that four men had perished in a blast at an Army depot. The investigators who arrived from the Pentagon came in twos and threes, all in civilian clothes to avoid arousing too much attention. They examined the ground but couldn't find anything besides some traces of dynamite, an obsolete brand used in mining operations before 1970. The avalanche had obliterated much of the evidence of Bryans' sabotage.

Bryans himself was gone. Long before the security agents reached Huntington, he'd driven north into the mountains with his rifle, camping equipment, a month's supply of food and shortwave radio. Every morning and night at the prearranged times he turned the battery-powered set to his special frequency for instructions and/or news of the war. He was baffled when there were no messages, no instructions. He was surprised when he heard nothing about the war either. Puzzled but patient, the perfect deep-cover agent who would never see Leningrad again waited. They would surely send new orders. They had to, for he had no idea as to what he was to do next.

13

The meeting with the Red Army Chief of Staff in the Kremlin could only be characterized as unpleasant. Extremely unpleasant might be more accurate. The bitter tone of the talk came as no surprise to either Strelski or Malchenko, since Marshal Pasimov was a tough old soldier who'd never been famous for his charm. Under the best of conditions he was barely amiable, and once the signal had been decoded with news of the attack on Headset it was inevitable that Pasimov would react angrily. He was so furious when they entered his office that he didn't even ask them to sit down.

"Telefon," he said harshly.

The two K.G.B. officers nodded, waiting for the full tidal wave.

"A harebrained scheme," growled Pasimov, and when he shook his head the late afternoon sun glinted on his glass eye. It was the right one, a replacement for the orb that died in Hungary during the street fighting at Buda. "It was a stupid harebrained scheme from the start," he judged.

"It was approved by the Red Army Chief of Staff," Strelski pointed out stiffly.

"He must have been drunk. I said that to the Premier this morning, and he agreed. . . . What the hell are you people going to do about this mess?"

"We've sent a first-class agent to eliminate the traitor," Strelski said.

"And he managed to silence that poor devil in the hospital. *Da,* I heard. Not too impressive when all you can report is that we've succeeded in killing one of our own," grumbled Pasimov as he shook his head again, "and this latest thing in West Virginia—awful."

"Awful," agreed Strelski.

The marshal stared at the two of them, suddenly pointed at Malchenko.

"Mal . . . Malchenko, right? You were a captain with a motorized infantry unit that went into Berlin with us in forty-five, right?"

"The marshal has an excellent memory."

"Cut the crap, will you? You were a damn good soldier, Malchenko. What the hell are you doing with these idiots?"

Malchenko shrugged.

"Internal security, at the moment," he answered.

"Of course it was you who exposed that fucking Stalinist conspiracy," recalled the marshal. "Nice work."

"I'm also one of the men who conceived Telefon," confessed the beefy colonel.

"You should have stayed in the Army," advised Pasimov.

"My mother wanted me to be a veterinary, but I didn't have the stomach for it."

The marshal sighed, suddenly gestured for them to sit down. "Look, we're trying to live in peace with the Americans," Pasimov explained. "We're trading with them, exchanging fiddlers and dancers and we're even planning a joint effort in space. They're willing to leave us alone if we leave them alone. Now you and your Telefon start making waves. It's got to stop."

"We're doing our best, Comrade Marshal," Strelski vowed.

"Not half good enough. At any minute the Americans will guess who's behind all this violence, and then it will really hit the fan. That's an American expression I learned from their Military Attaché."

"I'm familiar with it, Comrade Marshal, and I want to assure you that the K.G.B. is just as disturbed as the Red Army about this extraordinary situation."

The Red Army Chief of Staff jabbed his index finger towards Strelski.

"It isn't something tidy and under control like an extraordinary situation," bellowed Pasimov. "This is a fucking nightmare. The Premier has instructed me to order you to stop Telefon—immediately. Cut the wires. Rip it out by the roots. We don't care how many lives it costs."

Strelski's furrowed brow indicated his uncertainty.

"Spell it out for him, Malchenko," roared the marshal.

"It would appear that it is the judgment of both the Premier and the Red Army that the Telefon agents may be—in the last resort—expendable."

"You can't be serious," the K.G.B. general protested.

"Dead serious."

"You're talking about wiping out more than a hundred of our finest agents, people who'd be invaluable in case of war."

"Strelski—you are probably a terrific intelligence officer and a dedicated patriot," Pasimov said, "but there isn't going to be any war this year—probably not this decade. If we all act sensibly, we won't need a war with the capitalists for half a century. The Chinese—that's different. Nobody can predict that situation."

Strelski's eyes clouded over abruptly. He was staring out the window at the crenellated red-brick walls of the Kremlin, but he saw nothing.

"Strelski, the idea of Telefon was brilliant and you handled it masterfully," admitted the marshal. "I was wrong to call it stupid. It's the changed situation that makes it very, very dangerous today. Can you get those deep-cover agents out?"

The general hesitated, and Malchenko tensed.

"Yes, if necessary."

It was a lie.

"Fast?" demanded Pasimov.

"If necessary," Strelski lied again.

To protect the operation against a traitor or the remote possibility of infiltration by the Americans, Telefon had been organized without any cutoff switch or code phrase.

"Start pulling them out—as unobtrusively as possible," said Pasimov. "That's an order."

Strelski nodded.

"Let's hope you get them out fast enough," the marshal declared. "Otherwise—well, I'd rather not think about that."

It wasn't until they were back in the relative safety of Strelski's office—which was swept for "bugs" every week—that Malchenko spoke of the meeting.

"You shouldn't have lied to him, Pyotr. If he finds out—"

"I know I shouldn't have lied," said Strelski as he reached for the desk lighter, "but I'm counting on that bastard Tabbat to find the other bastard—and soon."

"You're dead if Pasimov finds out—and I may be too."

The general puffed at the newly glowing cigar, coughed.

"Aleksei, I was the one who lied and the marshal likes you from the old days—the good old days. I really had no choice. You must realize that the only alternative would be to send in assassins to destroy our own people—our finest agents."

"You're starting to sound like Dr. Frankenstein," warned Malchenko.

"These aren't monsters, dammit. These are wonders."

Malchenko turned to leave.

"They're turning into monsters every minute," he said. "The marshal is right. It was a great operation, but the price is getting too damn high. I helped get Telefon going, and I'm saying the risks are growing too fast. We've got to cut our losses."

"We can stall for a week or two," Strelski reasoned aloud.

"What if Dalchimski doesn't?"

There was a long silence. Finally Strelski opened a desk drawer, took out a bottle of Stolynichnaya vodka and two plastic tumblers. He poured an inch and a half of the colorless liquid into each, passed one to Malchenko.

"To Telefon?" asked the colonel.

"Too late for that. To Major Grigori Tabbat—may he be smart and lucky!"

They both drank. Back in the Kremlin, Marshal Pasimov was telling the Direktor of the North American Division of Red Army intelligence—the G.R.U.—that it might be necessary to liquidate 120 or 130 K.G.B. agents in the United States within the next two or three weeks.

"This sounds very serious, Comrade Marshal," said the military intelligence general.

"And very secret. Assemble your teams and stand by. Don't tell them anything, and that goes for your own staff as well. Not a word. I mean that literally."

On the 16th the first squad of assassins reached Mexico City. Two more units passed through Montreal's Dorval Airport a day later.

20

"Dracula?" asked the tall blond captain from the Office of Naval Intelligence.

"That's our boy," confirmed Colonel Jenkins. There were guards at the outer doors and more guards at the inner doors of this Pentagon conference room where Working Group Six met each week, but the fiery president of the Central Arab People's Republic was always referred to by that code name in here. Well, sometimes the Air Force spokesman used obscene epithets in talking of the dashing young North African major—but then, the Air Force was nursing a grudge because "Dracula" had closed the two U.S. fields in his hot and sandy paradise.

"Now what's he done?" asked General Donaldson, who not only represented the Defense Intelligence Agency but also carried the best-looking attaché case in the room.

"Guns for the rebels in Kenya."

"What rebels in Kenya?" demanded Timothy Katzman of the I. and R. unit at State.

"The ones this asshole is arming and training," Jenkins explained cheerfully.

"I thought he was arming and training the I.R.A.," said Donaldson.

"That was last month. He has a lot of oil money and a very short attention span," Jenkins told his colleagues.

"And he had lunch only last week with Henry," teased the O.N.I. captain.

"I'm going to take that remark in the spirit in which it was made," said Katzman.

"Nasty?" Jenkins suggested.

"Damn nasty. The Secretary of State will hear about this—when he next visits Washington," Katzman warned.

Annoyed by this levity, General Donaldson took charge as the chairman of Working Group Six. In sober tones he asked where the guns were coming from and what sort of weapons were involved.

"The usual light SovBlock hardware," Jenkins reported. "four hundred or five hundred AK-47s, maybe one hundred rocket launchers with antitank and antipersonnel ammo and at least a thousand mines. It's the stuff Moscow sent him three years ago. He's just got a load of new hardware that he bought from the French, so he's giving away the old crap."

"Any suggestions?" asked the general.

"A silver spike through his heart," proposed Jenkins. "It always works on vampires, they say."

"That's no way to speak about the head of a friendly power—with a lot of oil," admonished Katzman as he polished his horn-rimmed glasses, "and it wouldn't stop the guns anyway."

"Where the hell are they?"

"In a warehouse full of 'plumbing supplies' at Asmara."

Katzman clasped his hands together thoughtfully, hummed.

"A fire would be *nice*," he said softly.

"Any special kind?" Jenkins invited. "We offer a broad selection of fires. Electrical short-circuits? Cigarette dropped by dozing watchman?"

The O.N.I. captain looked dubious.

"There'll be one helluva blast," he said. "Can't somebody hit the truck convoy when it's out of the city?"

"Bandits?" proposed the general.

"Bandits are *always* good," Katzman agreed. "You stocking any bandits, Tom?"

Jenkins nodded.

"Up to size forty-six long. No problem. Twenty thousand dollars ought to cover it."

"Out of *your* budget, Tom," insisted the Navy officer. "We paid for that damn thing in Greece last month, and you know that you guys should have put up at least half."

Jenkins nodded again.

"We'll scrape together the cash somehow, and maybe we'll do something extra for Dracula himself. We just might let the Israelis hear about that next load of French hardware before it's loaded on the boat at Marseilles, and they'll—"

"I don't want to hear about it," declared the State Department spokesman. "Let's get on to something else. What about that Russian shake-out your girl spotted a couple of months ago? Was it really a massacre?"

"We don't say 'girl' anymore, Tim. That's sexist talk. Dorothy Putterman is a mature, responsible, creative analyst who's a credit to the Agency."

The O.N.I. captain was packing his pipe.

"That the one with the great knobs?" he asked.

"A boor might say that."

"She's a credit to your Agency all right. Well, was it a massacre?"

"We think so. Whole gang of key people crapped out in a couple of weeks. Some of them were old-fashioned hard hats, and Miss Putterman believes that there was probably some sort of Stalinist bunch resisting the peaceful coexistence policy."

"Were they all zapped?"

"Can't say, General. Quite a few casualties, including a hatful in the armed forces. . . . Something worrying you, General?"

Donaldson sighed.

"That number up in West Virginia has made a lot of people edgy. Somebody may have helped that avalanche," he said grimly.

"I'd check the nut houses if I were you," Jenkins advised. "It wouldn't make sense for either the Sovs or the Chinese to hit a target like that in peacetime. They wouldn't want to tip that they knew what the hell that base was. Sounds like an escaped loony to me."

"Could be one of those Kill for Peace groups," pointed out the U.S. Navy captain.

"Maybe. We don't figure that this was any spur-of-the-moment job. This installation's top secret—not like the C.B.R. base that weirdo tried to wreck near Denver."

The State Department man looked at his watch, and they all got the message. Internal Security matters belonged to Working Group Five. This committee—Six—dealt only with foreign problems and projects, and it was time to get on with the rest of the afternoon's agenda. There were eleven items to go, and the meeting didn't break up until after six.

When Jenkins reached C.I.A. headquarters the next morning, there was a message that Coltrane wanted to see him at once. It was probably some little chickenshit thing, but Jenkins went directly to the office of the Special Assistant to the Director.

"How's it goin', Tom?" Coltrane asked in tones that were barely perfunctory.

"Moving right along, Ben. Anything special on your mind?"

"Hot Rod for one thing—and that situation in Panama for another. Sure you've got them under control?"

"Doing our best, Ben. Appreciate your interest. Maybe you could get us some extra manpower for the Panama thing."

"The Office of the D.C.I. never meddles in that sort of question," Coltrane lied.

She was right, Jenkins thought. Coltrane was a turd. It wasn't just that this tall semi-bald bureaucrat was so crudely ambitious and jealous. The fact that he'd been feuding with Jenkins for more than a year wasn't the decisive factor either. It was simply a fact of life—widely recognized throughout the Agency—that Coltrane was a total turd. Nobody liked him, and most people didn't even think he was that smart.

"We'll cope, Ben."

"If you're short on manpower, why don't you pull that snotty girl off those computer analyses and give her something useful to do?" Coltrane suggested.

The hostility in his voice was unconcealed.

"She's getting to be pain in the can, you know."

"Dorothy Putterman, Ben?"

"Your damn Dorothy Putterman is stirring up some of our most diligent female staff with a lot of talk about prejudice in the Agency. She's trying to start a Women's Lib Group! We won't put up with that nonsense!"

It was preposterous. Coltrane was trying to get at him by sniping at his staff, a standard ploy in Washington in-fighting. Colonel Jenkins promised to have "a good talk" with her and "set her straight," assured Coltrane that Tall Turkey and Hot Rod were "moving okay" and Straw Hat would be wrapped up within a week. Then he left to confront Ms. Dorothy Putterman with Coltrane's fabricated yarn.

She was looking very well—quite businesslike but well—and yet a bit different. Colonel Jenkins kept his eyes resolutely fixed on her intelligent face as he recounted his exchange with the malicious Special Assistant to the Director of Central Intelligence.

"No point in arguing with that clown," Jenkins concluded,

"so I gave him a good grease job and pretended to take his phony story seriously."

At that moment a slight summer cold made her cough, and Colonel Jenkins' fixed focus fuzzed and widened. She wasn't wearing that swell new bra. She wasn't wearing *any* brassiere at all. That bastard Coltrane was probably right, and Colonel T. S. Jenkins faced this awful-wonderful old-new problem with very mixed emotions.

21

Tabbat was always full of surprises.

He rarely did or said what was predicted, and that was a major reason why he was still alive. It was 10 P.M., and they had just spent two civilized hours in a superior bar and restaurant called the Ginger Man. They'd timed it perfectly, arriving at eight to miss the crowd heading out across Sixty-fourth and then Broadway to Lincoln Center. Good drinks and light talk from a pair of relaxed bartenders named Danny and John, better-than-average food and draft beer, lavish desserts and superior service had all combined to put Barbi Gordon in a relaxed and tentatively sensual mood. Then he said it as they stepped out of the air conditioning into the heat.

"You know anyone in the F.B.I.?"

"I *hope* not," she replied emphatically.

They walked to the corner, appreciated the handsomely lit concert halls and theatres across the street and started south on Broadway. Halfway down the block he stopped to eye the illuminated fountain in front of the Metropolitan Opera House, then shook his head.

"What we *really* need is not an F.B.I. type but some sort of *cop*," he continued. "A nice *crooked* cop, greedy and not too bright. Has to be an inside man—not a street cop."

"Is that what they ordered on the radio this morning?"

"All they said was hurry up, please. Make us a miracle, Gregg, and find that fiend within the next week or two. . . . Hope you didn't mind being sent out when I was decoding, hon, but—"

"Rules are rules," she completed.

"Right. Now we need a crooked cop because it's going to take a large national organization to find this mother. There's nobody better at finding people than the cops because there's a couple of hundred thousand of them—and they're almost all plugged into the F.B.I. teleprinter network. That binds all those sheriffs and state troopers and other cops into a large national organization, with eyes everywhere."

His damp brow was furrowed in concentration as they strolled towards Columbus Circle.

"And you intend to sneak a 'wanted' description of Mr. Monster onto that teletype circuit?" she guessed.

He smiled.

"That's nifty," she said admiringly. "Also a little dangerous if that crooked cop suspects *why* you want this gent."

Tabbat shook his head.

"Not if he's the *right* sort of crooked cop. A good crook wouldn't blow the whistle. He'd just raise the price. Won't be easy to find the right man," he fretted.

"You know what they say," she answered. "You can never find a good crooked cop when you need one. . . . You're shooting dice with this whole damn mission, Gregg. How can you risk—"

"That's a *great* idea," he interrupted. "Let's find out about flights."

Unwilling to wait until they returned to the hotel, he found two public telephones—and the second one worked. After only twenty-nine rings he found himself talking to a female employee of United Airlines whose name was Debby. That's what she said, and she said it in a cheery-cheery voice that was acutely reminiscent of T.W.A.'s Miss Bleich. There

was a ticket clerk in London with a rather similar voice, Tabbat
suddenly recalled, and in Rio too. Perhaps it was a secret organization, or a bizarre cult.

"Four hundred and seventeen dollars each," Tabbat announced as he turned to his curious "wife." It was very humid.
"DC-8 departing at eleven-fifteen in the morning, five hours
in those friendly skies with macadamia nuts and the Mai-Tais.
Nonstop, they swear."

"First class?"

The man who was supposed to prevent World War III
stared at her indignantly.

"I should *hope so*," he answered. "We represent a first-
class power, and it would be an affront to tens of millions of
proletarians if Soviet spies rode in the back of the plane like
college kids or shoe clerks. Lenin would be spinning in his
tomb!"

"I wouldn't want to hurt all those workers' feelings, Gregg
—and certainly not Lenin's."

They were packing their bags at midnight. Dalchimski was
considering his next target.

22

Most of the airlines' terminals at John F. Kennedy International Airport have as much character as fluorescent lamps.
The only one with any class at all is the soaring birdlike structure that the late Eero Saarinen designed for Trans World. Unlike the functional boxes of the other carriers, it has the look of
flight. It gives the feeling of an airborne creature, confirming
the genius of the architect who dreamed it. The building that
houses United's ticket offices is neat, well lit, clean and func-

tional. In other words, it's sterile, plastic and devoid of thrills.

Tabbat wasn't seeking thrills that morning, even though he realized that he might find them. It wouldn't be the predictably trim and pretty ticket clerks or their crisply affable male colleagues who presented the danger. They would offer United's usual courtesy and efficiency, going through the automatic litany that left passengers—especially first-class passengers—with the comfortable sense that everything was under control. It was the private security agents doing the screening who might cause trouble.

"Creeps," he said.

The plastic panel behind the taxi driver was shut.

"What creeps?" she asked.

"Lunatics, fanatics—especially those goddam fanatics. Especially those heroes. Man, I hate those heroes. They've ruined flying. You can't tell what those amateur martyrs will pull."

He pointed at the photo on the front page of the *Daily News*.

"You mean the skyjackers, Gregg?"

"Yeah. Those Arabs are the worst. Trigger-happy patriots, blasting anyone in sight and accomplishing nothing. Between those bubble-heads and the other freaks—the freelance morons and paranoids just out of some looney bin—they've screwed up air travel for everyone. Cops and search machines at every damn airport I hit."

There was little traffic on the Van Wyck Expressway, and the sign announced that Kennedy was only half a mile ahead.

"Don't take it personally," she advised.

"I have to. They affect me personally. Do you know the problems I have moving with a gun from country to country? I'm a law-abiding civil servant, and I'm frisked as if I were some cheap hood. . . . The Israelis know how to handle those punks. They don't crap around with them. Armed agents on every El Al flight. Damn good security, and the kugel is great."

"What's that?"

"Potato kugel—sort of a pudding or stuffing with a crust on top. Best kugel and top security, terrific combination."

She giggled.

"Air France and S.A.S. have swell food too," he admitted,

"but no kugel. Lobster and champagne. Well, we're almost there."

The cab turned off, and six minutes of cloverleafs and signs later they reached the United terminal. The black porter who unloaded their baggage was visibly uneasy about the long thin case, and so was the crew-cut ticket clerk at the counter.

"Yes, it's a rifle," Tabbat said bluntly. "Hunting rifle. Can I check it through?"

The clerk sighed in relief.

"It's an expensive gun—so handle it carefully or you'll get an insurance claim," warned the K.G.B. man.

"Of course, sir. Here are your seating assignments. You did say you wanted to smoke? Right, 9A and B. Have a good flight, sir."

It wasn't over.

The fluoroscope-metal detector at the gate picked up the .22 pistol.

"Target pistol, unloaded," Tabbat explained.

"I'm afraid you can't take it aboard in your attaché case, Mr. Gordon," said the uniformed inspector firmly. "F.A.A. rules forbid it. You can pick it up when you reach your destination, sir."

"Wouldn't have it otherwise. You fellows are doing a fine job, and it's the least we passengers can do to cooperate. I'm backing you to the limit."

"Thank you. You can go through now."

The DC-8 was only half full in the first-class compartment. It took off exactly on time, climbed smoothly under the skilled guidance of one of those veteran pilots with twenty thousand hours and a wonderfully close shave. There were several trim stewardesses who displayed fine legs and unbelievable good-will, and the free drinks nine minutes after the large Douglas jet was airborne almost made up for the lack of kugel.

"You wouldn't want to tell me what you have in mind?" asked the woman who'd met him on the beach.

He shook his head.

"The less you know the better, hon. If something goes wrong and some people start asking you a lot of questions, I'll be safer if you can't give any answers."

She sipped her champagne.

"What can go wrong?"

"Everything. Murphy's Law—old U.S. Air Force cliché. Anything that can go wrong will. I'm with Murphy."

More drinks with those nuts from Hawaii that United has made a trademark in its "friendly skies." The cabin personnel worked doggedly to keep the atmosphere intensely "friendly," pouring drinks and serving lunch and talking up the five stereo channels on the headsets and plugging the movie. There was quite a bit of plugging in the film itself. It was a fast-paced Clint Eastwood picture. Three villains were gunned down in lurid color during the first four minutes, after which the action speeded up and the corpses multiplied like amoebas. There were a couple of marvelously endowed starlets who tried and tried to charm the pants off the Hero.

"They'll cut the good part," Tabbat predicted. "They always do on the planes—to protect the kids."

Sure enough, there was an abrupt transition and Eastwood was buttoning his shirt with splendid impassivity. His attention was already refocused on the pursuit of the Bad Guys, and he was going to Get Them No Matter What The Cost. Twenty-nine minutes and five corpses later, he did.

Fade out.

"More brandy?" asked the auburn-tressed kewpie doll.

Tabbat couldn't hear her. He removed the headset.

"Some brandy, sir?" the stewardess volunteered again.

"Thanks. How about you, Barb?"

"No, thanks. Two would make me sleepy. It's only three o'clock."

The cognac United served was a lot better than the Ukrainian garbage that the *Rezident* drank in Washington, and Tabbat sipped it appreciatively. He scanned the printed list of taped offerings on the five channels, grunted as he noted he'd missed the single Sinatra performance scheduled. "Come Fly With Me" was a good one—not the *best* but it was the upbeat songs that Tabbat favored anyway.

"Nelson Riddle," said the K.G.B. agent.

"Is this a game?" wondered his "wife."

"He did the arrangements for a lot of Frank's best recordings—a big talent. You probably never heard of Nelson Riddle. He could really swing. . . . I'm not knocking Axel Stordahl, of course."

"Of course," she agreed as if she knew what he was talking about.

"On the other hand, I was never too crazy about Gordon Jenkins. Jonathan Schwartz is right about him—too damn schmaltzy."

"Thank God," she sighed, "I know who he is—the disk jockey. Jonathan Schwartz on WNEW in New York?"

"He's more than a disk jockey. He has one of the *greatest* collections of Sinatra records and tapes in the world," Tabbat said reverently.

"Don't let it bother you," she advised. "When we get back to New York you can kill him and take the whole collection. It shouldn't be hard. He probably isn't even armed."

"Jonathan Schwartz has *unreleased* stuff. Fantastic stuff. Out-takes, things taped illegally at concerts or off broadcasts—fabulous things. . . . You know who his father is?"

"Frank's father? A man in New Jersey."

Tabbat shook his head impatiently.

"Schwartz's father."

"He wouldn't be Sam Schwartz who runs the St. James Theatre? *Bernie* Schwartz?"

"Bernie Schwartz is Tony Curtis," Tabbat scolded. "Changed his name years ago."

"No kidding? I thought Bernie Schwartz changed his name to Aretha Franklin."

"Jonathan Schwartz's father is Arthur Schwartz!"

"The composer?"

Tabbat smiled, nodded.

"You got it. He wrote some great tunes. 'Dancing in the Dark' and 'Something to Remember You By' and 'That's Entertainment'—a lot of *big* songs. Howard Dietz wrote his lyrics."

"Is that his real name?"

"Whose real name—Dietz?"

"I don't care. I'm just here for the ride. Let me know when we get to my stop, will you?"

Disgusted, Tabbat got up and went to the cubicle-lavatory. It was difficult to speak to a woman who was so ignorant and frivolous.

"You're not angry, are you?" she asked apologetically when he returned.

"No."

"I never took the course in forties and fifties songs, you see. The old movies—sure. But not those songs."

"Those were the best—but I understand. If you didn't take the course—well, nobody could blame you, Barb."

He could be kind when he wanted to.

"I do remember Axel Stordahl—I think. He was an orchestra leader and arranger, wasn't he?"

"Right. Passed away in Encino, California, back in 1963—classy guy."

Tabbat closed his eyes for a long moment, yawned.

"The Beatles don't count, Gregg? I know the Beatles," she volunteered.

"Leave it alone. We'll be landing in less than an hour."

He was probably irritated by the reference to Aretha Franklin, she decided. Maybe Aretha Franklin was just a great soul singer who didn't write or arrange songs. Bob Dylan? Neil Diamond? Stevie Wonder? No, she'd take his advice and leave it alone. He didn't seem to have much humor on this subject, and she was under strict orders not to annoy or frustrate him.

Fasten your seat belt.

No smoking.

Las Vegas.

Very hot—87 degrees in the shade.

No shade.

Almost dazed by the searing temperature and the glare, she followed him into the cool relief of the terminal. She stared.

"Never seem 'em before?" Tabbat wondered.

"Not in an airport."

"They're all over Las Vegas. It's a swinging town, Barb."

Swinging and clicking. The rows of slot machines in the terminal were whirring and rattling, every one of them absorbing coins as fast as the patrons could unload them.

"Gamblers?"

Tabbat scanned them contemptuously.

"Jerks. Jerks getting rid of their loose change before they leave. Lots of jerks in Vegas—not many real gamblers."

It was midweek, he explained, and the hotels in Vegas filled up with all sorts of conventioneers in on four-day "package" deals. The real gamblers usually arrived on Friday for the weekend, but these bourgeois boobs helped cover the overhead for the rest of the week. The hotels needed them, so relatively cheap deals were offered to bring in hordes of unsophisticated jerks who drank Scotch and ginger ale, wore the wrong clothes and sold a lot of washing machines in Minnesota. Or beer. Or swimming pools or Fords. Sometimes the conventioneers were orthodontists or electrical engineers, but the difference was small and the hotels didn't care anyway.

There are more than twenty-six thousand hotel and motel rooms in Vegas. Nobody here calls the city Las Vegas—not after the first hour in town. Las Vegas means "the meadows" and maybe there once were meadows here—perhaps back when the Paiute Indians roamed and raided the region. Some Mormons had settled in the neighborhood back in 1855 because Brigham Young had told them to, but the Paiutes didn't take that fine religious leader seriously and they hounded the Mormons out of the area. The U.S. Cavalry didn't push around that easily. The Yankee horse soldiers showed up in force during the Civil War to protect the trail west, and they didn't take any crap from the Paiutes at all. The troopers were in no mood to understand the "hostiles," being rather hostile themselves in the sandstorms and desert heat.

Vegas was founded—officially—in 1905 by some people who apparently had nothing else to do. The Paiutes had shipped out in a rather resentful mood, and the town dozed on for a quarter of a century until some student of human nature talked the elders into legalizing gambling in 1931. Today Vegas is a booming community of 300,000 God-fearing people who fear at 143 churches. There are 159 Boy Scout troops, about 1,000 "gaming tables" and a few more than 16,000 slot machines—including those at the airport.

A single hotel—the MGM Grand Hotel—has more rooms

than all of those in Wichita *combined*. Twenty-one hundred
rooms in one gigantic edifice that makes the Taj Mahal look
like a doll house: swimming pools and restaurants and shows
and superstars and crap tables and baccarat, the leggiest chorus
girls with the firmest bodies in the smallest costumes. Roulette,
free hors d'oeuvres, ice water—it's magnificent and very clean.

There are *two* Hiltons, the larger with 1,500 rooms and
suites and entertainment that stops just this side of human
sacrifices. Lovers of animal acts can get their kicks at a small
425-room hideaway named Circus Circus, and there's always
the Sands and the Sahara and Caesar's Palace and the Riviera
and the Thunderbird and the Tropicana. All come equipped
with belly-busting buffets, health spas and casinos. It is the
casinos that pay the tab, for gambling is the difference between
profit and disaster in this man-made oasis near the edge of the
Mohave Desert.

Tabbat told her about this over the insistent sound of the
taped music that gushed endlessly from the speakers in the
terminal, spilling out in mindless cycle like the pastel soft
drinks in those bubbling machines that hypnotize customers
in cheap snack bars.

"So it's sex that makes the wheels go round here," she
replied.

"I didn't say anything about sex. I was talking about
money."

"But money is sex, Gregg."

"You're bananas. Money is power," he corrected firmly.

"Same thing. It's elemental Freud—practically a cliché."

His eyes narrowed. She certainly hadn't learned that in any
Soviet school.

"Where'd you pick that up, Barb?"

"Barnard. My dad worked for the U.N. Secretariat back
in the early sixties, so I got in two years of college in New
York. Finished at *home*."

"Uh huh."

He waved at a taxi.

"Look, Gregg. Money is power is sex, which explains capi-
talism."

"You mean the rich are piling up the cash, and screwing the masses in the process?"

"That's a bit simplified, but you're on the right track. You're sort of a capitalist yourself."

The driver unlocked the cab's trunk fifteen feet away.

"Me?"

"In a manner of speaking," she said with a naughty smile. "You're out to screw *everybody*. Don't ask for the details. I only took one semester of psychology."

Her views of human behavior were unorthodox—even kinky —and far from the regular Moscow line, but that only made her interesting. She wasn't boring like those other broads he'd worked with in London and Algiers and Tokyo. They'd been technicians, good in the sack and well trained in how to get foreign men into compromising situations. They had little to say, however, and they couldn't talk about Freud.

"You're a maverick—like me," he said with a grin.

"No, you're unique. I've just got a few notions I picked up here and there, but basically I'm like a lot of other women at the Center."

The warmth vanished from his face.

"Don't say that," he ordered. "Don't use those words— *ever*."

"The—"

He interrupted before she could articulate "Center."

"There are people who know what that means. Don't *ever* make that mistake again."

They entered the cab.

The Center was the phrase that K.G.B. agents around the world used for their headquarters in Moscow, and there were thousands of F.B.I. and Army Counter-Intelligence agents who knew the expression. He was right.

"Sorry, Gregg. It was stupid of me."

"Where you folks goin'?" the driver asked over his shoulder.

"Versailles Chateau," replied Tabbat and the Chevvy rolled.

"Where's that, Gregg?"

"Strip."

"In the cab?"

He smiled again, but not fully.

"Our hotel is out on the Strip. That's Route Ninety-one. Choice real estate where the best hotels are situated. It's called the Strip," he explained.

"Nice?"

"Vegas nice. It's the high-rent district. Best and biggest everything."

Including the signs. It wasn't dark yet, but you could see those huge electric signs from more than a mile away. Each hotel and casino and pizza parlor had its own enormous sign, boldly demanding attention as it pierced the skyline.

"There's a downtown area too," Tabbat told her. "Main drag's Fremont Street. Lots of topless joints and slot machines —cheap thrills for the poor folks. That's where the old bags in house dresses and tennis shoes go to pump the handles on the one-armed bandits. You can find them in there at six on a Sunday morning, trying to grab for the fun they never had. They don't do any harm, and they're good losers. Most of them have been losers all their lives. . . . Christ, I'm getting to sound like some third-rate journalist."

"Not exactly. What's our hotel like?"

He yawned.

"Versailles Chateau? Contemporary plastic, with a lot of gold paint and bellboys from Montreal who lay on the French accent," he began.

As he spoke about the blackout drapes that would let you sleep all day after playing till dawn, the individual temperature controls on the cooling units, the steak house and Restaurant Louis XIV and other delights, his mind was on the mission again. The message from Moscow had made it bluntly clear that time was running out—fast. Something drastic might happen if he didn't nail Dalchimski soon. The operation could turn into a "wet affair"—K.G.B. slang for a bloody mission with loss of life. In addition to this mounting pressure, he had the new worry about the woman they'd provided. If she spoke of the Center, she might talk about wet affairs or maybe even mention the Collegium—the ruthless senior staff who set top K.G.B. policy.

No more mistakes.

After the next one, he'd get rid of her.

Nothing personal, but he couldn't waste any time running from the American security agencies because of her carelessness. He had to prevent World War III, a worthwhile project that should earn the Nobel Prize but was more likely to get him a bullet—from one side or the other.

"You here for the pharmacists' convention?" asked the driver when Tabbat completed his report on the hotel.

"Course. Just flew in from New York. Gonna be a real humdinger."

"You run a drugstore?"

"I'm not a delegate. I'm an exhibitor," Tabbat lied.

"Salesman? We get lots of them. Last week had the hardware crowd in. What're you exhibiting, mister?"

The big sign of the Versailles Chateau loomed three-quarters of a mile down The Strip.

"Enema bags," replied the man from the sea. "Jiffy Enema Bags—newest advance of American technology. They're *electric!*"

It took several seconds for the man at the wheel to comprehend the enormity of this extraordinary scientific breakthrough.

"Electric? Keerist—that's triffic. How you do it, mister?"

"Transistors," Tabbat confided. "We're beating the Japs at their own game."

The driver chortled and chuckled.

"Teach them little rats a lesson. They're not all rats. Had a Sony convention in over Easter. Some of them are damn fine tippers."

"Good and bad in every group."

Tabbat's profound insight into the human condition left the taxi man breathless—for five seconds.

"Good and bad in every group," he ratified.

There is no point in attempting to describe the splendors of the lobby of the Versailles Chateau. It is spacious—roughly the size of a high-school football stadium and apparently the work of a decorator who'd studied a lot of 1930s M.G.M. musicals and had a wild sense of humor. It would not be quite ac-

curate to call it Cleveland baroque, although some gentlemen
well known to both Ohio and federal law enforcement agencies
had substantial investments in this establishment. These were
indirect, via holding companies that controlled holding companies that controlled Panamanian corporations with Swiss
accounts, but the F.B.I. knew and respected the major share-
holders. Only eight years old, the Versailles Chateau had the
distinction of having its phones tapped—under a court order—
from the day it opened.

There are, of course, many fine hotels in Vegas owned by
perfectly honest people who pay their taxes, obey all laws and
traffic regulations and regularly worship at the church or
synagogue of their choice. Several of the city's largest inns are
the property of a chap who is said to be Howard Hughes, a
shy man who plays games of Monopoly with himself—using
real hotels. It is rumored that he also indulges in an occasional
game of whist with Judge Crater, but this has never been confirmed by either Jack Anderson or *The Hollywood Reporter*.

Well, the Chateau is posh, plush and rather comfortable for
anyone who doesn't mind fuchsia couches, purple Naugahyde
chairs, electric-blue drapes and semi-Alaskan temperatures in
the suites. When the American Psychological Association held
its convention here a couple of years ago, one Yale professor
suggested that the sleeping quarters might be kept cold to
drive guests out and down to the gambling, but he was only an
associate professor and something of a wise guy. Tabbat and his
aide checked in, unpacked their bags and flipped open the *Las
Vegas Sun* to see where the action was.

It was fabulous.

Sammy was in town.

Dean was working at another hotel.

Barbra was opening tonight.

Elvis was closing tomorrow.

Wall-to-wall superstars. Tabbat had secretly hoped that
Frank might be in town, and still cherished the dream that the
Chairman of the Board might fly in—perhaps in his private jet
—to surprise Dino or Sammy. Frank loved to play these little
jokes on his pals, Tabbat remembered. He was very warm and
whimsical and generous, a real stand-up guy you could count

on when you needed help. It would be good to meet him some day, for they would surely get along well. Tabbat was completely confident about this, and knew that it was merely a matter of time.

He was jerked back to immediate reality when she turned the radio dial to another station, and the room was awash in Neil Diamond's version of "Sweet Caroline." Nice song, but Jeezus.

"Let's get out of here," Tabbat said impatiently.

"Shall I change the station, hon?"

"Turn it off. I want to catch a drink downstairs in the Lounge."

As she dressed, he dropped the silencer in the right pocket of his jacket and slipped the newly reloaded .22 into the inside breast pocket. It was three inches deeper than usual, long enough to take the gun. Somebody in the U.S. *apparat*—perhaps Barb—had been thoughtful, and some tailor had no notion as to why he'd made this unusual alteration. The weapon fit unobtrusively, almost as well as it would in a shoulder holster.

They had drinks in the Lounge where a good trio was playing superior soft rock, and then Tabbat lost $190 at the crap table in the next room. The player who took the dice from him was a heavy, graying man in his late fifties, tanned and well dressed in expensive sports clothes. There was a trim nineteen-year-old strawberry blonde beside him. Maybe she was twenty, but surely she was his. Each time before he made a pass with the ivory cubes the older man patted her flank for good luck, and she smiled sweetly at this recognition of her magic. Magic or not, the man won $4,400.

"Awful," judged the woman who was Barbi Gordon this month.

"Vegas," Tabbat corrected.

They took a taxi to another hotel where they drank some more and saw a rising young comic perform in the Lounge. Tabbat explained that there was nothing minor league about the talent in Vegas hotel lounges. Important performers—stars in other cities but not quite the Big Name needed to headline a Vegas main-room show—appeared in the Lounge here and at other Strip establishments. At 8:10 Tabbat gave $10 to the headwaiter of one of this hotel's "five gourmet restaurants" and they sat down to an utterly undistinguished meal. The decor was red silk and splendid and the waitress wore clinging outfits that made the uniforms of Playboy bunnies look like diver's suits, but the cuisine was not peachy. Barbi Gordon said so.

"It doesn't get much better anywhere," Tabbat admitted. "Volume operation . . . steady flow around the clock . . . kitchens working twenty-four hours a day. Figure it that way, and they do pretty well."

The entertainment was a lot better. The finest nightclub acts in the world appeared in highly professional and expensively produced revues, slick shows featuring excellent musicians and beautiful showgirls and costumes that could only be described as fancy. The thousands of men and women in town for the two conventions—both the pharmacists and the plumbing supply group—had a marvelous time. Tabbat seemed to be enjoying himself too, although he'd disappear every forty minutes or so to make a telephone call.

"Found him," Tabbat told her at 2:50 in the morning.

She didn't bother to ask who, but faithfully trailed Tabbat to the taxi and closed her eyes until they reached the Tropicana —a "150-acre vacation wonderland Featuring the Exciting Folies Bergère in the spacious Theatre Restaurant." As they entered, Tabbat explained that she was about to meet a man named Jerry.

"I'm not going to ask," she promised.

"What?"

"Whether he spells his name with a G or a J."

"Good."

"I'm not going to ask *anything*," she said.

"You're learning," Tabbat approved and he gave her arm a warm squeeze. It wasn't much, but it was better than a pat on the ass and she was willing to settle for that difference.

Four minutes after they sat down at the table Tabbat had booked by phone, the elaborate French spectacle began with a blast of brass that could dislodge your contact lenses. The music was brisk and merry and the semi-nude French showgirls who pranced out were just as brisk and just as merry.

They were smiling resolutely. Even the silver and gold pasties on the tips of their impressive teats seemed merry, almost Christmaslike.

"I don't think they're all French," Tabbat confided.

"I'm not going to ask. Let's just experience the wonder of it all."

Wherever those girls came from, they had great figures. Jerry didn't. He was built like a gas pump, and looked just as hard. Some five-feet-eleven, he must have weighed 210 and his teeth were perfect. Great caps. He had played football in high school and for two years in college—until he was expelled on suspicion of dumping games at the behest of gamblers. Now he was the assistant security chief of one of the big Strip casinos—not the Tropicana. This was his night off, and he was visiting and waiting until his girlfriend—third from the right—finished her dancing chores for the evening. Jerry could apparently see in the dark, for he found Tabbat after the lights had dimmed and silently patted him on the arm before sitting down beside him. The production number ended, and the applause unfurled like a banner in the wind.

"Jerry, you're lookin' good."

"You're doin' all right yourself, champ," he answered Tabbat with a glance at Barbi Gordon.

He didn't seem to expect Tabbat to introduce her, and Tabbat didn't. In their frame of values, attractive women were necessities but not generally individuals. Tabbat had met him outside a brothel in the old part of Marseilles, and had—almost casually—beaten unconscious three North African thugs who'd been mugging the tipsy foreigner. It had been easy for a crack hand-to-hand combat and karate expert such as the spy to smash and batter the hoodlums, but Jerry saw it as a matter of moment and a debt of honor.

"In town for long?"

"Got in tonight. Lookin' for a guy who owes some money to a couple of friends of mine," Tabbat lied.

"You think he's here?"

Tabbat shrugged, gestured to a waiter to pour another set of drinks before the show charged ahead. It was close, but the waiter just made it.

A singer did five numbers—well.

More applause.

"Swell show," said Tabbat.

"First class. . . . Say, this clown—is he into you for much?"

"Forty."

"Forty, huh? Want me to spread the word?"

"I'm not sure he's here, Jer. I ought to ask the cops to find him. He's a missing person, way I see it."

Jerry found this notion amusing, grinned.

"That's funny. I dig that. Yeah, there's a sergeant I know downtown who could help you. He likes to help people."

"Like you, Jer."

"Hell, you're my friend. I owe you—champ. His name is Ted Beckam. Tell him I said he's a right guy."

"Would he mind if I left him an envelope with a grand, Jer?"

"Nobody minds a grand. See you 'round."

Jerry stood up and the lights went down and a bunch of healthy young women in feathery headdresses leaped out onto the stage as if they'd been goosed with electric cattle prods. The pharmacists in the audience went wild—discreetly. After all, pharmacists are professional men and known for their sobriety and self-control. Also their wives were there.

Tabbat was in excellent spirits as they stepped into the cab that would carry them back to the Chateau. He was humming softly—"Something's gotta give, something's gotta give, something's gotta give!" One of Mercer's best.

"Enjoy the show?" he asked dutifully.

"Who wouldn't?" she evaded neatly.

He reached over, patted her cheek tenderly.

"About that Jerry—" he began.

"No questions."

"He owes me one, or he thinks he does anyway."

Now she turned her head, kissed him briefly.

"No shop talk. I've had a fine evening, Gregg. I'm tired and I want to get to bed."

When they got to bed at 4:45, she wasn't tired at all.

23

Dalchimski liked the Berkshires. These green valleys and mountains in western Massachusetts were at least ten degrees cooler than it had been in Dayton, and the change from the hot city streets and urban clamor was definitely an improvement. He hadn't expected the American summer to be nearly this torrid, a full twenty degrees warmer than the Julys of Moscow. Comparing the Ohio weather with that of the Berkshires and looking up at the mountains on the horizon, he understood why this was a popular ski area in the winter.

He'd flown into Albany, moved on by bus to Pittsfield, where he'd rented the car. The auto rental agency had helped him get the room down Route 7 in the smaller town of Stockbridge, explaining that the Red Lion Inn was booked solid for every weekend through Labor Day but might be able to accommodate him for two days in the middle of the week. This fit nicely into Dalchimski's schedule, for he never risked staying anywhere for more than two days, even now. The sprawling, old-fashioned hotel had a gracious and almost historic quality, with big high-ceilinged rooms and a broad porch with rockers and a Swiss chef who knew his craft. The town itself was charming, with wide tree-lined streets, a surprisingly large public library and a small museum dedicated to the works of an American artist named Norman Rockwell. Dalchimski had never heard of him, but at least he could understand these pictures.

Even Stockbridge had been touched by the decay of capitalist society, however. There was a large building which housed a mental institution for the children of the rich, or so the high charges of $500 a week hinted. Nearby Tanglewood—only three or four miles up winding Route 183—offered the Boston Symphony Orchestra concerts only on weekends, with raucous rock groups dominating the midweek schedules. Fortunately there was a summer theatre within walking distance of the Red Lion Inn, and while the Russian didn't "get" all the sex jokes in the comedy about the psychiatrist and the nymphomaniac, he grasped enough to laugh a dozen times.

When he awoke the next morning, he looked at the Book. He had been considering his next target for several days, but he enjoyed studying the Book, which he found as exciting as some men might a collection of pornographic photos. Each name in the Book gave him an odd thrill, making him feel rich and furtive and wickedly potent. Of course, Dalchimski didn't admit any of this to himself for he saw his role as that of the righteous and avenging angel. Well, that wasn't it either, for he was a good Stalinist and that meant a fiery atheist. The paranoia and puritanism and repression in this bitter man combined to produce enough hatred to challenge half a dozen of the psychiatrists and analysts in the nearby institution, enough to fuel the boilers of the General Electric plant up in Pittsfield. All this had been acceptable and even useful in the U.S.S.R. of ten or fifteen years ago, but what had once been patriotism was now psychosis.

Times change.

Dalchimski wouldn't.

They couldn't make him.

He would destroy them all—with the Book.

He turned the pages slowly, savoring his treasures with a sly smile. It was delicious. He made his choice, shaved and dressed and walked downstairs. He turned left up the street past the country store and Nejaime's Market and the antique shop, stepped into the telephone booth. It was a fine clear morning, and he noticed three pretty teenagers stepping out of the drugstore across the traffic. He saw the chunky uniformed policeman directing the stream of cars, stopping the vehicles to permit an elderly man to cross. It was a traditional New England scene, much like those films of two decades ago.

He dialed the number in Indian Gorge, Texas, listened to the buzz.

"Bakery," said a man's voice.

"Mr. Archibald?"

"Yes."

"I wonder whether you have any of those nine-inch pecan pies that Mrs. Dempsey told me about," said Dalchimski.

There was a silence.

"Sorry, we're out," the man with the Texan accent answered.

The homicidal maniac hung up the phone, walked back to the Red Lion for breakfast. The pancakes were very good, and they were served with real maple syrup that added to the experience. Some places might skimp and serve the cheaper mass-produced syrups, but not the Red Lion Inn of Stockbridge. Dalchimski checked his watch as he rose from the table, and he left a generous tip.

It would be on the radio within a few hours.

24

When Tabbat and the woman beside him awoke at 1:50 that afternoon, the room was dark and cool. The blackout drapes were doing their job and the super-duper air conditioner was throwing enough cool to freeze 246 chicken legs, so the couple in the bed had no way of knowing that there was a sun in the sky strong enough to kill a Brahma bull. There was no clue in the extraterrestrial darkness that the temperature outside—out there in the Mohave—was actually 101 degrees Fahrenheit. The temperature was going to top 100 for a dozen hours a day during the next week, a prospect that might irk some Vegas visitors but would delight the canny casino owners since such heat would keep the tourists and convention types in the cool gaming rooms.

Tabbat opened his eyes, blinked twice and concluded that he couldn't afford the luxury of wondering where Nicolai Dalchimski was at this moment. Tabbat didn't have the time. He rolled out of bed, paused tenderly to readjust the light blanket that covered her and moved purposefully into the bathroom to prepare his body for the day. She'd slid back into sleep, he guessed accurately, and didn't mind a bit. After he'd showered and shaved, he used the privacy of the toilet to pry off the back of his American Express card and remove the snapshot that had been hidden inside the two sheets of plastic. Then he dressed and took a taxi to the auto rental office. He parked his cream-colored Olds outside the photographer's shop at half-past three, and met Ted Beckam at five.

Right in the police headquarters itself. Tabbat couldn't help but feel a bit uneasy as he waited in the reception area, for his body knew—absolutely *knew* beyond any doubt—that all police everywhere were his natural enemies. He wasn't comfortable with any of them, not even the Moscow militia types who were so servile to the K.G.B. In a certain sense, Tabbat had been born for a secret life outside the law and becoming a spy and assassin was just sensibly commercializing his neuroses. He looked around, recognized the familiar types of police bodies and faces he'd seen in thirty countries and the standard assortment of victims and fools who wandered in seeking help. Compared to all these clichés, he was a cool, shrewd, superior individual and he regained his poise and confidence.

"Very nice of you to see me so soon, Sergeant," Tabbat said when he faced Beckam in the privacy of the small, drably furnished office.

Ted Beckam was a big tanned man with a swell open smile. The clue lay in his clothes, Tabbat calculated. Sergeant Beckam was dressed just a little too well for a man who earned $16,000 to $18,000 a year, and Tabbat was confident that he drove a car that cost $1,500 or $2,000 more than the vehicles of other sergeants. Tabbat had no illusion that the whole Vegas force was corrupt, but he sensed that this one cop—this friend of Jerry's —was "flexible."

"Hope I can help," Beckam replied briskly like those good straight cops on television. "Jerry said you had a little problem."

"That's it. I guess you'd call it a missing person case. Might be amnesia."

The sergeant nodded compassionately.

"Who's missing, Mr. Gordon?"

"Bookkeeper who works for my family. He's sort of a second or third cousin, I suppose."

Beckam's eyes showed a new interest.

"This a Family matter, sir?"

The key word was "Family." He wanted to know whether one of the powerful Mafia outfits was involved.

"Yes—back East," lied Tabbat.

Beckam nodded again, trying to figure what was wanted and how much he might expect.

"This fellow disappeared a few months ago, Sergeant, and we're all worried about him. He could be here—or anywhere."

"Had ample funds?"

"Including some of the firm's payroll. We think that he lost his memory."

Probably lost his goddam marbles, calculated Beckam, for a man would have to be deranged to think he could skip with Mafia money. They'd spare no expense to track him down, and hit him. It was a matter of principle. Being a man of principle, Beckam respected this. He'd help, if he could avoid any direct link to the hit.

The man he knew as Gregg Gordon put a photo on the desk, extracting it from a thick white envelope which he laid down beside it.

"His name is Nick. Nick Dallo. He has dark eyes, only half a head of brown hair and stands about five-nine. He doesn't speak English too well. Talks with an accent. Weighs about one-eighty-five."

Beckam wondered how much cash was in the envelope.

"Been missing long?"

"Maybe two-three months. We've tried to find him ourselves, but we haven't had any luck. Maybe you could put out a missing person thing about him—on the teletype?"

The "flexible"—the English would say "bent"—sergeant was

impressed and amused. This branch of the Family had a lot of nerve, using the national police teleprinter system to hunt down a crooked crook.

"I'll ask my captain," Beckam promised.

He scooped up the photo and the envelope, left the room. Counting the cash in a cubicle in the john, Tabbat calculated correctly.

"We'll try to help," promised the sergeant when he returned with the photo—the copy Tabbat had just bought—in his hand. Beckam wasn't holding the envelope, however. The $1,000 was in his pocket, or his locker.

"We'll be grateful—doubly grateful," assured the spy.

Another $2,000 if you find him.

"All you want to know is where Mr. Dallo can be found, right? You don't want him arrested?"

"Hell, no, Sarge. He hasn't done anything *bad*. He's just forgotten who he is and where he belongs."

Maybe they'd find him back on the East Coast, Beckam thought hopefully. Down in Key West or Baltimore—far from Vegas. If anyone ever discovered the skeleton with its feet in the tub of cement, there'd be nothing to point to this distant city in the Nevada desert.

"Where you staying, Mr. Gordon?"

"Versailles Chateau. Lively spot. Has most everything."

"Bet it hasn't got a jai-alai court," Beckam challenged alertly. "Only the M.G.M. has that."

"I'm more interested in a rifle range. Thinking of doing some hunting when it cools off some."

Beckam studied him appraisingly.

Hit man?

He didn't resemble the usual hood, but then everything was changing these days. With all this Women's Lib crap and radical maniacs kidnapping people and half the White House soiled by the dirt of Watergate and other scandals, it was difficult to guess who might do what. Sure, this fella could be a hit man.

Beckam told him about the well-lit night range four miles away where one might shoot after the temperature had dropped to a mere 80, and Tabbat thanked him for the guidance.

She was not in the room when the K.G.B. operative returned to the Chateau, and at first he automatically suspected the worst. But she hadn't been killed or picked up by the F.B.I. A portly man had tried to pick her up at the pool where she'd been swimming and sunning, but he was simply a lecher who believed the rumors that there was a lot of easy tail in Vegas.

She didn't ask Tabbat where he'd been, and when he excused himself at 10 P.M. after dinner she didn't inquire where he was going. He drove out to the gun club that Beckam had mentioned, spoke persuasively and transferred some cash. They let him shoot for an hour, even sold him extra ammunition. It was still too hot to be comfortable, but Tabbat told himself that he was fortunate. He fired and fired and fired, with good results. Yes, this experience in night shooting with the new rifle could come in very handy. There was no telling where or when he might find Dalchimski.

It could be tomorrow night.

25

There was no word on the 6 P.M. news broadcast, and Dalchimski found this disappointing. The Americans were so swift and efficient in collecting reports on disasters. An apartment house fire in Chicago with fifty-three charred victims, a mad sniper cutting down seventeen people in New Orleans or Dallas, a school bus accident slaughtering sixty-two children in St. Louis or Kansas City—these tragedies were regularly rushed to the attention of the public with brisk and comprehensive reporting. Of course, foreign disasters that took 189 lives in

Tokyo or Rio were shunted off to the back pages and the final minutes of news broadcasts but Texas was part of the United States.

Was it being hushed up by the authorities?

The Soviet government routinely suppressed news of airline crashes or other events that might be embarrassing, Dalchimski reasoned, so perhaps the authorities in Washington were pursuing a similar policy. It wouldn't be easy to keep *this* secret, he thought as he decided to have his dinner at a highly recommended local restaurant. The detonation of forty nuclear warheads must surely have created such a tremendous explosion and fireball that it had to be noticed for a hundred miles.

Maybe they didn't all go off.

Perhaps the saboteur had been slain by the security unit at the Air Force's "special weapons" bunker.

Well, the eleven o'clock news would probably have some word on even that lesser event. Comforted by this and brimming with confidence in the prurient interest of the media in violence, Dalchimski drove up Route 7 to a charming little hotel named Orpheus Ascending where he enjoyed a superior French dinner and a piano player who excelled at Cole Porter and Richard Rodgers show tunes.

There was no mention of either Indian Gorge, Texas, or the nearby air base on the 11 P.M. broadcast. The former K.G.B. documents expert grew uneasy, began to speculate and worry. Something was wrong. It had worked every time before this, but now it wasn't going right. He started to pack his suitcase, determined to get away. If something was wrong, the safest thing was to flee—to move on swiftly.

No.

It would look strange if he checked out at midnight.

It would attract attention.

He didn't sleep much that night. After breakfast he paid his bill and drove the car back to the rental agency in Pittsfield. By 11 A.M. he was on a bus racing east on the Massachusetts Turnpike towards Boston. It had been a mistake to visit the Berkshires, for there was almost no air or rail service into that resort area. He'd be more mobile in a big city such as Boston, safer in the crowds and able to leave quickly for Chicago or

Montreal or Miami almost any time. A big and busy hotel in a large city would be much safer.

He glanced up—into the bosom of a plump young woman in a tight blouse. She was walking back to the "rest room"—an American euphemism that didn't detract much from the convenience of having a toilet on a bus. Russian buses offered no such amenities, but he didn't think about that. He wasn't thinking. He was reacting to the physical impact of the young woman. Something stirred involuntarily within him, reminding him of his loneliness and his body. He resented his body's needs and desires, and he glared bitterly at the woman who had forced this awareness upon him. His mission—his destiny—was much more important than any sexual appetites. He would not be distracted or deflected by a pair of firm young breasts—or anything else.

The Statler Hilton at Arlington Street on Boston's Park Square was big enough, and he felt much more secure in that large hotel with eleven hundred rooms. Still, he knew that something was wrong. When there was no report in the evening edition of the *Herald American*, his sense of danger began to grow. It was gnawing at him like some rodent with tiny sharp teeth, and pacing the room didn't ease the tension. He ate dinner in the room, afraid to leave the television set and not daring to go out because he dreaded what might be waiting in the street below. They could have the hotel surrounded. They might be toying with him, just waiting for him to emerge.

They'd never get the Book.

No matter how many K.G.B. operatives from the U.S. networks might be lurking outside the Statler Hilton in the night, they'd never recover the Book. He'd scout the streets around the building warily, and if he saw any sign of them he'd start telephoning immediately. He'd slip back into the room, barricade the door and began calling at once. Within an hour he could set off twenty, and by midnight he'd trigger the whole army—every one of them.

Shortly before ten he left his room and walked down the back service stairs—six floors. He scanned the lobby for several minutes, trying to determine whether any of this crowd of people could be his enemies. He had so many enemies. It wasn't only the K.G.B., but also the brutal fascists of the U.S. secret police forces. There were so many thousands of these savage thugs, hired killers employed by the capitalists to keep the workers enslaved. He saw a party of a dozen men and women joking and laughing as they headed for the door, and he decided to leave with them—to hide in this boisterous herd of bourgeoisie. They'd make perfect camouflage.

It worked. He got out into the flow of pedestrians, "strolled" swiftly away. Four times in the next fifteen minutes he checked to see whether he was under surveillance, and sighed with relief when he spotted no followers. It was difficult to be certain, for Moscow's agents were clever and skilled in trailing people, but —as far as he could tell—he was not being tracked. He walked on, wandered into a cheaper area where there were many bars and several theatres offering obscene films. Dalchimski had heard of this decadence, this obscenity that reflected the sickness of the West. Perhaps he ought to see just how sick these people were. The photos outside gave no specifics, but the titles on the overhead signs promised much.

He looked around again—still taut and vigilant. He stepped towards the glass booth, studied the fat tieless man whose face seemed to balloon oddly above the sign that said $5. Dalchimski hesitated. The porky man in the box office paid no attention, for he was used to middle-aged men faltering momentarily outside this grubby theatre. It hardly mattered to the ticket vendor, since he was on a straight salary anyway, and besides the uneasy middled-aged men usually got up enough nerve to enter.

Dalchimski didn't. He bolted. He walked away swiftly, strode a block in the heat until he saw a telephone booth just across the street. A taxi nearly struck him as he hurried towards it, but he dodged it and reached into his jacket for quarters. There would be no problem. Nicolai Dalchimski had always traveled with at least $3 in change from the moment he'd reached North America. He made it a point to be ready—at any hour—to be equipped to call.

He stared at the telephones. It was hot in the booth and the sweat was sheeting his body, but he was barely aware of his physical state. His mouth was dry. His heart was beating fast as he dialed the number in Texas. Perhaps it was foolish or even dangerous, but he had to know.

"Hello," said a woman—Texan and not too young.

"Mr. Archibald?"

There was a pause, a sigh.

"Guess you haven't heard. Mr. Archibald was in an accident."

What did she mean?

"Nothing serious, I hope."

"Mighty serious," she answered. "He was driving his car down the Interstate yesterday—over by the air base. Big trailer truck was coming down the hill behind him, and its brakes went out. Piled into him at seventy, knocked his car right into the gorge."

Dalchimski closed his eyes, and he could see the collision— the terrible impact—and the car falling, falling.

"Mr. Archibald—"

"Dead," she said. "It was horribul. Jest horribul. Never had a chance."

Ambush?

Had it been a trap?

This was exactly the sort of brutal "accident" at which the K.G.B. excelled, Dalchimski thought. They had experts, professionals trained for precisely this sort of sly execution. There was a special unit called Department V, ready to strike anywhere with expensive and ingenious murder tools. Was it possible that the Center had decided to liquidate its sleeper agents before Dalchimski could use them?

"That's awful," Dalchimski heard himself replying.

"Lord's will, I suppose. Were you a friend of his?"

"Not really—just an acquaintance. My name's . . . Tom Strauss. Well, please give my condolences to Mrs. Archibald."

"Sure will. I'm her sister."

Dalchimski hung up and stood there shaking, caught in a mixture of frustration and fear. If they'd destroyed Archibald, they'd be watching the others too—waiting to butcher them like hogs. There could be a battalion of Department V technicians spread across the land, killers smuggled in via a dozen

U.S. ports of entry during the past month. They might be looking for him too, each one of them armed with his photo and those guns that silently fired poisoned bullets. Even though he'd dyed his hair and grown a mustache, they might still recognize him. They were trained hunters, adroit at stalking. They'd slain many.

"Not me," Dalchimski said as he stepped out of the booth.

"How about me, baby?"

She had large breasts—even bigger than the girl in the bus. Heavily lipsticked and showing her legs in a garish green miniskirt, this plump woman—perhaps twenty-five or twenty-seven years old—was plainly a whore. She had a big knowing smile that was surely false, but the scent of her perfume and powder affected him anyway. He could lose himself in her cheap animal quality, escape from the K.G.B. for an hour.

"Looking for action?" she pressed in the flat accents of this state.

"A lot of action."

"How about a party? I've got a girlfriend—sort of my roommate. She's a blonde, and she knows a lot of tricks. You know what I mean?"

"Why not?"

It was crazy to throw all his caution away like this, but he wanted to do something crazy now.

"Fifty bucks? We'll give you a real good time."

She licked her lips, flicking her fat tongue at him in a preposterous parody of erotic promise. He was supposed to believe that this tart was seething with lust. Well, he didn't care. He needed a woman, and two would be even better. If the assassins were on the trail, there was little point in puritanical abstinence now.

The third-rate—no, fourth-rate—hotel was only a hundred yards away, and her roommate was a tall thin girl whose need for a bath was barely obscured by her cologne. It was difficult to tell whether she was a natural blonde in that dimly lit room. After Dalchimski had paid the $50 and disrobed, the two woman stripped and began to do the things they'd done so many times before. It was all a performance, but they worked conscientiously. Dalchimski's body surrendered.

"You from New York, baby?" wondered the brunette as she caressed him mechanically.

"Yes, but I was born in Holland."

"You talk like that," said the blonde.

The resumed their labors, and he responded again. He felt tired, and when he closed his eyes he drifted off before he realized what was happening. He must have slept for several minutes. When he was awakened by the passing fire engine, he opened his eyes suddenly. The brunette was still touching him, but the blonde was in the bathroom. He could see her through the open door, reflected in the mirror above the sink.

She was going through his wallet.

Dalchimski knew what he had to do. He reached out, seized the woman beside him by the throat and twisted—breaking her neck before she could make a sound. Then he got up, took a heavy lamp from the bedtable and unplugged it from the wall. He moved towards the bathroom as quietly as he could. The blonde finished counting the money—*his* money—and smiled at the total—$4,162. Some score! She was beaming as she turned to the doorway.

Dalchimski smashed her in the face with the lamp base, driving the smile back into her pulped flesh. She reeled, and he whipped the cord around her neck. She was dead ninety seconds later. Dalchimski picked up his wallet, dressed quickly and made an attempt to wipe his fingerprints from the lamp with the blonde's blue underpants. It didn't matter that much, he told himself as he left the hotel. They were only whores. No one would miss them. No one would even come looking until the smell of their bodies—decaying in the summer heat—soured the atmosphere of the hall.

By then, Nicolai Dalchimski would be gone.

He'd be one thousand miles away.

He'd be safe in a distant city, with $3 in coins and the Book that made him the most powerful man in the world.

26

Fifty or sixty years ago some canny observer of the corrupt ways of machine politics in New York City wrote an ironic and amusing article about the difference between honest graft and dishonest. Posing as an authority on the hefty Hibernian hustlers of the Manhattan combine known as Tammany, he explained that it was honest graft if you gave the building contract for a new school to a firm that paid you a bribe equivalent to 20 percent of the contract price and then overcharged the city by 50 percent. It would be dishonest graft if you took the bribe and didn't get the contract for the firm.

By these standards, Ted Beckam was an honest crook. He delivered what he had been paid for, and promptly. A dishonest crook might have taken Tabbat's money, never sent out the alarm on the missing persons list and then lied that no one could find Nick Dallo. There was a fair chance that a dishonest crook could get away with this, but there was also the risk that the Family might check with some other Family or with some bought clerk in the police of another city. In that case, there was a better than fair chance that Sergeant Beckam would suffer a very painful accident—perhaps even a fatal one. It wouldn't happen in Vegas. Every Eastern Family knew better than to do anything like that within the city limits, for there were rules and customs that had to be respected. Only animals or morons would hit a cop in Vegas.

All those God-fearing and tax-paying residents of this fine City of Churches would be horrified, for Law and Order are prized and cherished here. In this community of organized risk and chance the uncertainties of random violence are not to be tolerated. The dumping of corpses, or even such minor matters as the breaking of arms or the forceful theft of purses, might offend the conventioneers and tourists and honeymoon couples. Vegas is a swell place to visit, and the Chamber of Commerce is dead right when it talks about the sunshine, fun and safe streets.

So Beckam put it on the teletype circuit and had the snap-shot of Dalchimski sent out by telephoto. General Strelski would have had a three-megaton fit if he'd known that Tabbat had turned over a picture of the defector to U.S. police. Strelski was as predictably paranoid about the Americans and about standard K.G.B. procedures as many C.I.A. executives— Coltrane, for instance—were about Russians and the necessity for obeying regular U.S. methods. Yet Strelski's techniques wouldn't find Nicolai Dalchimski, and Tabbat felt no compunctions about trying anything that might work. If he succeeded, he'd be a hero and get a medal and a pay increase and a new, bigger apartment with the latest stereo-phonograph rig. Nobody would tell the Center about Tabbat's defiance, and if he stopped the Stalinist, they wouldn't care. If Tabbat failed, there would be nobody at the Center to listen. There would be no Center.

Through the wonders of modern science and a lot of tax money, the message and the picture spilled into many hundreds of police headquarters within an hour after Beckam accepted the $1,000. It generated no excitement or special attention. It wasn't sexy. There's nothing sexy about another man who's missing, for experienced police around the country—in big cities and small—realized that he'd probably left his wife for some crazy young chick or lost his marbles and decided to opt for the counter-culture. Some of the police had only a fuzzy idea as to what this counter-culture might be, viewing the key ingredients as drinking cheap wine, smoking grass and giving up real work to screw around in a rural commune where nobody washed or ate meat. Anyway, this was only a "missing person" alert, not a "want." It wasn't as if this Wop—or was the name Spic?—had stolen money, slashed nine throats or supplied guns to some militant gang. There was no warrant out, no heat.

Tabbat had considered a warrant, but rejected the idea as too dangerous. For one thing, Beckam might be understandably reluctant to expose himself to all kinds of risks by putting out a "want" if there was no warrant. The sergeant could crap his way out of any "missing person" beef by pretending innocence and swearing he'd been tricked, but there was no way to beat the other situation. Even if Beckam would have taken the chance, there was the additional threat that some cop somewhere might teletype back for more information or might get into a gunfight trying to "apprehend the suspect." No, this was safer.

So in fifty states all sorts of policemen—state, city and federal, brilliant and ordinary, fat and thin, old and young, hip and bigoted, ambitious and time-servers, tough and thoughtful and tough-thoughtful—began to look for Nick Dallo. Casually. Routinely. They were also looking for stolen cars, runaway teenagers, dope dealers, fugitive accountants who'd fled with payrolls, two-time losers who'd broken out of a prison farm in the next state, the drunken brother of the high-school principal, the burglars who hit the hardware store, assorted perverts, deaf-mutes who were lost and black radicals suspected of shooting at cops last year. They were simultaneously enforcing traffic laws, settling family quarrels, collecting drunks, chasing escaping bank robbers, tapping telephones, disarming mental cases, negotiating for pay rises, rushing pregnant women to the hospital, eating free lunches and risking their lives in various ways—all while not filling out assorted forms.

But they were looking, patiently and placidly, for the man said to be Dallo. A man named Dallo was arrested on a charge of indecent exposure in Athens, Georgia, but he proved to be only twenty-four years old and a graduate student practicing "streaking." His name wasn't Nick anyway. A motorcycle patrolman on the edge of Detroit thought that a man in a 1973 Imperial—dark blue with whitewalls—resembled the photo of the missing person. The driver turned out to be a vice-president of the Ford Motor Corporation, and a contributor to the mayor's election campaign. A San Francisco detective was only a little surprised when the man he interrogated on Russian Hill proved to be a five-foot-ten-inch lesbian with a good sense of humor. She laughed at him, instead of calling the American Civil Liberties Union.

The Akron, Ohio, constabulary reported to Beckam that they had recently arrested a fifty-nine-year-old man named Naxos Dallopolis as the head of a porno film ring, but the bleeding-heart liberal judge had thrown out the case and Mr. Dallopolis had left town with a pair of nineteen-year-old sisters—Gloria and Gretschen Derma. They were nieces of "Bearcat" Derma, who'd starred on the Oakland Raiders in the 1960s. Then there was the call from an irate lieutenant on the New Orleans force. His name was Nicholas Dallo, and what the hell was going on?

Tabbat kept shooting. He was at the range every night for an hour, polishing his accuracy. Then he'd go out to show his companion the town, taking her to a different hotel each evening to enjoy the entertainment and gambling. He never won or lost much, for he knew that the Center scowled at such capitalist diversion. This was just a way of passing time, he explained to her, and he gave her a concise course in the games and operating procedures. He told her about the odds and the protocol, and he spoke knowingly of the security procedures—including the armed men watching through two-way mirrors in the ceilings.

"I don't suppose anyone could rob these places," she answered in the Sands one night. "After all, they've designed the casinos with that in mind."

Tabbat sipped his drink, reflected briefly.

"Depends. Right crew, right equipment, right plan—could be done. There's no place that's *completely* secure. You might need an inside man—like that job on the Courier Center at Orly. What was his name? I read about it in the Chicago papers. Johnson—he got twenty-five years. Sergeant Johnson."

She remembered the case of the U.S. Army sergeant who'd photographed top-secret documents at the Armed Forces Courier Center at Orly Airport near Paris. That guarded vault had elaborate security systems, had been considered impregnable. Every major espionage organization in the world now included that classic operation in its training programs.

"Could you do it—here?" she asked provocatively.

"Guess so, but who'd want to? There isn't that much cash

in a casino at any one time—maybe six hundred, eight hundred thousand. I'd take a place with more cash and less security, a big bank with those nice sixty-year-old guards. That son of a bitch we're looking for did a bank job, you know, and I'm ten times better than he is."

"Of course."

"He's good enough—at his thing," Tabbat admitted. "At *his* thing he's very, very good. He's the number one maniac and champion telephoner in the world—hands down. . . . Well, how about another drink?"

"Coffee?" asked Colonel Jenkins at C.I.A. headquarters seven hours later.

Dorothy Putterman nodded, and they started down the corridor towards the cafeteria. Her devotion to principle impressed Jenkins, for this was the sixth consecutive day she was bouncing along without a bra. You had to respect a person who stuck to her convictions, the colonel told himself.

"Was talking to Ham," Jenkins announced softly.

Hamilton Roosevelt Feldman wasn't a colonel, but he was one of the senior civilian executives at the Agency. He had worked his way up in the power structure during the past fourteen years, and held the same rank as Jenkins in a parallel line on the Table of Organization. Not only that, he was paid $8,000 a year more—partially in tribute to his Ph.D. from the University of Minnesota. Ham represented the Central Intelligence Agency on Working Group Five, the inter-agency outfit that focused on counter-espionage. He knew a great deal about Tolstoi, Chekhov, Castro's sex life and the chess masters of the twentieth century.

"Tough," replied Ms. Putterman—aware that her boss was irritated by the intellectual pretensions of Hamilton Roosevelt Feldman and his extra $8,000.

"They're trying to put the pieces together on that thing in West Virginia and the nut who gunned his way into the Army base in Colorado. The F.B.I.'s all steamy about the fellow who died in the hospital at Leavenworth."

She shrugged, and Jenkins couldn't help admiring how they moved. It saddened him to think that he'd have to give up these simple pleasures, to purge himself of these obsolete attitudes.

"None of our business," she answered.

She was—as usual—correct.

"I told him just that, Dorothy. Probably all mental cases. That's what I said."

She shrugged again, and Jenkins swallowed hard.

"I wouldn't know, Tom. I'm not a psychiatrist."

"No, but you're a damn fine analyst. You've got a wonderful mind—aside from your great talent with the computer. Ham respects your mind a lot."

It was entirely possible, she decided, for. she'd run into Feldman on five or six occasions at concerts at the Kennedy Center. One had been all Mozart.

"What does he want?" she asked crisply.

"Well—if you've got a little time—would you talk with him and try to develop a computer program on this hash?"

She almost smiled at the humor in the odd situation.

"You want me to, Tom?"

"Not at the expense of our own stuff. Cotton Candy, Sand Shark and Hot Rod come first."

"Jaw Bone?"

"I forgot that. After Jaw Bone. There's no wild rush on this. Probably doesn't add up to a crock of snake piss anyway."

Now she smiled, broadly and in spite of herself. She usually found the colonel's efforts at rural slang tedious, but this whole situation seemed funny.

"End of the week okay?"

"Course. Goddam generous of you to pitch in, Dorothy."

She was a fine person, Jenkins thought as he opened the door of the cafeteria for her, and he'd defend her against that vulture Coltrane. It was outrageous that some jealous and ambitious bureaucrat should try to supress the efforts of intelligent women to assert their rights. Dorothy Putterman stopped abruptly, looked at him strangely and walked on. The colonel followed her into the cafeteria, saddened by the consciousness of his gauche sexist error. He wasn't supposed to open doors anymore. She'd explained all that two full weeks earlier.

27

Screw you, Hanrahan.

Anthony Scungilli began every day with that defiant manifesto. The great-grandson of a man who'd been the most
dreaded shot in Sicily, Scungilli wasn't going to let a fat slob
like Joseph X. Hanrahan—Lieutenant Joseph X. Hanrahan—
get him down. It was a year now since Hanrahan had slyly
arranged to have Detective Scungilli transferred to the Homicide Division, one of the least popular assignments in the
Boston Police Department. You had to work your ass off at
Homicide. You couldn't goof off, for murders attracted press
attention and the reporters were always putting the heat on you
to solve every killing in an hour and a half. If they'd done ten
minutes' worth of homework they'd know that police statistics
showed that the great bulk of solved murders were those involving family fights, and that most of the other killings weren't
solved at all.

Scungilli glanced at the photos on his battered desk, shook
his head. Whores. Couple of dead hustlers, that's all. Nothing
special about them at all. One—the blonde with the appendec-
tomy scar—had been busted twice last year. The other bimbo
had served three months in the winter, and had been treated
for V.D. when she entered the women's jail. A pair of strictly
ordinary clapped-up whores had been knocked off in a strictly
ordinary and fourth-rate hotel, and the papers had yelled as if
this were the Crime of the Century.

Fuckin' ridiculous.

Had to be some wacked-up guy with all kinds of hate-your-
mother problems or maybe sexual guilts left over from parochial

school. Tony Scungilli had no such guilts. He was a competent and hard-working cop who did his job well, went home to Revere for a good meal and banged his wife every night—'cept when she was out of action. He didn't fool around with outside chicks, not since he'd been married. A lot of guys did and that was their business, Scungilli had decided years ago. Very few of them seemed to suffer any guilts, but then they didn't go around wrecking hustlers. There were a lot of real good men on the Boston force, and Scungilli was quietly proud to be associated with them.

Except Hanrahan.

Screw you, Hanrahan.

Hanrahan had been after him for a long time, making jokes about his name. You didn't have to be no goddam Harvard professor to know that "scungilli" meant "octopus." Shit, it was on the menu of every damn Italian restaurant in town. Hanrahan didn't like Italians, and he didn't like Tony Scungilli most of all. What bothered the bastard most was that Scungilli was smart, was making tough cases that puzzled other detectives. Scungilli felt sorry for Hanrahan, a dumb-ass Mick who didn't know all that racial crap was over the hill. Someday that idiot Hanrahan would gun a Spade who'd turn out to be a minister or politician, and they'd hang the lieut by the nuts. The Commissioner would get the word from the Mayor, and that would be the end of Joseph X. Hanrahan.

This thing with the whores was ridiculous. Marie Banteau, twenty-four and a tramp out of Canada. Joan Miller, a local hooker who'd dropped out of high school at fifteen. The lab boys had gone over the room pretty good. Maybe not quite as perfectly as they do in the movies where they find every speck of dust, but they'd done their job. They'd found some traces of grass in an ashtray, a smear of dog crap on the corner of the rug, a gray hair beside the bed, $98 in cash and a mess of different fingerprints. Two of these belonged to the right hand of Nicolai Dalchimski, but how the hell was Scungilli to guess that? He was a detective, not a seer. Detective Scungilli had sent the assorted prints to the state capital at Springfield first, and they could only identify the two dead women. Then he'd sped the prints to the F.B.I.'s master national print file in

Washington. As he chewed vigorously on the gum he'd taken up when he'd abandoned cigarettes in March, he wondered whether he should have sent the Feds the dog crap too. They could tell exactly what kind of dog it was, he thought with a toothy grin. A six-year-old Ukrainian wolfhound who ate a lot of fish. Go check Lochober's and the Union Oyster House.

But it wasn't a dog that had killed the hookers.

It was either a man or a member of one of our female Olympic squads. Strong, much stronger than most women. He'd demolished most of one broad's face with the lamp base, and that took plenty of power—or craziness. Or both. Maybe it was a pimp, Scungilli speculated. There weren't as many in Boston as in some other towns, but there were some and they could get rough with the hookers. No, it was almost unheard of for a pimp to kill and then there was the $98 in cash. A pimp would have taken every penny.

The phone rang.

He picked it up, heard that the Feds' report was banging in on the teleprinter now. "Be right down," he said, welcoming the opportunity to stretch his legs. Tony Scungilli was no damn martyr and he sure didn't miss those years of foot patrol, but he often found himself stiff and cramped behind a desk—looking for an excuse to walk. Four minutes after the telephone call he stood reading the printout from the District of Columbia.

Zero.

Unknown.

Whoever it was who'd left those prints had never served in the U.S. armed forces or been arrested in any of the fifty states. But he might be picked up again on some charge—anything, even drunken driving—next week or next month. Scungilli would be ready.

"Put out a 'wanted on suspicion of murder' on this louse," he ordered. "May be armed and dangerous. Hold in connection with two homicides of known prostitutes, Boston."

Then he returned to his office to resume calling the mental institutions within two hundred miles. He'd already checked a dozen, working from instinct that a disturbed man—perhaps one recently released from some asylum—had killed the two victims. It was drudge work, but a lot of cases were solved this way. Even if he found some clue as to the possible identity of the perpetrator, the bastard could be anywhere by now—maybe as far as Hawaii. It depended on how much money he had.

With more than $300,000 in cash and American Express checks, Nicolai Dalchimski was standing at the corner of Broadway and Columbus. Not in New York, in San Francisco. He'd eaten a seafood dinner on Fisherman's Wharf, turned down a taxi driver's suggestion that he ogle the transvestites at a nightclub famous for its female impersonators and made his way to The Condor. He'd found a music-and-news weekly in the cab on his way in from San Francisco's airport, read an article that mentioned the silicone-expanded bosom of a top-less dancer named Carol Something who starred at The Condor. Something had changed in the repressed Stalinist since his sexual collision with the two tarts in Boston. It was as if a dam had broken. Now he wanted greedily, and the huge teats of Carol Something drew him to this intersection. It was the right place. The two-story sign of a woman in a bikini had red lightbulbs where the nipples should be, and he felt none of the qualms that had kept him from the obscene film in Boston.

He had made up his mind about a number of things.

The next "sleeper" he'd awake would be the woman who believed she was Lorraine Damann, and had been running a boardinghouse in Ithaca, New York, for more than a dozen years. After that, he'd set off four more at two-day intervals. Then he'd call all the others, twenty an hour. The wave of destruction would terrify and arouse the whole country, would force the Pentagon to hit back. Once the U.S. missiles and bombers were on their way, the traitors in the Kremlin would have to fire their own rockets. Both of these evil regimes would be scourged by the greatest conflagrations since the planet was born—burned and gutted.

Nicolai Dalchimski would not be present for the holocaust, however. He'd make all the final calls from a booth at Miami Airport, and he'd be on a plane to Rio before the war began. He'd already figured out exactly how much change he'd need, and added in an extra $10 as a precaution. Yes, he had the situation under control and the fact that they were hunting him

wouldn't make him panic. He was smiling when he entered The
Condor, and he was smiling when he emerged at 2:10 in the
morning. Carol Something's body had done its job, and now he
would find a woman. There would surely be several in the
nearby streets, and even if his choice went through his wallet
she'd only find $130. He wouldn't have to kill her. It had been
a mistake to destroy the other two, and he wasn't going to
repeat that blunder and arouse the San Francisco police. The
larcenous pair in Boston had merely been bad fortune, he told
himself again.

His luck had changed.

This time he met an attractive and sleepy-eyed black woman
who gave him half an hour for $30, and nothing more. No
trouble, just professional service. He didn't have to kill her,
which was something of a relief. Maybe he'd be as fortunate
tomorrow night, he thought hopefully as he flagged a cab, and
he wouldn't have to slay that woman either.

28

For those who like colleges, Ithaca is a great town. Cornell,
which has grown to be an important university since it was
founded in 1865, is four times bigger than Ithaca College but
each has its charm. The town itself is set in an attractive area
in upper New York State, on heights overlooking the Cayuga
River. Cayuga is an Indian word reflecting the Algonquin—or
is it the Iroquois?—who used to pad around these parts in
terrific hand-made moccasins, a tradition that today's better-
dressed Cornell and Ithaca students maintain. They are a
minority, however, frequently oppressed by the Torn Sneaker
Tribe which has scourged so many campuses in the past decade.

Most of the visitors who pass through are seeing their children or have some other connection with the two colleges, and they generally stay at the Holiday Inn or the Sheraton Motor Inn or the Howie Johnson. Those are transients who can afford rooms going for a minimum of $15 a day, plus taxes.

Students can't cope with these prices, so they bunch up in apartments or rent rooms at boardinghouses such as the one operated by Mrs. Lorraine Damann. It was three storeys high, had nine rooms for rent and was only a five-minute drive from the Cornell campus. There was a lawn in the front and a porch, and there were tall leafy trees that provided essential shade in the hot months. Even here on the breezy cliff above the river it got much more than warm in July and August.

There had been a Mr. Damann for two or three years back in the early sixties. Gunther Damann had perished of acute and totally unexpected trichinosis or ptomaine or something. Whatever it was, it came from a tainted sausage and anchovy pizza and carried him off swiftly. Mrs. Damann, a roly-poly lady with lots of motherly feelings and a gift for dressing badly, ran the boardinghouse and cooked and dabbled in pottery. She had a wheel and a kiln out in the garage, and often appeared with clay-stained hands and a rueful smile. Her food was wholesome, adequate and not too costly, and she only sold her ceramics and pots at the annual Christmas Bazaar of Our Lady of the Immaculate Conception Church.

She was a homebody, and rarely left the boardinghouse. Her neighbors accepted and understood the fear of driving that had come over her after Gunther's death, and they helped out by picking up the food she'd ordered by telephone from the same market she'd been patronizing so many years. People help each other in Ithaca. It's that kind of town, proud of its quiet and its gardens. There's an active Nature Club and a chapter of the Bird Watchers League. Mrs. Damann had been treasurer of the League since 1969, being reelected unanimously every spring. Attending those meetings one night a year was just about the only time she went out, and on those occasions she always did something rather odd. She made sure that one of the guests—she never called them lodgers—was home and ready to take any telephone messages. She insisted on keeping a pad and pencil by the phone, and limited the guests' calls to no more than ten minutes. That was a house rule.

There was a simple explanation. She had an elderly sister in Canton, Ohio, who was in poor health, and if her sister tried to reach her it was important that the phone be free. This was one of Lorraine Damann's "little fibs." She had two brothers in Odessa, and a sister who was Deputy Director of the Institute of Arctic Medicine in Murmansk. Her other "fib" involved the demise of her husband. Gunther Damann had served in the U.S. Army Engineers during the Korean War, and he'd noticed that some of the clay she stored for her pottery smelled a bit like C-3 plastic explosive. When his curiosity had failed to subside, it had been necessary to get rid of him. She'd done it quite automatically and had since forgotten it—in accord with the hypnosis.

Now it was a balmy Thursday night. The guests always looked forward to Thursdays, for that was the evening she served her special stuffed pork chops. She was proud of her stuffed pork chops, which she generally served with watermelon rind she'd pickled herself. The head of the Cornell School of Hotel Administration had once rated those pork chops "outstanding"—roughly the equivalent to a star in the *Guide Michelin*. At 6:30 P.M.—just as Mrs. Damann was carrying the platter of chops into the dining room—the phone rang. A helpful instructor in the School of Agriculture & Forestry saw that her hands were full, so he picked up the instrument and took the message.

"It's a man named Ryavec from New York," he announced. "Wants a room—double room—for three nights starting on the eighth."

Mrs. Damann put down the platter.

"What's his first name?" she asked curtly.

"Alfred . . . no, Albert. What'll I tell him?"

"Yes."

"You want to talk to him?"

"It won't be necessary."

To the amazement of all the guests, Mrs. Damann simply left her special pork chops and walked out of the room. The hungry people at the table assumed that she'd be back from the kitchen with the watermelon rind in a minute, but she never returned. Instead, she went to her kiln and picked up two boxes of "clay," which she proceeded to load into her rarely used car. She drove away. The guests all looked at each other, dumbfounded.

She drove eleven miles, parked the car by the side of the road. She removed a suitcase from the trunk, carried that bag and the "clay" three hundred yards into the woods—directly to a manhole cover set flush in the earth. She took a tool from the suitcase, pried up the metal and found herself facing another steel plate set in concrete. This didn't defeat her, however. She formed a charge of the C-3 plastic, inserted an NO-9 detonator and set the fuse for one minute. Then she walked sixty or seventy yards, waited for the explosion to blast open the steel plate. It did. She returned, approved her work and looked down into the narrow shaft at the cable. Now she took a pair of rubber gloves and a twin-bladed cutting tool—something like razor-sharp pliers—from the valise. She climbed down the ladder built into the wall of the shaft, put on the gloves and attacked the cable. She tried and tried to sever it for half an hour, sweat pouring from her and stinging her eyes. She failed.

The metal sheath that protected the cable was too tough. She climbed to the surface, took a heavy glass bottle from the suitcase and descended again. Carefully—so carefully—she poured the colorless liquid on a three-inch section of the sheath and watched the acid eat through the outer layers. Then she finished her job with the cutters, chopping the cable in two.

Alarm lights flashed. In a cavern dug into a mountain near Colorado Springs, Colorado, and in a strange building jammed with electronic gear near Thule in Greenland, men responded quickly and profanely.

"What the fuck's wrong?" said Captain Francis Bostikyan of the North American Air Defense Command in Colorado.

"What the fuck's wrong?" said Lieutenant Paul W. Rifkind of the U.S. Air Force's Ballistic Missile Early Warning System in the Arctic.

This sharp language was pure reflex, for both knew that the situation signaled by the flashing lights and the beep-beep-beep of the alarm wasn't critical. Ten years ago it might have been much more serious if the main land-line linking the radar outpost to NORAD headquarters had gone out of action, but now there were other communications circuits including those built into the satellites put up during the past two years. These alternative circuits would kick on automatically in case of such failure. They did. Within ten seconds after the break, they were functioning. Fifteen seconds later Captain Bostikyan put down his cigarillo and picked up the gray telephone on the wall of his glass-walled office.

"Maintenance," he said, looking out at the huge twenty-by-sixty-foot world map on the far wall of the NORAD command post. "Maintenance, we've got a Dingbat on the main Bee-Mews land line to Thule. You'd better run a circuit check and get out a repair crew."

He scanned the enormous plexiglass "display panel" which showed all the vital facts on North American security. None of the three biggest radar stations—Thule or the ones in England or Alaska—showed any signs of incoming rockets, nor was there any alert coming in from the planes or ships on electronic patrol. Just a breakdown somewhere, not an attack.

The NORAD maintenance experts began an immediate series of tests, sending signals over sections of the cable all the way from Colorado to Hudson's Bay. It took seven minutes for the detectors to identify the site of the trouble as Charlie 44, a segment near Ithaca, New York. By 7:55 a crew was loading its gear into a repair truck thirty miles away. Lorraine Damann was driving north by that time, moving at a steady and law-abiding fifty miles per hour towards the rendezvous point near the Canadian border. Shortly before dawn she reached the point on the southern shore of Lake Ontario where the pickup was to be made. She walked down to the beach, peered into the darkness for some sign of the helicopter.

The sun rose.

It was pink and lovely, doing wonders to the sky as the colors changed to gold and the darkness died.

She waited, unaware that no aircraft would fly her to safety. She waited and waited, hour after hour. It grew very hot and the sun burned her eyes, but she waited.

In Vegas Tabbat awoke and decided that he'd better check with Beckam. Tabbat was edgy and tired of waiting. Unlike parachuting or hand-to-hand combat or sniping, it wasn't one of the things at which he excelled. He got out of bed and turned on the radio, listened to the latest scandal from Washington and shook his head. There'd be more bad news any day or any hour, and that last message from the Center indicated that time was running out for both Tabbat and his mission.

The K.G.B. wasn't very good at waiting either.

29

There are people who'd say that the atmosphere of the Lucky Dude was incongruous, but the truth is that it wasn't much more peculiar than a number of its rival spots on Fremont Street. There was a country trio up on one end of the stage working its way through the combined repertories of Johnny Cash and Loretta Lynn, and at the other end a twenty-year old go-go dancer was shaking and wondering how her son was doing back home in Helena, Montana. Three waitresses with tired feet moved around in circles—and in yellow hot pants topped by silver lamé halters—unloading beers and rye and gingers to the minority of patrons not busy pumping the handles of the slot machines.

This wasn't the Strip.

Not by a long shot.

This was where the lower middle class came to gamble for smaller stakes at less glamorous games of chance. Sixty-year-old women in comfortable shoes and stretch pants with little stretch left migrated here like lemmings. They carried paper cups filled with quarters, and they rammed the coins into the machines with a speed and determination bordering on the furious. If they or their white-haired husbands with the arthritic hands were enjoying themselves, it wasn't visible. They were working, working at having a good time. Everybody had a good time in Vegas. That was why you came here.

Tabbat watched them for a minute before he wandered over to the machine where Beckam was going through the motions.

"You're five minutes late," joked the policeman. "Cost me three dollars waiting for you."

Tabbat, who'd been ten minutes early but spent a quarter of an hour checking out the block for watchers, chuckled mechanically. "I'll make it up to you," he said and handed Beckam a $50 bill. Some men might have passed a $100 note, but that probably would have made Beckam greedy.

"Any news?"

Beckam shook his head, dropped another quarter into the slot and cranked again.

Nothing.

"Might take a couple more days, Mr. Gordon. They're out looking for him—all over the country. I've got the local force on the job too. No stone unturned, you know."

"That's good of you. My Family's getting a little impatient though."

Beckam nodded, inserted another coin.

"Patience is a virtue—seek it if you can. Seldom found in woman—never found in man," he chanted. "Learned that in first-year high school."

He pumped again, and this time a rain of coins poured into the cup—$12 in quarters. He beamed.

"My luck's changed. Maybe yours will too, Mr. Gordon."

"Soon?"

Beckam started filling his jacket pocket with his winnings.

"Can't tell. Maybe you could help it along. Offer a reward."

He was greedy. That didn't bother Tabbat. It was a good sign, for a greedy person will do what he's paid to do and the spy had plenty of cash.

"Two thousand?"

"Ought to do it."

A larger sum would have been a mistake, for it would have signaled that someone or something terribly important-illegal was involved. Just $2,000 would whet the sergeant's appetite. It was unlikely any other cop would see a penny of it, not more than half anyway. When it was over, Beckam would ask for another $1,000. Tabbat would pay it—to keep him happy and quiet.

"Suppose I leave it with you," Tabbat offered as a gesture of good faith. "I'd feel safer that way. I happen to have just about that much with me."

Beckam said he had to "take a leak," which set up the passing of the money in the men's toilet. "I'll put this on the wire right away," he pledged as they left the building. "Call you soon as I get word. Where'd you say you staying?"

"Versailles Chateau."

"Riiight. Hope to have good news soon. Know how a Family worries 'bout a missing relative. Awful feeling."

It was in the rented car driving back to the hotel that Tabbat heard the strange report on the 5 P.M. news broadcast. Vacationers fishing in a launch off Sudus Point, New York—a little town on the south shore of Lake Ontario—had seen a woman waving at them from the beach. She appeared to be in some trouble, but the water was too shallow and there were rocks so they asked the local police to look into it when they docked an hour later. A radio car was sent—with startling results. As the police vehicle drew near, the middle-aged woman pulled a gun and killed the officer at the wheel with two shots. The car spun out of control, crashed into a parked coupe that later proved to belong to a Mrs. Lorraine Damann of Ithaca, New York. The other cop rolled out of his wrecked car, slid under it an got off four rounds as fast as he could. One slug from his .38-caliber Smith and Wesson revolver tore a hole in her chest, three inches below her throat.

But that wasn't what killed her.

She had taken some kind of poison. Officer Joseph Melita, who had a broken shoulder and a marvelous stubborn devotion to duty, had seen her swallow the pill. Officer Melita, only twenty-five years old and the father of five, had no idea why. His partner—Officer Burford Denver, thirty-eight and father of four—would get a hero's funeral. Nobody in Ithaca—where Mrs. Damann was known as a quiet widow—could explain her mental breakdown.

Ithaca-Damann-BMEWS cable. They were one in Tabbat's mind, a single entity on the list. He could still remember the goddam phone number, which didn't matter. Mrs. Damann's troubles were over. She'd died just as heroically as the unfortunate cop. She was off the hook. Tabbat wasn't. What's more, he could sense that it was going to get worse—soon.

Although Dalchimski had meant to wait forty-eight hours between incidents, he couldn't quite resist making another call the next morning when he disembarked at the Houston Airport. It was a bit self-indulgent, he thought, but he couldn't control himself that well these days. The addition of the bacteria to the water supply at Homestead Air Force Base south of Miami would have an interesting effect on the B-52 crews of the Strategic Air Command, and hopefully the news would not be suppressed.

It wasn't, although the Associated Press accepted the S.A.C. story of tainted food which killed one navigator and left more than 130 ill—too ill to fly. Neither Tabbat nor the *Rezident* bought the story, nor did the U.S.A.F.'s Office of Special Investigations. The number of such "incidents" could not be ignored. Somebody was making war on the United States, and Somebody had to be punished. The "alert" level was raised at every U.S. air base—as a precaution. If any more attacks came, they must be beaten off and the U.S. Air Force must be ready to hit back.

30

The telephone rang, and Tabbat seized it.

"Mr. Gordon?"

"Yes."

"I think I've got some good news," Beckam said.

"How good?"

"He's in Houston."

Tabbat's face lit up and broadened in an instant.

"Are you sure?"

"Just about. An airport cop spotted him an hour ago. Says Mr. Dallo's dyed his hair and grown a mustache. Can't imagine why he'd do that."

Don't be smart, you bastard.

You aren't being paid all this money to needle.

"Certain it's him?"

"Well, he looks like the picture and he talks with an accent. He's registered at the hotel as Karl Martin Beller, and he's acting edgy. Hardly goes out of the room."

"He's confused and ashamed. He'd been seeing a psychiatrist, you know," Tabbat improvised automatically.

You had to hand it to these East Coast Mafia boys, thought Beckam. They were real smooth. Dallo or whatever his name was would get a quick and quiet sendoff, probably end up at the bottom of the Gulf talking to the shrimp.

"Which hotel?"

"Right at the airport," Beckam replied. "Room three-oh-five. I told the Houston police to keep an eye on him. They've got a man covering the lobby. You just ask the desk clerk to page Mr. Law, and he'll pick up a house phone."

The bad joke was unimportant. What counted now was

the next flight to Houston. Tabbat thanked the sergeant, phoned a travel agent and found there was no scheduled service to the Texas city for six hours. He chartered an "executive jet" —a Lockheed six-seater that was airborne in fifty-five minutes. Sixteen hundred dollars of the cash she'd brought from the *Rezident* produced instant service, and by 3 P.M. Tabbat, his woman and his rifle were entering the air terminal in Houston. Served by fifteen airlines, it was seething with people—healthy, tanned people.

Tabbat cut his way through them like an infantry lieutenant leading a bayonet charge. As they entered the lobby of the Host Hotel, he turned to her abruptly.

"You got a gun?"

She blinked, wondering whether he wanted her to or not.

"Yes."

"Good. I'll go up. Take a look at his picture."

He showed her the photo, and she nodded. She'd feared that he might be annoyed about the .32 automatic, even though the Colt was a U.S. weapon and she had a perfectly forged license to carry it. It was a relief that he approved. Tabbat had to be kept happy, for his mission was crucial. They'd told her that in the bluntest terms.

He walked to the house phone, asked that Mr. Law be paged. The name boomed out of the speaker again and again— ten times. There was no response. Tabbat insisted that the call be repeated, and after another two minutes they saw a sharp-featured man of about thirty—dressed in a light blazer, sport shirt and checked pants—hurry to another house phone ten feet away.

"Law," he said.

Tabbat put down his instrument, turned to the detective.

"My name's Gordon. Where the hell've you been?"

"Had to take a leak," apologized the plainclothes officer. "You the dude from Vegas?"

"Yeah."

"Your uncle's upstairs. Amnesia, huh?"

"That's it. Thanks a million, officer. How's the Widows' Fund?"

The detective peered, saw Tabbat reach for his wallet.

"Oh, no. Thanks, but we're not allowed to accept contributions. You'd have to mail a check to headquarters, sir."

The "sir" was the best part of it. He said it with such solid sincerity, better than John Wayne.

"What's your name?" Tabbat asked with one eye on the elevator shafts.

"Williams. P. D. Williams."

"You're a credit to the Houston force, Officer Williams. I'll take it from here."

Williams smiled in awkward appreciation at the compliment, hitched up his $22 pants.

"Be glad to help. Sometimes they get violent, sir."

"No, he's a pussycat. Thanks."

The detective left. Tabbat checked, saw her—with the rifle case beside her chair—seated where she could scan the exits. He took the elevator to the third floor, found the door marked 305 and glanced up and down the corridor. He drew the .22, held it flat against his thigh. He wouldn't need the silencer in this hotel, for the sign in the lobby had boasted every room was sound-proofed. He knocked on the door.

He would shoot Dalchimski immediately.

A bullet in the belly would be Tabbat's opening remark, and after that they'd talk about the Book. With animals such as Dalchimski, a slug in the guts was the only way to communicate.

He rapped again, ready to mumble "Room Service." If this wary beast was holed up, he'd probably be having his meals in the room and be used to Room Service by now. There was no sound, and Tabbat didn't like that.

"He's gone."

Tabbat turned to face the uniformed black maid.

"Left bout five, ten minutes ago, Officer."

She was looking at the gun.

"Wha'd he do? Somethin' bad?"

"Child molester."

"Dirty dog," exclaimed the maid righteously.

Tabbat rammed the weapon back into his jacket, hurried down to the lobby. The room clerk confirmed that Mr. Beller had just checked out—with no forwarding address.

"Goddam cops with weak kidneys!" Tabbat told Barbi Gordon bitterly ten seconds later. "We *almost* had him. Come on!"

They searched the airport, hurrying up and down for more than an hour before Tabbat stopped—sweaty and panting. Wherever the son of a bitch was, he wasn't at this airport. The K.G.B. agent was right. Dalchimski was boarding a plane at Houston's other airport, a DC-8 bound for Cleveland. He still wasn't sure whether that man he'd seen eying him in the lobby was one of Them, but it was time to move on anyway. He couldn't take any chances now, not when he was doing so well. His work would be finished in a few days, he thought happily. *They'd* be finished, all of them. Just considering it made him feel strong.

Tabbat felt exhausted. She had never seen him looking so tired, so weak and worn. Seated beside him on the plastic chairs with the crowds swirling by, she studied the fatigue in his eyes. He looked spent, like a football player who's been on the field for a grueling sixty minutes of a very tough game—and lost. She wondered what she could do or say to comfort him.

"You look bushed, Gregg," she said—and she patted his hand.

The way she used American slang—that was good. He sighed, grateful to have such a well-trained assistant. He realized that he wasn't used to women who were tender, who cared. This one cared, or seemed to anyway. Compassion was an unusual quality in his world, he reflected. That was probably because it could cause trouble, make an agent let his guard down or forget the dangers.

"How about some coffee—or a drink?" she suggested.

"In a minute. . . . We *almost* had him. It was him. I *know* it was him."

"You'll find him again."

The fatigue was in every bone and muscle. Even his eyes hurt, and he closed them for a moment—just a moment.

"It's crazy," he said with a yawn. "I'm in a crazy business. Can't afford to close my eyes when I'm dead tired, or I might be dead dead. Any place I am—any second of any day—somebody I've never seen before might kill me."

He spoke softly, but the anger was so sharp that it was tangible.

"I'm getting tired of all this," he told her. "I've been at it for a long time, and I used to enjoy the excitement. I was never afraid."

"You're not afraid," she assured him loyally.

"I'm afraid we won't get this maniac in time. He's wasted so many people, butchered so many—for nothing. He thinks he's the avenging angel. I think he's a disease, and I hope it's not catching. I don't want to be like him. That's what I'm afraid of—after all these years."

"Gregg—"

They both paused, for a harried blonde with two small children suddenly dropped into a seat only three feet away.

"What's that?" demanded a fair-haired boy of ten or eleven.

Tabbat yawned once more.

"That a rifle, mister?"

"Don't bother the gentleman," urged his mother.

"Looks like a rifle case. You a hunter? My dad hunts deer. What do you hunt?"

"Roaches, pubic lice, moths."

The woman sat up, glared.

"Leave him alone, Billy. He's nasty."

"You're damn right I am," agreed Tabbat, and then he wearily rose and led his woman to the nearby bar. "When this is over," he said, "I'd like a month's vacation on one of those peaceful Caribbean islands. Not a swinging one like Puerto Rico or Jamaica—a quiet one like St. Maarten. I know a great hotel called La SaManna, good beach and terrific food. We could just bake in the sun, and forget about killing people for a while. Maybe those masterminds back home would forget about us for a while. That would be nice."

Tabbat would have been unhappy if he'd known that Marshal Pasimov was thinking about him at that moment. It had been a mistake for Strelski to have Tabbat memorize all the names and telephone numbers, for now he was a fourth copy of the Book. This was dangerous, for he wasn't equipped with a destruct-device and the Americans might take him at any time. The safest move would be for the G.R.U. killer teams to put Tabbat under surveillance at once, to be ready to destroy him swiftly—if necessary.

The Red Army Chief of Staff picked up the telephone, gave the orders and turned to the memorandum about the new water-purification pills to be issued next year. They were a distinct improvement over the old ones, tasting much less unpleasant. "Good," wrote the marshal across the first page. He prided himself on being a humanitarian, always sympathetic to the needs of the common foot soldier. Unlike some other top officers, Marshal Pasimov had never forgotten his humble origins.

31

"I don't like it, Pyotr," said Malchenko with a frown.

"*You* don't like it? I don't like it either—not a bit," replied Strelski.

"It stinks—worse than your cheap cigars. The whole thing stinks."

Strelski leaned back in the big chair, rubbed his face and realized that he'd better shave before dinner. It wasn't that often that he was invited to meet with the Collegium, and he'd better look his best.

"You think Pasimov's up to something, Aleksei?"

"Damn right, but I'm not exactly sure what. Whatever it is, it's wrong. Even if all he really wants is a progress report from Tabbat, I don't like it. Anything can happen if Tabbat communicates with the *Rezident* in Washington. Suppose they've turned one of our people at the embassy?"

Strelski opened the desk drawer, pulled out a cigar.

"You think there's a double-agent in our *apparat* there?" he asked

"How the hell would I know? If I thought there was, you can bet your ass I'd have done something about it. There could be, Pyotr. If we've penetrated the C.I.A. and their Air Force Intelligence, those bastards could have turned one of our people—maybe even that thug of a *Rezident* himself."

The general groped in his pocket for the box of wooden matches, found it.

"Unlikely—but possible. Never underestimate the other side, any of the other sides. There are quite a few these days."

"Do you have to light that damn thing?"

"Yes, I do. Good for my nerves. Reminds me of a Polish whorehouse, and that soothes me."

Malchenko shook his head. Nobody was perfect, but this habit of Strelski's of quoting his own words at you again and again was one of his least pleasant quirks. The general lit the panatela, puffed.

"I'd open a window, Aleksei, but the security people just sent around another hot memo reminding everyone that the Americans have excellent long-range microphones."

"Shit, *we're* the security people."

The general smiled benevolently.

"Aleksei, we live in the kind of world where even the security people have security people. It's already 1985, even if nobody knows it."

Malchenko's stomach rumbled—so loudly that the man behind the desk heard it.

"Eating in the staff cafeteria again?" he jested in an effort to ease the tension.

"I've had belly trouble for nearly a month, and I'm not sleeping much either. This latest thing isn't going to help. If we do what Pasimov wants and The Other Side has penetrated our U.S. *apparat*, we'll be handing them Tabbat on a fucking plate."

"Not what the Red Army Chief of Staff *wants*, what he's ordered."

"On a fucking plate," Malchenko repeated furiously.

"You like Tabbat, don't you?"

"Yes. He's a human, not a robot. That's got nothing to do with this though. Tabbat's memorized the whole damn list. That's what worries me."

The general puffed again.

"He's got his little pill, hasn't he?"

"Sure, but then what do we do about Telefon?"

Strelski rubbed his chin again, nodded.

"You're a good Socialist, and you've got a good mind, Aleksei, and I suspect you've got some other thoughts about this situation."

"You want me to say it straight out?"

"You usually do. Tact isn't exactly one of your strong points, comrade. I'm not criticizing you. I value your directness."

Malchenko stood up, waved away the curl of smoke.

"All right. I think they mean to kill him!"

"Good thinking."

"You think so too?" Malchenko asked in open surprise.

"Of course. That was my first reaction when the order arrived. The marshal wants to close out the entire operation—quickly and totally, and without alarming the Americans. Next year he may feel sorry that he did, but right now he's what the American conservatives used to call a 'peacenik.' Funny, isn't it?"

"Not to me. I'm not looking for war either, but I don't see anything amusing about killing one of our own agents."

"I'm not sure you appreciate the gravity of the situation, Aleksei."

"What the hell are you talking about?"

Strelski ground out the cigar savagely.

"Not one. Many more than one," he said in grim tones. "If I may be as blunt as you, the *whole damn Telefon network*."

"More than a hundred and thirty people? They'd massacre them all?"

"Massacres seem to be coming back into fashion, Aleksei. Remember, we wiped out more than that number of Stalinists only a couple of months ago."

"I can't believe it. Are you sure?"

"Not entirely," Strelski responded with a shrug. "I can tell you that our people at the airports have reported some unusual movements of G.R.U. commando types out of the country—men who've handled wet affairs in the past. They were all heading west, more than fifteen of them. There could be others."

Malchenko leaned across the big desk.

"You really believe this?"

"I do."

"And you're going to let them get away with it?"

The general gestured towards the chair behind his old friend.

"Sit down, Aleksei. Look at me. I'm not very handsome and I don't have any personal protector in the Central Committee —not anymore—but I'm an unusual man. I'm a career K.G.B. officer who's fifty-nine years old. I've survived all the feuds and purges. Men tougher and smarter than me were slaughtered when they destroyed Beria, when the Red Army killed the head of the entire K.G.B.—supposedly the most powerful man in the entire Soviet Union."

"Pyotr—"

"Aleksei, I'm fifty-nine and I want to be sixty. I've been a Party member for thirty-one years, but if I defy the Red Army Chief of Staff head-on, I'll never see sixty. Perhaps—if I were extremely lucky—I might just possibly spend that birthday and the rest of my life as the deputy chief of guards at some remote prison camp in Siberia. I probably wouldn't be that fortunate, and if they liquidate me as a traitor to the State my family would be ruined. No pension, no apartment, no jobs. They'd be beggars, or maybe end up as street cleaners."

Malchenko sat down, didn't answer.

"You think I'm a coward, don't you, Aleksei?"

"I understand."

"You think I'm a coward."

"I'm thinking about Tabbat and the others."

General Strelski belched.

"My stomach's not so good either. Well, Tabbat's just as smart as we are, Aleksei. He'll spot this trap in a minute, and he'll cope. He's a better survivor than I am—better than either of us."

The colonel nodded in agreement. Tabbat was much too

cunning, too jungle-wise not to sense the danger. Tabbat had no illusions, trusted no one. He'd know what to do.

"What do you think he'll do?"

"Something clever and—if necessary—quite violent. I wouldn't want to be the men they send after him, Aleksei. Those men are going to die long before I do, and there's still the chance that Tabbat will find the degenerate with the Book. Remember, it was you who said he's the best agent we have."

Malchenko's belly growled once more. This time the general reached into his pocket, took out a green roll of mints.

"Try a couple, Aleksei. One of our women who works as a maid at the U.S. Embassy stole them from their Assistant Naval Attaché. They're called Tums—good for the stomach."

Malchenko put two in his mouth, grimaced at the odd taste.

"You suck 'em or chew 'em?" he asked.

"Whatever you like. Now get out of here and have that message coded for broadcast to Tabbat. It'd better go out to-night."

Tabbat and the woman had returned to Las Vegas, and he heard the instructions on his shortwave receiver in the car. He'd driven out of the city because he knew that reception would be better. Even so, he could barely discern the words aimed at him by the Soviet Union's most powerful shortwave transmitter. When he got back to the hotel room, she looked up hopefully.

"Good news?"

"Bad," he answered and then he walked into the bathroom to take a shower and figure out his next move.

32

It isn't easy getting into the headquarters of the Central Intelligence Agency. Entering the agency's computer room is even tougher. Just being a C.I.A. employee or even a senior official with a key to the executive incinerator isn't enough to gain access to this super-sensitive "security area." You've got to have a good reason to penetrate these guarded portals, and if it's good enough you'll be awarded a special pass which will be checked by the faithful, vigilant and earnest men who defend the entrance. Just to keep everyone on his/her/its toes, the color of the special pass is changed from time to time at irregular intervals to confuse and thwart any and all enemies. There is a special unit of especially wary and devious people who handle special matters such as these special passes. This unit isn't to be confused with the Special Projects Unit, of course, since the Special Projects Unit—which is different from the Special Research Division—is different.

Smirking will not be tolerated, nor will disrespect. Just be grateful that all these hard-working people are there breaking their humps to protect the country, serving day and night. The C.I.A. never sleeps, never even dozes and—when necessary—makes house calls. These are almost always outside the continental U.S.A., and the service must be good because there have been very few complaints. The details are, of course, classified, since they relate to matters of "national security." Unless you're a medical student or write Vincent Price movies, they probably wouldn't interest you anyway. As a matter of fact, the computer center setup isn't any of your business either.

It was/is part of Dorothy Putterman's business, and she had

the correct pass. There was a sign on the wall that said RESTRICTED AREA, and next to the sign was a two-inch-thick steel door in which was set a small window of bullet-proof glass. Just beside the door was a telephone hanging on the wall, and beneath that was a slot or slit some three inches wide and half an inch high. Above the door was a closed-circuit TV camera, and it was triggered by a photoelectric cell some sixty feet down the corridor. When a visitor was still twenty yards from the door, his or her body broke that invisible beam and a buzzer sounded inside the metal barrier. It wouldn't work to try to slide under the beam, for the floor was wired to a pressure alarm. Ms. Putterman walked through the beam and, in the officially approved procedure, paused, giving the security men inside a chance to inspect and identify her.

"It's the one with the lungs," announced one of the alert and perceptive guardians.

If his partner didn't answer, it wasn't because he disagreed with this thoughtful description but rather because he suspected that there might be a hidden tape recorder nearby. There was a rumor going around that the National Security Agency—the eavesdropping and codebreaking crowd—had concealed microphones in the disinfectant dispensers above their urinals, and everyone knew that the C.I.A. was a lot more clever than the N.S.A. at this sort of thing.

Ms. Putterman walked to the wall phone, picked it up and identified herself in a clear, articulate voice. Then she slid her card into the slot—just as people do with those money machines built into the outer walls of banks. There was a certain amount of whirring and buzzing and then a click, after which she removed the card and put it back in her purse. Now there was a hum and the steel door slid open, closed behind her fifteen seconds later. She didn't go to the big computer, which some inventive chap had nicknamed Bertha, or to either of the three medium-sized models. She marched to the simplest, which was known as Simon. All right, the humor isn't much and the literary style dreadful, but the C.I.A. is still dynamite in the nitty-gritty of cloak and dagger. Dynamite.

The simplest was a little $290,000 number done up in basic black, without pearls. Ms. Putterman had her notes complete and her "program" ready, so she fed the first "program" into the computer, waited a bit before going on to the second and paused again before adding the third. The basic problem that she was putting into Simon was merely a question of possibilities and probabilities. That was the first question she wanted to answer for Feldman and the hard-noses of Working Group Five. The Air Force representative on Five was a Brigadier General Norman Meggleston, sometimes called—behind his back—"Megaton" Meggleston since he'd been a resolute advocate of an all-out "preemptive strike" during his recent three years with the Joint Chiefs of Staff. A number of people tended to underestimate him because he had the crewest of cuts and the most terrific tennis game in the Pentagon, but Meggleston was no dope. The fact that he was the toughest and most aggressive man on Five didn't mean that he wasn't fiercely realistic, and this time—although no one else on Five knew it yet—he was right. All these incidents weren't just coincidences. A large professional and clandestine organization was trying to injure the ability of the United States to defend itself.

Or to make war against a foe, which—to classic military thinkers—added up to the same thing. General Meggleston was a classicist who'd given up smoking twelve years ago, did an hour of calisthenics every day and kept a pilot's .38 in his desk in case the Pentagon was attacked. He wasn't the least bit reluctant to face the unpleasant; he welcomed it. Trouble exhilarated him, and he was convinced that these incidents added up to serious danger. It was—in large part—his pressure that had inspired Feldman to ask for the computer run by the C.I.A.'s shrewdest analyst. Unlike Coltrane, Feldman admired Ms. Putterman and her mind and—to tell the truth—he too felt that something might be wrong.

She ran the programs three times, checked and rechecked. Then she reached into her purse and took out another set of programs related to one of the projects she'd been discussing with Colonel Jenkins. This set she ran through five times, and when she was finished she glowed with a big fat smile. She put the programs in her purse, and reread the two printouts before she dropped them both in the "burn basket" beside Simon. The contents of this trash container would be incinerated that evening, burned to fine ash in a wonderful fire machine that had three separate screens atop its chimney to prevent any morsel or scrap from floating out into the sky.

She left the computer center with a gracious "Thank you," walked purposefully to Jenkins' office on the floor above.

"You look like the cat that," he judged from the triumphant expression on her rosy face.

"I am the cat that. I'm afraid that Feldman and his colleagues may not be too thrilled by what I've found. Simon says that the odds are about fifty-six thousand four hundred to one against this particular set of coincidences. You going to tell him?"

Colonel Jenkins reflected, pursed his lips and finally nodded.

"Guess I'll have to. He's out with a bad cold, but he should be back in a day or so. This kind of lousy news can wait, I suppose. Lord, it's certainly going to get Meggleston all steamed up when he hears it at next week's meeting of Five. The Air Force is already goddam nervous, according to the grapevine."

He was sorry the moment he'd said it, for he knew that she resented the things he learned via the grapevine. She was convinced that she should have access to these tips too, even if she was younger and a woman.

"Fine work, Dorothy," he said to compensate for this "discrimination."

"I've got something else. Maybe this'll improve things for us with Coltrane."

She put the piece of paper on his desk.

"Well I'll be screwed, glued and tattooed!" said Colonel Jenkins in uncontrolled reversion to the argot of his college days. "Fan-goddam-tastic. This looks *real* fine, Dorothy."

"I should have figured it earlier, but we didn't have enough data," she explained.

"Don't be so modest. I'm going to put you in for a promotion."

"I was due for one ten months ago."

Coltrane had held it up, and she knew it—but Colonel Jenkins wasn't about to admit that. She'd go bouncing to the Personnel Director yelling "sexism" or some other crap.

"There's been a freeze on, you may recall," reminded Jenkins.

"Balls. You'll get this Hot Rod computation out to the field?"

"Sure thing, and I won't forget Feldman either."

She left humming a tune that the colonel didn't even bother to try to identify, although he'd taken a year of music at college and played clarinet in the band. It had to be Mozart. It always was.

33

The man they'd picked to kill Tabbat was code-named Leon. He was a G.R.U. agent who'd operated in many countries during the previous decade, always as Leon or something like that. Leon is a fairly useful and sort of interchangeable name, since it could be French or Belgian or Spanish or Argentine or American or several other things. He hadn't been born Leon, but his favorite uncle had been named Leonid—the one who'd lost both legs in a World War II tank battle at a city then known as Stalingrad. Before the Great Revolution Stalingrad had been Tsaritsin, and after the shakeup of the 1950s it was renamed Volgograd or something like that. Leon never paid much attention to all these political matters, since he was far from intellectual and didn't clutter his mind with ideological questions. He wasn't a simple farmer, you understand. Leon came from Baku, an oil-focused city of 870,000 on the Caspian Sea. He was a high-school graduate, thirty-three years old and blessed with a nice head of curly brown hair.

He was a calm person, fond of dogs and dried fruit and

swimming. He'd been a sergeant in a Military Police unit for two years before somebody picked him for G.R.U. training, and when his instructors found out that he had a natural aptitude for languages they sent him to special courses in German and English. He was an excellent shot with all sorts of small arms, the 9-millimeter Walther P-38 pistol and the 7.62 NATO FN automatic rifle and Britain's L2A3 submachine gun, as well as Communist weapons and U.S. guns. He was more than competent with knives, and he had stamina and patience. He couldn't crack safes or break codes or seduce secretaries in foreign government agencies, but he could follow and he could kill.

There wasn't much call for an assassin in the G.R.U., since the K.G.B. was much more into such wet affairs, but Leon got enough experience to earn several promotions. Between these lethal assignments—which he neither liked nor loathed—he served as a courier for important papers, as a bodyguard for people in danger and as an instructor for G.R.U. recruits. There were at least a dozen men and two women in the K.G.B. who'd killed more than Leon had, but they were obviously unsuited for this job. No one in the K.G.B. could be trusted in this matter and Leon was already in Montreal, waiting for orders to cross the border to eliminate the deep-cover agents.

Waiting didn't bother him at all. He was comfortable in a second-rate hotel favored by salesmen, equipped with enough cash to enjoy the city. He was always in his room from midnight through 9 A.M., from eleven to one and then from four to eight. He watched television, read paperbacks and perused copies of stimulating monthlies such as *Oui*, *Penthouse* and *Cavalier*. He'd tried *Playboy*, rejected it as too wordy and pretentious. The city was so warm that he didn't mind spending most of his time in the air-conditioned room, stretched out near the telephone with a bag of dried apricots and pears. He munched away, confident that his superiors would tell him what to do and when. Taking orders and killing people were two of the things Leon did best.

When the phone rang at 11:15 A.M. and the man's voice asked for Madam Bicard, Leon politely explained that this was not her room. Then he departed immediately for 1198 St.

Catherine Street West to meet Albert Einstein, Elizabeth Taylor, Maurice "The Rocket" Richard and Jesus Christ with twelve hungry friends. Brigitte Bardot was there too, topless and unashamed, and protecting her stood a figure with a terrific resemblance to Boris Karloff in his "Frankenstein monster" gear. The figures were all wax, for this was Montreal's popular Ville Marie Wax Museum with exhibits courtesy of Madam Josephine Tussaud's London workshop. The word "Madam" in the phone call had set the place for the rendezvous. It was a simple code.

Leon studied the Bardot statue earnestly, decided that it had an attractive elfin quality but the girls in *Penthouse* had better breasts. Leon, who wasn't much of a judge of character or art, clung to the naive old-fashioned view that bigger is better. Some people forgave these limitations because he was a splendid marksman and relentless tracker, and these were the people who'd sent him to Montreal and told him to go to 1198 St. Catherine Street West and stand with a pair of sunglasses in his left hand within fifteen minutes after someone telephoned "Madam." It could have been worse. Soviet intelligence used many more elaborate identification schemes: perhaps a copy of the *Reader's Digest* in one hand, a pack of Camels in the other —and wear a blue bow tie. Leon hated that one, since he was awful at tying a bow. This was easy.

He saw her walking towards him, and hoped that she was the contact because she had a nice young face, a trim figure and the assured manner of an airline stewardess. She was a stewardess and flew on a Western European carrier's transatlantic service, which permitted her to indulge her revolutionary sympathies and earn an extra $500 a month as a courier.

"Leon? It's me, Karla. How's Bob?"

"Fine. What do you hear from Aunt Lisa?"

After the exchange of correct sign and countersign, they strolled out to the busy street that was filled with tourists and shoppers despite the August glare. She chatted, lit a cigarette, offered him one and then walked away—leaving the pack with him. When he got back to his room, he found the photo of Tabbat and the orders to proceed to the Sheraton-O'Hare Motor Inn near Chicago's main airport. The brief message on the back of the picture was explicit. "Armed, experienced, very dangerous." It should be a challenge. The question of who this man was and why he had to be liquidated didn't occur to Leon, for those were political abstractions and he had the very real problem of getting a seat on the next flight to Chicago. A certain Red Army colonel once said to a colleague that you could tell Leon to go kill a bear in the zoo, and he'd do it. That colonel is a fine judge of character, even though he does drink a bit too much.

When Leon unpacked his bag in the O'Hare motel that evening, he double-locked the door and drew the drapes carefully. After removing his clothes from the large valise, he hung them up and then opened the false bottom built into the suitcase. Wrapped in plastic so they wouldn't clink against each other were a number of pieces of metal, some flat and some tubular. Leon began to put these together.

The results were impressive.

In less than two and a half minutes he was holding an L34A1 submachine gun—the silenced version of Britain's standard L2A3 used in Her Majesty's armed forces. With the stock extended, it was 34 inches long—including a murderous-looking 7.8 inch barrel. The fat silencer casing which covered the barrel jacket masked the gas escape hole in the barrel, and there were three settings on the firing mechanism. Before he snapped in the 34 round, staggered-row box magazine, he flipped the switch to "S"—the safety position. A more dashing fellow might have tried "R" for semi-automatic fire or "A" for fully automatic, but that would be pure braggadocio. He knew that this weapon could spit out 9-millimeter parabellum slugs at a rate of 550 per minute, that its spiral diffuser extending beyond the barrel worked. Leon had slain twice with this very gun. Leon would have preferred the Soviet 7.62-millimeter AKM assault rifle, which was nearly a pound heavier, but *they* preferred that G.R.U. agents on this sort of mission operate with foreign hardware. If anything went wrong, that would make it a bit easier for the U.S.S.R. to deny any link. That's why all the men sent to destroy the Telefon deep-cover people were equipped with British and West German weapons.

It was a lot of crap, of course. Leon knew this, and he suspected that his superiors probably realized it too. They had a passion—a compulsion—for these childlike games which were unlikely to fool anyone, but they also had authority and Leon did not question authority. He had never even told anyone that this stunt with foreign guns was a lot of crap. Leon was no mastermind, but he was shrewd enough to know that merely seeming to differ could be unwise if not dangerous.

He put the sling around his shoulder, jerked the L34A1 up into firing position. "Okay," he said to himself in the full-length mirror on the closet door. He didn't bother to check the .38-caliber Walther PPK pistol in the quick-release holster strapped to the calf of his right leg, and he wasn't even going to take the throwing knife from the lining of his other bag. If his target was armed and experienced, the odds were that Leon would never get close enough to use it. He disassembled the rapid-fire gun, concealed it and flicked on the television. Then he sat in the armchair, took off his shoes and tie and waited for the image to jump from the screen.

Indians.

Probably Apaches, he judged. Leon was a connoisseur of cowboy and Indian films, and after having seen so many he was a knowledgeable scholar of war paint and clothing. He could tell a Sioux feather bonnet from a Black Foot headdress as quickly as many anthropologists. Now the Indians were firing and shouting as they attacked the stagecoach, and Leon sighed contentedly.

This was the part he liked best.

They would call soon with further instructions, he thought as the battle raged. They always did, so all he had to do was wait and enjoy the movie. It was one of the good ones, made before the Americans had grown guilty about their capitalist-imperialist abuse of the native tribes. There was a lot of violence, the Indians were bad and they lost. There was something comforting in that, and Leon slept extremely well that night after the film ended.

34

The freak fires that knocked out the main generators and central control tower at the Naval Air Station near San Diego didn't get too much space in the *Las Vegas Sun*. It wasn't any reflection on that vigorous daily, however, since no one died and the base's energetic fire department had extinguished the blazes within half an hour. The new emergency generator installed last year had kicked on automatically, to the delight of both the base commander and the General Electric Company, whose hardware was involved. G.E. had barely fought off a very attractive bid by a Japanese firm with mixed cries of "dumping" and "buy American," so it was a relief when the generator confirmed the reliability of good old Yankee workmanship. Tabbat read the two-paragraph story on page five, and only his eyes showed the impact.

But she saw it in his eyes.

She was getting to know him—perhaps too well. They both understood that it made little sense for professionals to get involved with each other. In a day he might be on his way back to Moscow, and in a week she could be heading towards Tokyo. In a month—or a minute—they might both be dead. Aware of this, she couldn't help asking anyway.

"What is it?"

"Our boy."

He tapped the article and she read it.

"He didn't do too well this time," she said consolingly.

"What about *next* time? Do you know what fantastic goodies this son of a bitch has on his shopping list? Can you *imagine* the terrible destruction he can trigger—with just a call?"

She shook her head.

"I don't, Gregg—and probably I shouldn't."

"Then there's the other devil," Tabbat continued, as if speaking to himself. "He must be over the border into Mexico by now, driving like a bat out of hell to get out of range of the nuclear explosions. . . . It's all right. You can ask. What nuclear explosions? I'll tell you. From the goddam missile warheads. Okay, ask the next question."

He was very angry.

Besides, she wanted to know.

"What missile warheads?"

"That's the big fucking joke. That's the snapper. The warheads on the rockets that haven't been fired—the ones still sitting in their silos and on their launchers five hundred miles west of Vladivostok. Hilarious, isn't it?"

"Maybe—if you know the joke. I haven't heard it myself."

Tabbat lit a cigarette, inhaled and coughed.

"If you're lucky, you won't," he told her. "It's a real sick joke. For a lot of people it's been fatal."

"Maybe the cops will find him again, hon."

"The odds are a thousand to one against it. It was a miracle that they spotted him once."

"Maybe if you raised the reward?"

"I've thought of that—another two or three grand. Might attract too much attention, get somebody curious. Could make Beckam jumpy too. A reward that big would make him think that somebody important's going to get hit—very important. That could involve headlines, the F.B.I. or anything. Too rich for his blood. That's what he'd say."

"Even if he did, you couldn't be much worse off—and he might say yes."

"Okay—that's Plan G."

He ground out the cigarette.

"What are A to F, Gregg?"

"I wish I knew."

He reached for another cigarette.

"You're smoking too much," she reproved.

"And enjoying it less. That's not all. Our friends back home are getting cute. They'd like to have a chat, so I can tell them whether I'm doing my homework. What am I—a school kid?"

"Maybe they're worried, hon."

His bitter laugh was brief, staccato.

"Maybe—but I think they're cute. Not cute enough to fool me. I can smell their stunts. Don't forget, I've worked with these bright boys for a lot of years, and they know how I work too. On this job, we all agreed that I'd play it solo. Well, me and you but nobody else. Now I'm supposed to phone that Armenian animal."

"If it's an order—"

"It's a stunt. They're switching plans. They're changing gears, and I'm not going to get caught in the grinder."

She'd never heard of a K.G.B. agent defying the Center.

"What are you going to do?"

"About what, Barb?"

"The message."

"Never got it. Lots of static yesterday. Better have my receiver checked at a radio shop, I suppose."

She looked at the man in bed beside her.

"Gregg, they'll repeat it. They'll keep repeating it."

"Maybe I'll have better reception tomorrow. Today I'm busy figuring out what the maniac will do next. There has to be a pattern."

"Why don't you write down everything you know—all the hard facts? Set them up in columns, and maybe you'll see some correlation."

He leaned over, kissed her and then took a pad from the bed table."

"I've tried that at least nine times, maybe twenty-nine," he said, "but once more won't hurt."

He groped in the drawer, found the pencil and started making his lists. He began with the American names of all the agents whom Dalchimski had already detonated.

Zero.

He checked the first names and last names, forwards and backwards. He went over the combinations three times before he gave it up, shrugged

"I'll try their real names," he said as he began a new list.

He wrote the eight names swiftly, repeated the process—up and down.

"Four times. I checked the list four times, and there's nothing."

"Then there has to be something else. You say there's a pattern. I believe you," she encouraged.

"Ah, the love of a good woman. Right, I'll go with the states."

Colorado.

Maine.

Wisconsin.

Kansas.

West Virginia.

New York.

Florida.

California.

"*Merde*," he said. "Bet you didn't know I spoke French so well."

"You've got a great accent. What's next?"

He sighed.

"I've never tried the list of installations."

"Why not?"

"Why not?" he agreed.

This took more time. Twice he stopped and swore as he hesitated over the names of the specific targets, and then he cursed again when he was done.

"Nothing," he announced grimly. "Not a goddam thing. Makes no sense at all."

He tore the pages into bits, burned them in the ashtray.

"I'm going to the can," he said.

"Gregg—"

"I do my best thinking in the can," he told her as he rolled out of bed.

"Really?"

"No—but I couldn't do any worse."

She lay there wondering for several minutes, finally heard the toilet flush and the sound of water running in the sink. When he emerged he was wearing a bathrobe—the one she'd bought for him a few days earlier. She picked up the pad and pencil.

"What're you doing?" he asked.

"I'm going to write down the next list. There has to be another one, and you know it."

"You're getting to be a nag—just as if we were married for years."

She smiled for a moment, then frowned seriously.

"You've tried cover names and real names, states and installations. What else is there?"

"Phone numbers?"

"Call them out."

He did, and it was another total failure. Even when they changed the numbers to the corresponding letters of the alphabet the results were negative.

"What else, Gregg?"

"You're a real fanatic. Say, were you ever a schoolteacher?"

"None of your business. Your business is the next list. What is it?"

"You sound like my mother."

"Screw your mother. What about the inspiration you were supposed to get in the john? They told me you were one of the best—one of the smartest. Earn your money, champ."

"No, you don't sound like my mother. She was nicer. Names, states, installations, phone numbers . . . we could try towns, I guess. Yeah, the towns where the installations were."

She wrote them down.

Denver.

Augusta.

Lac du Flambeau.

Chanute.

Huntington.

Ithaca.

Miami.

San Diego.

"Read them again," he ordered.

She obeyed, and he nodded.

Then he grinned.

"Well I'll be a son of a bitch," he said loudly. "I think we've got him. I think we've found the son of a bitch's pattern. They said they'd wipe out his name, and now he's writing it across the United States. Denver—D. Augusta—A. Lac du Flambeau—L. Chanute—C. Well, well, well, we've got your goddam number, Comrade Dalchimski."

She glanced at the list.

"This spells out Dalchims."

"Which leaves k and i," Tabbat explained. "There's only one k in the Book, and that's where he has to strike next. We've got him. Let's move."

They disembarked at the Detroit airport at 4:20 P.M., Tabbat made his phone call, and at 5:35 they took off on the North Central prop-jet Convair that would bring them to Kalamazoo, Michigan—a city of eighty-six thousand people, four banks, a Fisher Body plant and an Upjohn pharmaceutical factory.

One of the eighty-six thousand was a man named Conrad Bernard Temko, proprietor of a chemical supply firm. Its telephone number in the 616 area code region was 345-9989. Tabbat knew those hard facts as well as he knew the mission that had been assigned to the deep-cover agent, but he wasn't nearly as sure about how he'd handle the meeting. How do you tell a reputable businessman that he's actually a saboteur for a foreign power, a Communist power? After you tell him, how do you convince him that you aren't crazy? Temko would never believe it. He might even summon the police.

There was one way, Tabbat reasoned as the Convair rose from the Detroit field, but that was terribly dangerous. Tabbat would have to speak the trigger-phrase, utter the coded message that would destroy the fiction—and life—of Conrad Bernard Temko. Once those words were spoken, that character would vanish as if written out of the script of some soap opera series. But that wouldn't solve the situation completely, for once this man reverted to his identity as a K.G.B. commando, he'd be motivated by a tremendous compulsion to complete his assigned mission. They'd built that into him when they programmed him so expensively and thoroughly all those years ago. Now there was little if any chance that anything Tabbat could say about a change in plans or new orders would reflect Temko from his "duty."

Tabbat would try, mentioning the names of the senior K.G.B. people who'd created Telefon. He'd speak Russian to him, quote manuals, use the shop talk of the intelligence organization. If that didn't work, Tabbat would use force to knock him out or cripple him. If necessary—and as a last resort—he'd kill him. These were the bitter thoughts that troubled the K.G.B. agent as the loudspeaker delivered the pilot's announcement that the plane was approaching Battle Creek on its flight west. Tabbat was still troubled at 6:10 when the Convair landed at Kalamazoo.

35

"You're sure he'll be there?"

"I'm sure," Tabbat replied as they waited for the Rent-a-Car girl to complete the forms.

"It's after six, Gregg."

"That's why I phoned him from Detroit. When he heard about a possible seventy-thousand-dollar order, he was more than willing to stay. We've got an appointment for a quarter to seven."

"Be finished in a jiffy, sir," promised the young woman in the green uniform and the cheerful demeanor so typical of the helpful people who stood behind airport counters.

"It's nearly twenty after, Gregg."

Barbi was right, he realized. He couldn't afford to be late. Arriving early would be even better, so he told her the address and asked her to meet him there as soon as possible in the rented car. He'd go ahead by taxi—right now. The cab was one of those large roomy ones made by the Checker folk, a heavy vehicle with surprising agility. The driver was simply superb. He was competent, knew the route to Oak Street and refrained from the Chamber of Commerce talk that taxi types frequently offered in smaller cities. It wasn't that this chauffeur couldn't have told him *plenty* about Kalamazoo and the eighty-three fine lakes nearby and the Nature Center and the symphony orchestra. The driver had a solid seven minutes of good material *easy*, maybe nine if he covered the four savings and loan associations and the three bus lines and the art center. The man behind the wheel mentioned none of these, for he had years of experience in "reading" passengers and he knew—just knew—that this fellow had other stuff on his mind. If you understood people, you could see it plain as day.

They reached the whitewashed cinderblock office-and-warehouse, Tabbat paid him and the man said, "Have a good day." As the cab pulled away, the K.G.B. agent noticed the gray Pinto parked in the driveway and wondered what sort of person this Temko was. He earned enough from this firm to afford a more expensive car, but perhaps his wife had the more costly set of wheels—maybe a big wagon to haul groceries and move the kids to school and dancing classes and Scout meetings.

The deep-cover agent could very well be married, have a full and normal family. There could be three or four kids and all the rest—everything that went with the solid and conventional bourgeois life somebody had programmed him for so long ago. Tabbat shrugged, hoped that he wouldn't have to kill him. Then he tried the door, found it open and entered the outer office.

He faced a woman in her mid-thirties. She was seated at a desk, putting the final touches on her lipstick job. She seemed pleasant enough, although the beehive hairdo was at least eight or ten years out of style and betrayed her age. She glanced up, saw him across the bulk of her IBM electric typewriter.

"Mr. Callender?" she asked, using the name Tabbat had picked before the call from Detroit.

"Yes. Is Mr. Temko in?"

"I'm terribly sorry. He had to step out for a minute."

Alarm bells rang and sirens sounded in Tabbat's mind.

"You're expecting him back? We had an appointment, you know."

She tried to smile reassuringly, failed.

"I know. . . . Something came up."

The sirens screamed louder now.

"Was it a telephone call?"

"Something unexpected. I'm sure he'll be back."

She was trying so hard to protect her employer, but Tabbat still had to fight down an impulse to hit her. Why couldn't she answer a direct question directly?

"This . . . is . . . very . . . important. Was it a telephone call?"

"Ah . . . I think so. Yes, he had a call ten or fifteen minutes ago. You say that's important?"

"Only if it was from a man with a foreign accent."

"That's who it was. Is something wrong?"

Tabbat answered with a question.

"And Mr. Temko left immediately, hurrying out as if he had something extremely urgent on his mind?"

She nodded.

"What's this all about?"

"Just a bad practical joke, I hope," Tabbat lied. "That man with the accent is a bit loony. I'll get over to his place and calm him down before there's any trouble. That your car out there—the Pinto?"

"Oh yes. Mr. Temko drives a green Pontiac coupe, a seventy-five. Can I give you a lift? I'm leaving in three minutes."

"I'll phone for a cab."

She pointed to the telephone, excused herself and vanished into what had to be a toilet. Tabbat instantly dialed the operator, asked to be connected with the police.

"Police headquarters."

"This is an emergency. No joke. It's life and death. There's a maniac on his way to the Doolittle Electronic Labs. He's driving a green seventy-five Pontiac coupe, and he has explosives. He's heavily armed. I repeat—this is no joke."

"Who is this?"

"Captain Gregory of Military Intelligence. He's on his way

from Four-ninety-nine Oak, left ten or fifteen minutes ago. This man is extremely dangerous, homicidal."

"Jeezus Christ!"

"I'm on my way after him. I'd suggest you notify your radio cars and alert the Doolittle security people. Tell them I'll be there in twenty minutes."

He saw the toilet door open.

"Is he some Commie nut?"

"That's exactly it," Tabbat replied truthfully and slammed down the phone.

He assured the secretary that a cab would pick him up in a few minutes, so he didn't mind waiting outside if she had to go. He watched the Pinto glide out of sight, and then he started cursing. He swore in English, Russian, French, German, Spanish—and a bit in Arabic. It didn't help much, but it passed the time until Barbi arrived in the rented car.

"Everything okay?"

"Shit, Dalchimski phoned him ten minutes before I got here. Two can play at this telephone-weapon game. I called the cops."

He saw her slide over, and he entered and took the driver's seat.

"The cops? What can they do, Gregg?"

He clicked his safety harness shut, started the engine.

"Stop him. Wound him. Kill him. I don't give a damn. They can blast him into dog meat for all I care. I told them he was a homicidal maniac, loaded with guns and explosives. I hope they believed me."

Crank calls were as routine to the Kalamazoo police as they were to cops in all the other cities of the world, but something in Tabbat's voice had convinced the desk sergeant this was a real crisis. Every radio car was warned to look out for a dangerous mental case in a green '75 Pontiac coupe, and four were ordered to try to head him off on the highway that was the most direct route from 499 Oak to the laboratories. The Security Officer at Doolittle was warned of the danger.

He set the gongs ringing, boomed the warning over the speakers in the eight guard posts—including the one at the main gate. A heavy truck was parked across the in-driveway, sealing it off like a roadblock. Magazines clicked into a score of automatic weapons, and then the guards at Doolittle heard the distant howl of sirens. The security men saw the growing green dot being chased by two blue ones. A pair of police cars raced down the road in hot pursuit of the Pontiac, hurtling at eighty miles an hour towards the defense installation.

"Open fire!" crackled the voice on the speakers.

Four M-14s hosed the coupe with metal, destroying the windshield, wrecking the engine and punching a dozen holes into the suddenly late Mr. Temko. Instant horror followed. Gasoline and oil spurted from the machine, and crimson gouts blossomed on the defaced wreck that had been a popular local businessman. With a very dead man at the wheel, the Pontiac surged forward on sheer momentum and smashed into the truck.

There was a fire.

Four others erupted within seconds.

The guards ran, and then the car blew up as the flames touched the jets of fuel. Another and much larger explosion followed swiftly, throwing a piece of the hood, the entire left rear door and most of the back half of the coupe in a wide arc. Chunks of the one-time Mr. Temko rained down like charred snowballs. The destruction of man and machine was so terrible that it would take two days to identify the body with any certainty, and then primarily by dental charts.

The terrible scene would have thrilled the man whose call had precipitated the carnage, but Dalchimski was more than four hundred miles away and couldn't see it. Tabbat was only eleven miles away, driving west towards Chicago at a steady fifty miles per hour. There would be questions and perhaps inquiries about strangers, so he guided the rented sedan away from Kalamazoo for eighty minutes before he dared stop. Hopeful that the roadblocks were behind him, he studied his watch and then turned on the battery-powered shortwave receiver.

The message was the same, only more imperative.

He was to report within the next two hours.

36

As anyone in the spy business can tell you, secret agents communicate with each other and with their superiors in eighty-three different ways. Some people say eighty-four because they believe that Ingmar Bergman movies are filled with coded messages, but that's a lot of rubbish and Sweden doesn't do much in the cloak-and-dagger game anyway. On missions in foreign countries, the "black" operatives of most sophisticated nations tend to go in for such standard items as microdots and miniature shortwave transmitters that are often referred to as "music boxes." Some of these are remarkably small, like the one used in Egypt by the Israeli captain who posed as a former S.S. colonel just before the Six Day War of 1967. A lot of these small jobs are equipped with tape recorders and super-speedy senders that can squirt out three hundred characters in fifteen seconds. The early models were developed by the Abwehr for use by German agents in 1939–45, and were some-times called "cigar boxes." Much-improved versions are still very popular with the K.G.B. today, for the set can send twelve hundred miles and transmit so fast that radio-direction teams have almost no chance to get an accurate fix.

Tabbat didn't have such a transmitter for several reasons, one being the special situation of his infiltration in scuba gear and another his acute reluctance to run unnecessary risks. He didn't send postcards adorned with double-talk messages to mail-drop addresses in neutral countries, although a lot of other agents did from time to time. He didn't slip trick phrases into classified advertisements in the *Times*—any *Times* in any city—or blink out messages with a flashlight from the top of a seaside cliff. Nobody's done that for at least twenty years.

He had been given several special emergency procedures for use in special emergencies, phone numbers to call at certain times on certain days and addresses to which he might send telegrams containing camouflaged messages. On the basis of his past experience, the numbers to be called would be those of public telephone booths in second-rate movie theatres or suburban bars or on the edge of a busy highway. There were certain people who worked these circuits on the prearranged schedules, presumably lower-level agents who could be bullied into shivering in some rainswept booth on the Pennsylvania Turnpike at a quarter to one in the morning. The idea was hardly exclusive, of course, for a number of Mafia executives and senior drug traffickers had been operating with those methods for fifteen years.

It was now 8:36 P.M. on a Wednesday night, and the mastermind-imbecile who'd set up the contact schedules had provided for an 8:38 connection via a booth at a drive-in movie a few miles south of the District of Columbia. The first part was easy, for Tabbat remembered the area code from his previous trip to the States fifteen months earlier. He sat in the pizza parlor's phone booth, watching the cook expertly flip the dough until 8:37 and then started dialing—slowly and carefully. He clicked out the final number just as his watch showed 8:38.

"Room five-nineteen," he said as if he were speaking to a hotel operator.

"That's Mr. Dawson," replied a voice that might have been Armenian. The accent was very slight.

"Mr. David Dawson?"

"The line is busy."

Now they could speak, having tested each other with the recognition and danger signals.

"Please report on sales."

"We almost had a very big sale in Houston a couple of days ago," Tabbat said. "Missed it by ten minutes. Could have wrapped up the whole deal."

"How about the competition?"

"Extremely busy. I suppose you've heard about what happened in Kalamazoo a couple of hours ago?"

"Not yet."

"You will. I'm going to have to talk to Nick about these crazy phone calls."

"Where?"

"Where he's going to be the day after tomorrow. I'll see him there," Tabbat announced.

"Can you be sure? The General Manager is very worried about this situation."

"Tell the General Manager that Nick's spelling out his name, and I figure he'll hit Indian Gorge."

"Impossible. He's already tried that. It was a dead loss. Besides, he can phone from anywhere."

"It won't work," said Tabbat. "He'll have to talk to this prospect in person. I'll let you know how it comes out."

He could almost hear the gears and wheels in the other K.G.B. man's mind.

"Fine, fine. Anything we can do to help?"

"Just keep your other salesmen out of the territory. I wouldn't want them to scare him off."

"Sure, sure. Where are you now?"

Tabbat hung up the phone, rejoined the woman in the car.

"Son of a bitch wanted to know where we were," he grumbled as he started the engine.

"You didn't tell him?"

"No, but I may have told him too much anyway. He'll be transmitting this home in an hour, and they'll be able to figure out the same thing I did. There's only one more "I" on the list, and our compulsive maniac needs that to finish spelling out his name. It has to be Iron River," he explained as he swung the car into the highway traffic.

"You didn't tell him that, did you?"

"No, and he didn't ask. That's what makes me nervous. Of course, I hung up before he could ask. . . . No, I don't like it."

"You had to call, Gregg."

Tabbat flicked his high-beams on and off irritably to signal the driver of an approaching car to dim its glaring headlights.

"I don't know. Maybe I had to, but I don't like it. They're playing games. If they weren't, why would he do something as stupid as asking where we were—and on a nonsecure phone?"

"Gregg—"

"They'd better not try any ding-a-ling stunts," he said bitterly. "I've had enough crap. This is our last shot at Dalchimski, and I can't let anyone screw it up. If we blow this one, we won't have any idea as to where he'll hit next. Could be the Pentagon, S.A.C. headquarters at Offut, the Atlantic Fleet command post in Norfolk—even the White House. Maybe all of them in one goddam day, and the Americans won't sit still for that."

"I'm certain they realize that, Gregg. Don't worry. They won't meddle."

At five minutes after ten that night Leon received orders to proceed to Iron River, Wyoming.

37

The entire state of Wyoming has a population of less than 355,000 people, which is probably less than the number of Los Angeleans who wake up with a hangover on a Sunday morning or Chicago housewives who resent their husbands bowling with the boys one night a week. The name Wyoming means "large prairie place" in Algonquin, but it is rather unlikely that the Algonquin ever got this far west—even at the old air fares in effect back in 1890 when Wyoming was admitted to the Union.

Wyoming also has some outstanding high spots, including the Rocky Mountains, which dominate the western half or two-thirds of this spectacularly beautiful state. There are also the Tetons and Yellowstone National Park. Among the grounds for divorce are "indignities" or the husband being a "vagrant" or impotent or insane for five years, which is longer than most marriages last in a lot of more crowded and urbanized states. Three large rivers have their sources here.

A fourth and smaller river has its headwaters in the Rockies too, and because of the high mineral content in its valleys this body of cold clear water has been designated the Iron River. There is a lot of good skiing and hunting and fishing in this region, some increasingly popular vacation lodges and dude ranches and a number of important holes in the ground some twenty to twenty-five miles from the town of Iron River. These are not sources of coal, oil, iron or gypsum—with which Mother Nature blessed Wyoming in abundance before she hit it big doing television commercials. These are silos, underground missile installations for intercontinental rockets of the U.S. Air Force. There are other I.C.B.M. complexes in Wyoming that are better known, but the eighty nuclear-tipped Minutemen weapons of the 102nd Strategic Missile Wing were just as dear to the S.A.C. Battle Staff in that massive bunker outside Omaha.

They also held a warm place in the hearts of senior Soviet commanders, and that is why Iron River and its neighboring rocket complex had been placed on the Telefon list. There was nothing malicious in this decision, for the conscientious professionals who'd drawn up the target list had included nine other strategic missile wings. They certainly hadn't selected Lieutenant Josef Kalchova for the assignment. He'd been recruited and trained by the K.G.B. because he was a strong and determined young officer in an engineer battalion who already spoke superior English. In addition, Kalchova was a good skier from a small town along the Finnish frontier. He'd fit into the Iron River scene easily, they calculated, so they nurtured him on cheeseburgers and Cokes and Coors beer and hot chili and football scores and the records of the U.S. Olympic ski teams back to 1948 when Sweden took the Winter Games at St. Moritz and Gretchen Fraser grabbed the Women's Slalom gold medal for the U.S.A. with a time of 1:57:2. When Barbara Cochran repeated that triumph in 1972 and set a new record of 91.24 seconds, Doug Stark—that was Kalchova's name now— bought beers for all his friends.

He had many friends among the 2,108 people in that valley. Doug Stark owned one of the two places in town where you could get a full meal and honest drinks and cheery company. It was called The Dougout, and it had grown nicely since he'd bought the place in 1962 and changed the name from Pete's Pit. The purchase had included Pete's prized recipe for barbecue sauce, so the regulars stayed on and new customers multiplied. The Dougout wasn't anything large or grand, and it never got quite so busy that people had to call ahead for reservations. It was just a pleasant establishment on the edge of what passed for the town of Iron River, a restaurant that could serve forty-five or fifty people and a bar that accommodated about half that many. The cook was an ex-bronco buster named Marlon who'd retired from the rodeo circuit after his eighth broken bone, and the two waitresses were a red-headed thirty-six-year-old widow named Dolly and a Mexican-looking girl everyone called Lupe. That wasn't what her parents had christened her twenty-five years earlier, but the family name was Velez so a lot of clowns tacked on the Lupe to celebrate the film star Lupe Velez of the 1930s. They pronounced it "Loopy," which she was. Aside from tolerating that nickname, she took no crap from anyone and changed lovers two or three times a year.

Among the fortunate men who admired Marlon's cooking, Dolly's friendly manner and Lupe's terrific passion for life were ranchers, local and state police, miners, Iron River storekeepers and a group who'd become officers and gentlemen by Act of Congress. Commissioned and noncommissioned types attached to the 102nd were among the regulars, and during 1971 and early '72 Doug Stark saw a great deal of a female captain who was deputy communications officer for the Air Force complex. In fact, he'd seen almost all of her with the exception of the back of her teeth. It hadn't quite worked out—or maybe it worked completely out—and she'd been transferred to another missile outfit in California. Nobody ever knew exactly why Doug Stark didn't marry her. He never quite figured it out himself. He wasn't aware of the fact that he'd been deep-programmed to avoid any situations that might cause him to be investigated or checked for security. Wedding an officer engaged in sensitive missile work might have generated some risk, so his subconscious had intervened.

Shortly after she'd left, Stark had done his tour with the voluptuous Loopy and then he'd met a woman named Donna Pickall who'd come out from Sacramento to teach school. Donna Pickall had become Donna Stark in 1974, a union that was widely welcomed in the valley. Like her husband, she was an accomplished skier, devoted to the outdoors life, friendly and fond of the recordings of Joni Mitchell, John Denver, Judy Collins and Carly Simon. She played a tolerable guitar on Friday and Saturday nights, adding to the cozy atmosphere of The Dougout.

Unlike her husband, she didn't own a tripod. She enjoyed riding the mare he'd bought her as a wedding present, and she didn't mind living in the comfortably furnished apartment above the restaurant. The Dougout was a mile from the gas station and grocery which most people considered the heart of Iron River, and it faced some of the most splendid peaks in the region. She had magnificent views to enjoy, an affectionate husband who didn't look nine years older than her and a healthy life free of the pollution and problems of urban existence. The Starks were far from rich, people said, but they were well fixed and happy.

It was 5 P.M. when the Gordons reached Iron River. They'd flown into Cheyenne and come the rest of the way in a pair of Hertz cars. Tabbat had insisted on renting two vehicles to be sure of transportation in case one failed. He was grim, focused and determined—calculating all the possibilities with a cold professional expertise. This was going to be the last chance. If Dalchimski stuck to the forty-eight-hour cycle, they could get to Iron River in time to prevent him from setting off the agent who believed he was Doug Stark. Tabbat had a plan, and he went over it in his mind again and again as the two cars moved west through the summer heat on the concrete ribbon that unrolled across the prairie to the mountains that were barely visible on the horizon.

The peaks were much larger as the K.G.B. team entered the

valley, and when Tabbat saw the first signs announcing that Iron River was eleven miles ahead, he pulled over to halt at the side of the road. She stopped her car behind his, rolled down the window beside her when he approached on foot.

"You've got the drill?" he asked.

"I'll go ahead and register at the motel."

"The *White Eagle* Motel," he emphasized. "That's just three hundred yards from The Dougout."

"I know," she acknowledged patiently. "You phoned them and they told you they don't serve food but guests can eat at The Dougout. We've been over it seven times."

"Eight's better. Check in and tell them I'll be along in an hour or so. I'll be scouting the area to find the right spot for later."

"For after dinner when it's dark—right?"

"Right. Keep your eyes open. If anything unusual happens, try to reach me on the walkie-talkie. It has a range of two or three miles, if we're lucky."

"We'll be lucky, Gregg."

To her surprise, he leaned in and kissed her—just for a moment. Then he returned to his tan Ford, drove away. She found the White Eagle Motel without any difficulty some twenty minutes later. The single low building consisted of an office with a counter, an armchair and a vending machine that offered five kinds of cold soda. Beside the office were fourteen rooms. Each had its own air-conditioning unit, twin beds, the other basic furniture and a bathroom with shower. Skiers found these rooms adequate in the winter, but business was slow now and Mrs. Gordon was greeted with enthusiasm. Tabbat didn't join her until twenty to eight.

"Where've you been?" she wondered. "I was getting uneasy. I tried you five times on the radio."

"Checked out the town and went up the valley to the dam. That's why you couldn't reach me. I was out of range," he explained as he unbuttoned his shirt.

"The dam?"

"Dunbar Dam. That's his goddam target. If that goes, everything and everyone in the valley will drown."

"Oh my God."

"The rocket silos, the crews, the command post and a couple of thousand civilians—including us. Nineteen minutes. Nineteen minutes after he blows the dam this whole valley will be under ten feet of water, billions of gallons. Neat, huh?"

She shook her head in shock and dismay.

"I agree," Tabbat said as he turned on the cold-water tap on the sink. He splashed water on his face, reached for a towel.

"Let's eat," he said.

"Did you find the right spot?"

"I think so. Let's go."

"Go with the ribs," advised the dark, pretty waitress ten minutes later.

"Are they good, miss?" Tabbat tested.

"Everybody calls me Lupe."

"Are the ribs good, Lupe?" he repeated amiably.

"Specialty of the house. We've also got the best damn steaks in this part of the state, and you could eat worse chili. You could eat a lot worse chili."

Tabbat ordered the ribs with a side order of chili, and Barbi Gordon put in for a medium-rare sirloin. The "Bullshots" they both sipped while the food was being prepared were excellent, and the atmosphere in the restaurant-bar was pleasantly convivial—the other patrons were clean, nice-looking and neither grossly drunk nor excessively loud or abusive. Tabbat noticed the number of Air Force uniforms, said nothing. He spoke mechanically about the drive, the scenery, the normal inanities. Then he noticed a handsome-looking man of about thirty-eight giving some instructions to the other waitress, and he nodded.

"That's the boss," Tabbat said casually.

"That's Stark?"

"Has to be. Want another drink?"

It was when they tried to catch Lupe's eye that Stark noticed the signal, strolled over to take the order.

"Can I help you?"

"Are you Mr. Stark?"

"Most folks call me Doug. We're not that formal in these parts. What can I do for you?"

She looked at him, saw nothing but easy affability. It was difficult to believe that this man was capable of drowning several thousand people. Stark walked away, relayed the drink order and sipped a bourbon at the bar. The food which Lupe brought was unlikely to win any stars from the itinerant inspectors for the *Guide Michelin*, but it was hearty and honest and better than the fare at many metropolitan restaurants of infinitely greater pretension. The warm atmosphere and genial interplay between Stark and his customers added to the experience, and Barbi Gordon commented on the friendly tone of the place. Tabbat was scanning the room, first checking entrances and exits and then eying the blackness outside the windows.

"Would you excuse me for a second?" he asked, and rose without waiting for her reply.

He went to the men's toilet, locked the door from the inside and raised the window. He wriggled out easily with the agility of a well-trained acrobat, dropped to the ground and crouched low as he circled to the telephone wire that linked The Dougout to the line on the roadside poles. He did something with a small metal tool, reentered by the same window and was back at his table by the time the coffee arrived. That was 9:40.

At 10:20 Nicolai Dalchimski began dialing in a phone booth in a movie theatre in Phoenix, Arizona. There was no answer. He returned to his hotel on North Central Avenue, called again at 1:05. Irritated, he left word with the room clerk to awaken him at 7 A.M. and went to sleep. Dalchimski had a low tolerance for frustration, and his night was filled with fitful turnings and vaguely troubled dreams that left him unrefreshed in the morning. It was annoying, he told himself as he shaved, but nothing to worry about. Despite this, he cut himself twice. With tiny crusts of congealed blood defiling his sullen moon face, he dressed and hurried downstairs to the booth at 7:25.

There was still no answer.

He barely tasted the big breakfast he'd ordered, downing the grapefruit juice as if it were medicine and chewing the bacon with only remote awareness that his jaws were working. The scrambled eggs and toast could have been on someone else's plate, and most of them remained on his as his mind circled that telephone up in Iron River. The number was right.

He knew that, but decided to check it again with a long-distance operator as soon as he'd finished the coffee. She recited the same number, and he dialed again.

There was no answer.

Something was going wrong.

38

The sound of the throbbing engine jerked Tabbat awake. At times such as this he never slept heavily, for his survival experiences and training combined to prohibit any complete relaxation during periods of danger. The situation at Iron River was critical in itself, but that noise overhead was even more provocative. He hated helicopters. He associated them with the police and the F.B.I., and a moment after he sat bolt upright he charged across the room to turn on the radio he'd bought in New York—the one he'd tuned to pick up F.B.I. frequencies. He manipulated the dial slowly and carefully, searching for those voices mouthing cryptic phrases he dreaded.

No.

He looked out the window into the morning glare, his tired eyes smarting as he peered up until he spotted the chopper gliding lazily north towards the town. It was much too far to see whether the whirlybird carried the markings of any government agency or military unit. Perhaps it was an Air Force chopper, a S.A.C. bird moving some missile crew or maintenance team to one of the silos or back to the fortified bunker that was the 102nd's command post. The rotorcraft could be transporting wealthy hunters or fishermen, or perhaps geologists with electromagnetic gear on some aerial survey.

Tabbat didn't think so. Something in his viscera told him that this helicopter was a hostile thing, a threat. He didn't say this to the lovely young woman who looked at him sleepily from across the room. She might not have understood, and he was in no state of mind or emotion to explain. His instincts told him to hate this flying machine, and he would have killed it like some poisonous snake if he could have done so.

He watched this thing—the enemy—until it drifted out of sight. Then he sat down, yawned and rubbed his eyes. The slump of his shoulders signaled fatigue like some sagging banner. She saw that the pressure was finally starting to wear him down.

"You sleep all right, Gregg?"

"I slept fine—but not enough. I had a little errand to take care of at four. Took half an hour, and then I was restless for a while."

"At four?"

"Took out some insurance. We need at least forty-eight hours of no phone service to The Dougout to bring the maniac here. I did some work on two of the insulators on the lines. That ought to buy us the extra day. If it doesn't, I blow up the main cable downtown."

"You're serious?"

"I'll level this whole town if I have to. Crazy, isn't it? I'm just about fed up with all this blasting and killing, and the only way I know how to stop it is more violence. Maybe I'm not too bright."

"You're very bright, hon You're the best in the business—but you're tired."

"And very angry," he agreed. "Don't worry. I'll beat him. I'm a great competitor."

He took the last cigarette from a pack, crumpled the red wrapping and struck a match.

"Do you know why I'll beat that bastard—all the bastards?" he asked bitterly between puffs.

"Because you're smarter."

"Save the crap. I'll win because I'll make fewer mistakes. I'm more professional, more disciplined, more careful. I check on everything—twice. You're going to help me. Get dressed. I want to find out about that chopper, and you're going to do the recon for me while I watch The Dougout from here."

He was still watching the road for a telephone company repair truck at 10:50 when she returned to report. The helicopter had been chartered to bring in a sportsman-hunter, a man who was at least ten years younger and several inches taller than Dalchimski. The sportsman was staying at the Wyoming Lodge on Route 111, about three miles north. He was registered as John Leonard, and had rented a jeep for a trip into the mountains.

"I don't believe it. This isn't the right time for hunting. Too damn hot," Tabbat reckoned aloud. "Did he come alone?"

She nodded.

"Doesn't *prove* anything. The others could be here already."

"What others, hon?"

"Jeezus, I *told* you the F.B.I. travels in bunches. Did anyone meet him?"

She shook her head, handed him the carton of black coffee.

"You need this," she said gently.

"You're right about that. I could use three of these," he admitted as he opened it and watched the steam rise. "And five more hours of sleep wouldn't hurt either."

He sipped the coffee.

"According to the register, this Leonard's from Salt Lake City."

"I like you," he answered, "so I'll pretend you didn't say that. For Chrissakes, according to the register we're Mr. and Mrs. Red White and Blue from New York. Maybe he is John Leonard from Salt Lake, but I can't afford to believe that. He could be working for that Armenian creep in Washington, or maybe some other creep. There are a lot of creeps around, you know, and the biggest goddam creep of all should be joining the party shortly."

Dalchimski was in a phone booth at the Phoenix airport, making his seventh attempt to reach Douglas R. Stark at The Dougout. When nothing happened on his direct dialing, he sought the help of the operator in Iron River.

"I'm sorry, sir," she announced after a series of beeps,

whistles and clicks. "There seems to be something wrong with that line. It's been reported to our emergency service, and they hope to get to it tomorrow."

"Tomorrow?" Dalchimski complained scornfully.

"I'm sorry, sir," she chanted. "Our repair crew is short-handed at the moment, and the men on duty are working on a problem that's come up at the police station."

"I see."

"If your call is an emergency, sir—"

Dalchimski didn't answer, for they were announcing his flight north. He boarded the plane without any idea as to the reason for the failure of phone service at the Iron River police headquarters.

Two sabotaged insulators.

Tabbat's insurance.

He'd counted on the likelihood that the police lines would receive priority from the repair crew. Dalchimski wouldn't have the patience to wait. He wasn't an agent, just a deranged lab man with a terrible obsession that was going to destroy him. Tabbat sat in the motel room all day, watching the restaurant with binoculars through the slatted blinds. He had the rifle across his knees, and his focus was such that he barely heard the music on the radio behind him. There was limited reception in this region, and a single station to serve the small population. Whoever owned it was a fan of Country music. Hour after hour that was all Tabbat heard—aside from the customary commercials for tires and toothpaste and powdered soup. Tabbat had a great deal of stamina, and he took it for a long time. He didn't complain or criticize at one o'clock when she brought him a couple of sandwiches from the diner in town, and he didn't grumble when she handed him a can of root beer at four.

Hour after hour, and not one Sinatra recording.

Not even Tony Bennett or Nat Cole.

At 5:35 he finally yielded to his discontent.

"Tell me," he said, "is there *really* someone named Conway Twitty?"

She recognized the name of the Country star whose recording had just filled the room, and she nodded.

"There is, Gregg."

He considered this for several seconds.

"Why?"

The woman had no answer.

"Is that his real name, Barb?"

"No, he took it five or ten years ago—I think."

Tabbat reflected for another ten seconds, digesting this extraordinary piece of information.

"Why?"

She laughed softly, and he felt better for a little while.

39

When no telephone company truck appeared by 8 P.M., Tabbat decided that it was unlikely any repair crew would show up until morning and he put down the rifle. It wasn't that he was unprepared for a night action. The flare gun and rockets he'd bought at the Chicago sporting goods store rested only a yard from his feet. No, Dalchimski would probably come after dark all right—but not tonight.

"Tomorrow night," Tabbat told her as they left The Dugout after dinner.

For a moment her confidence in him wavered, and she wondered whether it was wise to count entirely on one man to stop Dalchimski. Even an agent as tough and clever as Tabbat could err, could falter for a second or simply fail through bad luck. Maybe she should have called for help. They'd come in force, at once. They too were competent professionals, equipped with excellent weapons.

"He'll come tomorrow night," Tabbat repeated in the car.

"You're sure?"

"Reasonably sure."

"And you're sure you want to do this alone?"

"It's the only way. Don't you get cute with me, Barb," he answered in a voice that had suddenly hardened.

"I was merely asking. After all, for one person to—"

"Two people," he corrected. "You'll have a very important role in this plan. I'm counting on you."

"Whatever you say. Then you've got it figured out?"

He swerved the car to a halt in front of their motel.

"There are still a couple of things bothering me," he announced. "I'd like to know more about that sportsman from Salt Lake City, and I'd sure sleep better if I knew where he's got the tripod."

"What tripod? I didn't hear anything about Leonard having a tripod."

Tabbat shrugged, turned off the motor.

"He doesn't. It's Mr. Stark. There could be quite a bit of trouble if the wrong people find it."

"Of course," she responded archly.

"Then it would really hit the fan," he continued. "If they found one of our tripods here—man, that would be something!"

"I suppose you're right. I'm not a camera bug myself."

He blinked in surprise.

She didn't know.

She didn't have any idea as to what he was talking about, and that explained the irritation in her voice. She wasn't going to ask because he'd forbidden questions, and that was probably adding to her annoyance. She was too young to know about tripods—at least the model that Stark had.

Where?

They'd have to find it before they left Iron River, and Tabbat would have to tell her. He'd explain it tomorrow, after dinner. That was when Dalchimski would come—sometime after dark. He wouldn't risk showing his face during the daylight hours, and he was smart enough to realize that Stark would have a much better chance of destroying the dam sometime between midnight and dawn. Still, you couldn't be sure that Dalchimski hadn't already reached the valley. The son of a bitch could be out there anywhere, perhaps even in the lodge where the man who called himself John Leonard was registered.

"We'd better take turns tonight," he said after they'd entered their room. "Four-hour shifts. Okay?"

"Turns?"

"Watching The Dougout. They should be closing soon, and if Dalchimski is coming tonight he'll show sometime late. I'll take the first shift."

Neither of them had the time or the interest to make love that night. He didn't even watch her sleep, something he'd come to enjoy. His attention was centered on The Dougout, and the highway leading to it. The only time it wavered was when he brooded about the tripod, and he was still thinking about it when he woke her to take the watch at four.

He didn't dream about the tripod, though.

He had a small nightmare about a telephone truck, and she heard him tossing restlessly as the sun's first rays glowed at the distant edge of the valley. She let him sleep until ten, staring at the road and wondering how and when Dalchimski would come. Perhaps he wouldn't come at all. Maybe he'd sense the trap and just wait it out until the phone was repaired. If he did, thousands of people—including those in the White Eagle Motel —would die.

40

When the telephone truck didn't appear by noon, Tabbat went over his options once again. There was a good chance that the repair crew would roll up this road sometime before sunset, and he had to decide what to do to insure that Doug Stark never got that call.

He could sabotage the main switchboard in town, perhaps

by sending her in to place an incendiary device or small bomb.

He could wait in ambush somewhere down the highway, shoot out the truck's rear tires with the silenced pistol and send it spinning into the ditch.

He could gun Stark himself, an act that might seem extreme to humanitarians but one that any cloak-and-dagger operative for a major power would recognize as justifiable. The wounding or killing of one man—himself a pro in the business—to prevent World War III and tens of millions of deaths certainly made sense. It was the surest and most logical of the options.

"I'm not going to do it," he finally decided.

"What won't you do, Gregg?"

"You'll do it, and if it works nobody will get hurt."

It worked, and nobody was hurt. She drove into Iron River, found a phone booth and called the Repair Service with word that it wasn't necessary to send a crew out to The Dougout because the line was all right again. The operator thanked her, promised to notify the truck immediately by radio. The service truck was less than a mile from The Dougout when the driver heard the message, and he turned the vehicle around just about twenty seconds before he would have come into range of Tabbat's rifle. Watching through the scope on the hunting gun, the K.G.B. man sighed as he saw the truck circle and move away.

Then Tabbat resumed his grim vigil, studying every vehicle and watching for a jeep that might be driven by a man who claimed to be John Leonard. At 3:50 a canvas-topped jeep came into sight, moving at an uneventful forty-five miles per hour. Tabbat didn't get a good look at the man at the wheel, but the driver didn't seem to be anyone Tabbat knew. He certainly wasn't Dalchimski, and he didn't stop or even slow down as he passed The Dougout.

That didn't prove a thing.

A trained agent wouldn't show any interest in the target during a recon run, and if this John Leonard was either F.B.I. or one of the *Rezident's* crew he'd be very well trained. That wasn't necessarily bad, so far as Tabbat was concerned. He was used to coping with experienced professionals, and he could anticipate their tactics and thinking. It was deranged amateurs such as Dalchimski who were so difficult to predict. Tabbat was confident—*fairly* confident—that he could handle the professionals, unless the woman betrayed him. She'd worked in the U.S. *apparat* for months or years, taken orders from the Armenian without question. Even though she'd been instructed to obey Tabbat, there was still the risk that she'd revert.

He'd know tonight.

Dalchimski would come, and perhaps this John Leonard with others. If Leonard interfered, he'd perish with Dalchimski. This was the end of the line, and Tabbat had no thought of mercy for anyone who threatened the conclusion of this bizarre and exhausting mission. Stark was another matter. He was a victim and an ally, and Tabbat was determined to save him. Now he thought about the woman again. What was keeping her? Was she calling someone else? She seemed so loyal and loving, but what did he really know about her? Not her true name, her age, where she grew up or what her family was like, what lovers she'd had or even the sports she'd played as a child. Even what little she had told him could be a lie, part of her "legend." Every K.G.B. "illegal" operating in a foreign land went equipped with a complete and wholly false "legend"—a life story as untrue as the forged identity papers. Whoever she was, she wasn't the person described in the "shoe"—the counterfeit passport supplied by those technicians at the Center. It was ironic to consider. Perhaps Dalchimski had prepared her "shoe" himself.

Her return interrupted this train of thought. He told her about the truck and the jeep, congratulated her on the success of her call to the phone company. They went over the plan for the night twice, and then he checked his weapons and equipment carefully. He was going to be ready, perfectly ready. *They* would overlook some detail, make the one mistake. His eyes flicked back and forth to The Dougout as he prepared. He saw Stark drive off at 4:15 in a green Porsche that wasn't new but still had plenty of power, and at 5:10 he watched him return from his errand with an armful of packages.

At 7:40 Tabbat sent her off in her car to circle the town and he drove the other rented vehicle to the restaurant.

"Alone tonight?" wondered Lupe as she took his drink order.

"She'll be along in a bit."

Several customers—a few couples, two groups of Air Force officers and three lone men—wandered in during the next quarter of an hour. Tabbat glanced out the window beside him now and then, sipping his Margarita calmly until he spotted the parked jeep. It was the same one. His eyes swept around the room, wondering which of the men might be John Leonard. Across the room the assassin whom the G.R.U. often called Leon chewed on pieces of barbecued chicken—carefully ignoring Tabbat's wary scan. Leon was in good spirits, ready for his night's work. He'd spotted Tabbat ten minutes earlier, and now Leon was enjoying his dinner. He'd found his target, and there was no way for Tabbat to recognize him.

She arrived at five minutes to eight, and was pleased to find Tabbat smiling. She was glad that he was in such a cheery mood. That signaled that everything was going well.

"He's here," Tabbat said evenly in a low voice.

"Who is?"

"The man who drives the jeep. Didn't you see it outside?"

He downed another ounce of the Margarita, savoring the salt ring as if nothing were wrong.

"Lots of people drive jeeps, Gregg."

He laughed as if she'd said something witty.

"It's him. I smell him. I can see him too—over there. Don't look, for Chrissakes."

She didn't. A moment later, she saw the reflection in the window.

"How can you be sure?"

"He's working too hard at his dinner. His eyes never come up. Ever seen him before?"

She shook her head.

"Probably a friend of your Armenian pal," Tabbat said as he picked up the menu. "Sure you haven't come across him?"

"Never."

It was impossible to tell whether she was lying.

"What are we going to do, Gregg?"

The "we" meant nothing. She'd say that in any case.

"We're going to order a terrific dinner—the works. We've got all the time in the world."

Customers came and went, and it was dark outside by the time they finished their main course. Tabbat glanced up again —as he'd been doing every few minutes—as if to signal the waitress. The man was gone.

"He's split," Tabbat announced.

"Where?"

"Doesn't matter. He'll be back."

Just before ten Tabbat paid the bill and they strolled out into the hot night. He walked a bit unsteadily, which wouldn't have surprised anyone who'd noted how much he'd drunk.

"I don't think you'd better drive, hon," she said.

"I'm sober as a judge," he answered indignantly.

"As a judge who's half sloshed."

After a brief and classic wife and husband wrangle, he yielded and climbed into her car. The car backed up out of view of those seated by the windows, moved down the short driveway and headed for the White Eagle Motel. The remaining patrons trickled out of The Dougout during the next hour and a half, with a trio of missile men the last to leave. They were boisterous enough to indicate that they'd had at least a few drinks themselves, calling out a merry farewell to "Loopy" who smiled patiently from the doorway. The waitress and the rest of the employees departed shortly before midnight, and a few minutes later the dining room darkened and lights appeared in the apartment upstairs.

There was almost no traffic on the road. Only an occasional car swept past during the next hundred minutes, moving at speeds which suggested either the high spirits of youth or the distilled spirits of blended whisky. At 1:50 a car cruised by at a more moderate pace and it returned a few minutes later. The driver parked it ten yards from the car Tabbat had left behind. It was a man. Tabbat could see his feet. He'd dropped out of her car hours earlier, rolled under his and drawn his silenced pistol. He'd waited for a long time on his belly, sweating and enduring the bugs.

It had to be Dalchimski.

Tabbat heard the pounding on the door, inched forward to hear and see better. There was still a tiny chance that this was some friend of Stark's or perhaps a hungry customer—or a thirsty one who didn't give a damn about the hour. But the man appeared to be quite steady on his feet, and the knocking didn't communicate the passion of a drunken fool.

A square of light cut down from upstairs. Someone was awake, presumably descending. Tabbat was breathing harder now. He released the safety on his gun, tensed for the confrontation. What did the bullfighting *afficionados* call this? The moment of truth? Yes, this would be the moment of truth all right.

He heard the door open five yards away.

"What the hell's going on here?" Stark demanded. "You bombed or something? We've been closed for hours, Jack."

"My name isn't Jack."

The voice that went with the feet was low and foreign.

"Come back at noon tomorrow."

"I have a message for you."

That did it. Tabbat rolled out from under the car, raised the gun and aimed it carefully.

"Dalchimski!" he shouted.

The man hesitated for a second or two, turned and reached into his jacket. It was the goddam maniac. Tabbat shot him three times, the silenced gun making soft coughing sounds. Two bullets hit him in the chest. The third pierced his forehead, creating a weird hole like a third eye. The son of a bitch fell, and Tabbat rushed forward. He had to get the Book.

He stopped in his charge when he saw the look in Stark's eyes, for he instantly understood: Dalchimski had spoken the code phrase.

"Lieutenant Kalchova," he said quickly. "I come from the Center. I'm here for the K.G.B.—Colonel Malchenko and General Strelski. The mission has been canceled. The man at our feet is a traitor to the Soviet Union, an enemy of the State. Telefon is off!"

The man who'd once been Doug Stark stared at him suspiciously, and Tabbat repeated the litany in Russian. He explained that he was sent with the authority of the Red Army Chief of Staff to destroy this Nicolai Dalchimski, a Stalinist conspirator who'd plotted the murders of members of the Central Committee of the Party.

"I see," Stark replied slowly in English.

"Good. Now I've got to find that book."

Tabbat searched the corpse quickly, discovered something flat and hard and rectangular in the jacket pocket. He reached down, grasped his prize and smiled in triumph.

That was when Lieutenant Kalchova dropped him with a single perfectly-executed karate chop, and Tabbat toppled across the body of the man who'd wanted to start World War III. Tabbat was semi-conscious when he heard the roar of a car motor, and still on one knee when he saw the green Porsche race up the highway—heading north.

The dam was north, and Stark was on his way with the tripod. Tabbat had the Book, but Stark had the tripod and the terrible determination that they'd deep-programmed into the Telefon agents. He wasn't Stark anymore. That name was as obsolete as "tripod." No one in the Red Army called the miniature atomic weapon a "tripod" anymore. The model itself was no longer in production, for much more efficient devices were now available. Still, the old-fashioned tripod had the blast power of five thousand tons of high explosive—more than enough to breach the Dunbar Dam. Inspired—and frightened—and more than a bit enraged by that thought, Tabbat staggered to his car and set out after the speedy green Porsche.

41

He knew where he was going. Tabbat had reconnoitered the roads between The Dougout and the dam, found the most direct route two days earlier. The saboteur would probably take it, for they'd programmed him to destroy the target as quickly as possible. What Tabbat didn't know as he pressed down the gas pedal was what the woman would do.

"Juliet to Romeo. Juliet to Romeo," called the walkie-talkie on the seat beside him.

Tabbat picked up his set, pressed the "send" switch.

"Go ahead. Go ahead, Juliet."

"He went by here ten seconds ago, heading north at high speed. Heading north."

She thought that the driver was Dalchimski, Tabbat guessed, but that didn't matter. What counted was whether she was still under Tabbat's orders.

"Proceeding north. Proceeding north. Follow immediately."

She'd be the back-up gun in the back-up car. That was the plan. She'd been watching in her car—lights out—up near the motel. If Tabbat failed, she was to kill the maniac. Now the problem was a different maniac—they had to view Kalchova as out of his mind—but the plan was the same. Time would be the problem. Four switches had to be closed—in the correct sequence—to start the timing mechanism on the "tripod." The delayed-action detonator would set off the warhead three, seven or eleven minutes later, depending on how this weapon had been rigged.

But there was also the possibility of an instantaneous explosion. This was probably one of the models built with an override, a fifth switch for suicide missions. If so, the lead that Kalchova had and the speed of the Porsche offered a grim prospect. There was still the threat of the man in the jeep, who might be in some other vehicle by now. Tabbat would have switched to a car to get more speed and a new profile. He assumed that any other professional would do the same.

Tabbat raced north at sixty . . . sixty-five . . . seventy miles per hour, grateful that this part of the route was straight-arrow concrete across the floor of the valley. He peered ahead for the tail lights of the Porsche, thought he saw the red specks far ahead. Then they vanished just at the point that the highway changed to a lesser road that twisted and circled through the foothills, and Tabbat guessed that Kalchova had switched out his lights to throw off pursuers. He'd probably test-driven this five hundred times without ever knowing why, the crazy

bastard. This was his turf, and he had the advantage of knowing the terrain far better than Tabbat.

Or the man who called himself John Leonard.

He was out there somewhere.

Where?

"Juliet to Romeo. Juliet to Romeo. We have company. Repeat, we have company."

Tabbat glanced into his rear-view mirror, saw the beams
and picked up his radio.

"Romeo to Juliet. Is that you behind me, or is that the
company?"

"That's the company. One man in a car. I'm in third place,
about four or five hundred yards behind him."

"Stay there. Stick with the plan. Do you read me?"

"Okay. Okay, Romeo. Be careful."

Tabbat didn't answer. He couldn't. The road abruptly
changed to curves, and he dropped the radio to steer with both
hands. His eyes flicked to the dashboard, saw that they'd covered a bit more than eight miles. Only three or three and a half
to go, he computed, and Kalchova still had a significant lead.
Now the question was whether the "tripod" was in place, or
was the saboteur delivering it?

He had to have it in the car.

He couldn't run the risk that someone might stumble on it,
and it wouldn't be safe to expose it to heat and rain and snow
over the years. No, he had the goddam thing with him.

Where would he place it?

Tabbat swore as he fought to keep control of the car, straining to keep it on the road and cursing as the curves forced him
to reduce speed at fifty. Even at that, it was a sweaty battle to
stay on the twisting road and avoid spinning off into the bould-
ers that waited in clusters to destroy him.

He kept computing.

The base of the dam was much too massive, and might
survive even so powerful a blast. The smart thing to do would
be to get up on top, set the detonators and drop the weapon
into the water. The water would magnify the shock waves,
smash the dam as if it were plaster of paris. Convinced that
this was what Kalchova would do, Tabbat made his decision as

to how to stop him. It was a calculated risk, but Tabbat had no choice. He couldn't go stumbling around in the darkness trying to find the saboteur. He had to estimate where he'd go, and hope his reckoning was right.

Now the road grew curvier and bumpier as the surface deteriorated, and then it was gravel. After three hundred yards of bucking and twisting, he swung around a turn—and nearly crashed into the Porsche. It was parked, empty. Tabbat didn't hesitate. He stopped his car, opened the door and leaped out. He took the rifle from the floor, swiftly removed it from the case and laid the weapon across the hood. Then he grabbed the flare gun, loaded it and jammed a spare rocket in his belt.

He looked up at the Dunbar Dam, towering above him two hundred yards away.

Where the hell was Kalchova?

There.

That had to be him—a small figure moving across the rim with something in his arms.

Tabbat heard the car coming up behind him, decided that he had to trust the woman. If she meant to betray him, this would be the time. Tabbat looked up, felt sorry for Kalchova and fired a flare. As soon as it left the fat pistol, he reloaded immediately and automatically.

Then he raised the rifle. The darkness vanished abruptly as the phosphorus ignited, throwing a bright and brilliant light. The flare started to float down slowly. Tabbat saw Kalchova put the atomic bomb down, bend over to do something.

He shot twice. The first bullet spun the patriot away from the tripod, and the second knocked him to his knees. On all fours, Kalchova started back to the warhead. Strelski would have been proud of him, Tabbat thought angrily. Then he shot him through the head. Lieutenant Josef Kalchova fell off the Dunbar Dam, having died needlessly in the service of his country.

"Shit!" Tabbat said.

That was when Leon stopped his car forty yards away, shoved the L34A1 out the window and opened fire. Tabbat staggered, dropped face down. Leon looked at the body, remembered that he was to look for the Book. He stepped out and walked towards the dead man. Suddenly he heard the sound of a vehicle closing fast, and he spun and dropped into a professional shooting stance. The lights of the woman's car blinded him for a moment or two. She was coming at him. Leon swung the submachine gun towards the beams.

And Tabbat rolled over. The flare gun was in his fist. Leon had missed with that first hurried burst, but Tabbat didn't. The rocket tore off the back of Leon's skull. Leon had made one mistake, and Tabbat hadn't.

The woman rushed forward.

"Are you all right?" she asked urgently.

He nodded, despite the searing pain of the bullet that had creased his left side. She hadn't betrayed him. Everything was all right. They made their way to the top of the dam, collected the "tripod" and dropped it into the water where it would never be found.

Everything was all right—at last.

42

By morning—long before the bodies were found—Mr. and Mrs. Gregg Gordon were 215 miles away, across the state line into Utah. They turned in the rented cars, reached San Francisco by plane at three o'clock. Shortly before five she stood beside him at the entrance to Gate 16 as Tabbat waited to board the jet that would carry him to Tokyo on the first leg of his triumphant trip home.

With the Book.

They would be exultant at the Center, and he would be

rewarded and honored. Stopping Dalchimski was a miracle in itself, but bringing back the Book was the crowning achievement.

"That ought to teach them not to meddle," Tabbat said as he thought of the assassin someone—probably that vicious Armenian—had sent to kill him.

She nodded.

"But it won't," Tabbat continued pragmatically. He had so few illusions left. Aside from this loving woman beside him, there were few in his trade whom he could trust—and he was leaving her in a few minutes.

"It doesn't matter, hon. You did a terrific job. You're a hero. You'll get a promotion and a medal, maybe even some new Sinatra records and a better stereo set," she said warmly.

She was sweet, loyal, loving.

"I wish you could come with me," he said as he put his arm around her affectionately.

"I've got work to do here."

"Too bad we never got to take that vacation in the Caribbean, Barb. Maybe we'll run into each other again."

"Maybe," she replied with a touching smile.

The last call for Japan Air Lines Flight 11 sounded, and he squeezed her shoulders. Tabbat had never found saying goodbye so difficult before.

"Gonna miss you," he said truthfully.

"I'll miss you too. I've learned a lot from you, Gregg. You're leaving a woman who knows a lot more about Frank Sinatra—among other things. I'm going to get all the records."

He squeezed her shoulders again, then took eight $50 bills from his wallet.

"Buy them with this. Don't argue with me, Barb. I wish I could give you something better, but we haven't had any time for shopping."

The other passengers were moving past them, and suddenly their privacy was gone as a knot of people bunched up nearby.

"There's something I'd rather have than the money, hon," she said softly.

"What is it?"

"I'll take the Book."

As she spoke he felt the pressure of her .32 against his side.

"No tricks, Gregg. Don't move an inch or you're dead," she said in a tough, quiet voice.

"Don't be crazy. I'm taking it to the Center."

"The Book's going to Washington, Gregg."

"To that goddam Armenian?"

She shook her head, and now he felt another muzzle bore into his back. He couldn't see the face of the man who held it, but he wouldn't have recognized him in any case. Tabbat had never seen this man, who'd been in the Army Hospital at Leavenworth as a security man for the telephone company.

"Gregg dear, I have a little confession to make. The lady who was supposed to meet you on the beach—she had a small accident. She's resting comfortably—in Langley, Virginia."

He tensed under the impact.

"Don't try it," she advised. "There are nine guns on you. You'd be dog meat before you could do anything, so don't do anything."

He looked around, saw the hard faces of the "passengers" clustered around them.

"Langley, Virginia? Then you're with The Other Side?"

"Gregg, look at it this way. We were after the same thing. We wanted to save lives and prevent a war. We wanted to stop that maniac and get the Book. We've known that such a book existed for seven years—seven goddam years. We couldn't find it. We didn't have anybody quite as bright as you."

"Thanks," he acknowledged bitterly.

"But we did have a very bright woman named Dorothy, a computer analyst. She came up with several of the answers, and she was the one who discovered that Dalchimski was spelling out his name."

"So that's why you kept bugging me to try new lists and new combinations?"

"That's it, darling. Even after you'd mentioned his name, we didn't have the list of targets or agents. That was in your head."

"And I thought that you were just—well, basically—a good piece of ass. I guess that's what you'd call a male chauvinist number, right?"

"Nobody's perfect, honey. Now stand nice and still while I take the Book."

She removed it from his inner jacket, and a well-dressed black man stepped forward to put it in a metal attaché case. Four other men formed an immediate cordon, escorted him away.

"And now I suppose I'll get twenty years at Leavenworth," Tabbat speculated.

"You'll get on that plane, hon. You've done a wonderful job—for both countries—but we really don't need any more K.G.B. agents at the moment. We're going to collect more than a hundred and thirty of them during the next twelve hours."

"Poor bastards."

"We'll take good care of them, Gregg. We see them as an investment. They should be useful when we have to work out an exchange with your people. One more thing—the money."

"What money?"

"That twenty thousand or more of the thirty the U.S. tax-payers supplied. That cash you got in New York—there must be at least twenty thousand left."

Tabbat smiled engagingly.

"I can't go home broke," he charmed. "How about a thousand for cab fare?"

She laughed at his impudence, took all the cash from his wallet—and returned $1,000 to him.

"You've got a lot of nerve, Gregg. Have a good trip home, and don't come back. Please don't *ever* come back."

He could see that she liked him, and that pleased him immensely. It was reassuring to know that even an American woman who was his foe would respond to his virile sophistication.

"The man in the hospital? Did you really—"

"You'll never know, Gregg."

"That creep with the grease-gun at the dam?" he wondered.

"Not ours. One of *yours*. We played it by your rules, and we certainly didn't want to scare you off before you had the Book."

He reflected for several seconds, wondering whether a

bullet or a medal would be waiting for him in Moscow. It would come as quite a surprise when he discovered that the Red Army Chief of Staff was personally delighted that Telefon was over, that Marshal Pasimov's protection and admiration prohibited any punishment for the loss of the Book.

"Time to go, Gregg. No hard feelings?"

He shook his head, turned towards the exit to the aircraft.

"You *were* a good piece of ass," he said mischievously.

"So were you. Goodbye, Gregg."

He walked to the plane, and seven armed employees of the Central Intelligence Agency watched as the big jet swooped down the runway and into the afternoon sky.

The man who'd been at the Kansas hospital turned to the woman, complimented her on her remarkable success as a double-agent. There was something patronizing in his tone, some trace of male condescension.

"You'll get a promotion too," he joked, "for being a good piece of ass. Well, this is an historic moment. We've just wrapped up a very tough case, and we've saved many thousands of lives—and we're about to round up a small army of the best deep-cover agents in history. Somebody should say something quotable, something historic."

She didn't hesitate.

"I'll say something historic."

"Yes?"

"Don't fuck around with Dorothy Putterman!"

43

"You're going to be amazed at what Pasimov said," Strelski announced two days later.

"I guess I will," said Colonel Malchenko.

"Aren't you going to ask?"

"You'll tell me anyway."

The general opened the humidor on his desk, took out a Havana, remembered and put it back in the box.

"Thanks," Malchenko acknowledged. "You're in fine spirits, I see."

"I always feel good when I hear that I'm not going to get shot—and neither are more than a hundred and thirty of our agents. The marshal was pleased, and the loss of the Book didn't bother him that much. He said that Telefon was obsolete anyway."

"Did you agree?"

"A general always agrees with a marshal. If you live long enough to become a general, you'll discover that. By the way, I think you're going to be a general before long. Pasimov's taking it up with our bosses. That's good news. You should look more cheerful, Aleksei."

"I find the loss of a hundred and thirty good agents depressing."

"But we've had our victories this month too. The Americans went ahead with that information we fed them about those guns in Asmara, and they wiped out the shipment. Now our Arab allies will be furious with the Americans, and we can be pious and sympathetic. Those stupid Americans have no idea that we are the people who tipped them."

Malchenko nodded mechanically, and his stomach rumbled.

"I've got something for that, Aleksei. Better than Tums."

"The Tums were pretty good."

"Our agent in the embassy says that she hears these are *definitely superior*."

"Sounds like a Yankee television commercial. What the hell are they?"

Strelski was fumbling in his desk drawer, finally raised his right hand in victory.

"Rolaids!"

"Better than Tums?" Malchenko asked suspiciously.

"Definitely! Now, let's get down to business. Tabbat's got his new tape-deck and record player, and he's off with some blonde from the Air Force for two weeks' vacation. I've got a new mission that should fit him to a T—when he returns."

"What is it?"

"It's terrific. It's brilliant. I'd say it's even more ingenious than Telefon!"

Strelski waited for his question. Colonel Aleksei Malchenko reached across the desk for the stomach tablets.

"Is it okay to take two of these?" he asked.

Early the next afternoon there was a small ceremony in the office of the Director of Central Intelligence in that heavily guarded and elaborately protected fortress-headquarters in Langley. The D.C.I. was present, and so were his Special Assistant and Colonel T. S. Jenkins and Ms. Dorothy Putterman.

"I've explained to the F.B.I. and the various Pentagon intelligence outfits why we couldn't let them in on this Telefon deal," said the D.C.I., "and I think they got the message. I told them that the White House was pleased by the way we handled it. That ought to cool them down."

"It certainly should," Coltrane agreed loyally. "We've done a fine job on Hot Rod, a first-class job."

Colonel Jenkins hoped that Dorothy wouldn't hit him, for Coltrane had contributed little except to meddle and harass her. Coltrane had been skeptical from the outset. Jenkins' eyes drifted to her rosy face, were suprised at her smile. If only she'd control herself in the face of his prejudice and provocation—just for a few days—she'd get that extra $3,500 a year in addition to the medal.

The D.C.I. made a brief speech expressing the warm appreciation of the Agency and the President, and then he gave Coltrane the medal to pin on her chest. It was quite an impressive medal—the highest the C.I.A. had—and quite a chest, Jenkins thought. Coltrane stepped forward with her best smile, pinned it on her blouse—over the left one.

"Congratulations, Dorothy," he said in his most sincere tones. "We're all proud of you, girl."

She looked up, smiled and spoke. Her remarks were brief, but meaningful.

"Turd!" she said in clear ringing tones.

As Colonel Jenkins winced, the D.C.I. looked puzzled.

In the stockade of a U.S. Army base in the mountains of Georgia, a remote and isolated facility used for training Special Forces men and Rangers, scores of civilians—well over a hundred men and women—wore similar expressions. Without warning, they'd been seized by federal agents and brought here from all over the country. No one had told them why, or what this weird situation involved.

"Can't you explain this?" a middle-aged bartender from Norfolk—not far from the naval base—queried one of the guards through the barbed wire. The military policeman didn't know himself, but he wasn't about to admit his ignorance.

"Ask your friends," he answered rudely.

"They're no friends of mine. I've never seen any of these folks in my whole life. They're all strangers."

The sentry walked away, and the man from Norfolk shook his head sadly. It was difficult to believe that this could happen in the United States, he reflected. *Goddam*, this was the kind of thing they did in Russia.

THE SWEENEY

Ian Kennedy Martin

Jack Regan is one of the Heavy Mob.
He's also a loner, intolerant of red tape and
insubordinate to his superiors.
And he just happens to be the best detective in
Scotland Yard's crack Flying Squad.

When Regan receives orders to co-operate with
Lieutenant Ewing, over from America to trace a cop
killer, Regan is pursuing his own case and ignores
them. But he soon discovers that Ewing is as tough as
he is – and a dangerous clash of personalities
develops. As the two cases begin to merge into a
sinister and violent network of IRA provos and
murderers, the two men close in for the kill . . .

Ian Kennedy Martin is the creator of Thames
Television's enormously popular TV series, starring
John Thaw.

THE ULTRA SECRET

F. W. Winterbotham

'The greatest British Intelligence coup of the Second
World War has never been told till now'
Daily Mail

For thirty-five years the expert team of cryptanalysts
who worked at Bletchley Park have kept the secret of
how, with the help of a Polish defector, British
Intelligence obtained a precise copy of the highly
secret and complex German coding machine known
as Enigma, and then broke the coding system to
intercept all top-grade German military signals.
Group-Captain Winterbotham was the man in charge
of security and communication of this information.
Now he is free to tell the story of that amazing coup
and what it uncovered.

'A story as bizarre as anything in spy fiction . . . the
book adds a new dimension to the history of World
War II'
New York Times

'Military historians, like the general reader, will be
astonished by this book . . . Group-Captain
Winterbotham cannot be too highly commended'
The Listener

'Superbly told'
Daily Express

THE SEVENTEENTH STAIR

Barbara Paul

The velvet silence of the tower hung like a pall around her . . . she lay, drenched in a chill sweat of terror, straining to hear the sound that had woken her . . . then it came again . . . a low sobbing cry echoing through the lonely chateau.

Rosella Eastwood was summoned to Paris by her guardian, but when she arrived she found no one to greet her, only a will bequeathing her the Chateau de Louismont in the Loire Valley: a place of hated childhood memories, where she had to face the hatred of the Louismont family, the agony of loving a man who could never be free, and the evil secret of the west tower.